DATE DUE

JUN 0 7 2019			
			PRINTED IN U.S.A.

COLD WHITE SUN

COLD
WHITE
SUN

Sue Farrell Holler

Groundwood Books
House of Anansi Press
Toronto / Berkeley

Groundwood Books / House of Anansi Press
groundwoodbooks.com

We gratefully acknowledge for their financial support of our publishing program the Canada
Council for the Arts, the Ontario Arts Council and the Government of Canada.

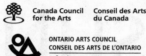

Library and Archives Canada Cataloguing in Publication
Holler, Sue Farrell, author
Cold white sun / Sue Farrell Holler.
Issued in print and electronic formats.
ISBN 978-1-77306-081-1 (hardcover).—ISBN 978-1-77306-082-8 (HTML).—
ISBN 978-1-77306-083-5 (Kindle)
I. Title.
PS8615.O437C65 2018   jC813'.6   C2017-907517-9
C2017-907518-7

Map by Mary Rostad
Jacket design by Michael Solomon
Jacket photographs by Egor Ukoloff, *Sun Dogs over Calgary*; and Audrey Scott /
UncorneredMarket.com, *Friendly Face at the Gondar Market — Ethiopia*

Groundwood Books is committed to protecting our natural environment. As part of our
efforts, the interior of this book is printed on paper that contains 100% post-consumer
recycled fibers, is acid-free and is processed chlorine-free.

Printed and bound in Canada

With gratitude to my cultural reader Kalkidan Getaneh, for her support and assurance that I
got things right, and to Lila Balisky, who provided comments on an early draft.

MIX
Paper from
responsible sources
FSC® C016245

To those who know what it is to be alone and afraid.

When the author and I began work on this story, I was hurt, confused, and didn't understand what had happened to me or why. I was angry, but I didn't know why I was angry and I didn't know where to direct it — my country, my family, the set of circumstances that caused me to flee Ethiopia, or a combination of all three. My underlying anxiety was senseless but I couldn't let it go.

Sharing my story and watching it develop as a work of fiction helped me see my past in a different context. This perspective has changed my heart and my mind and brought me peace.

ተስፋዬ

— *Tesfaye*

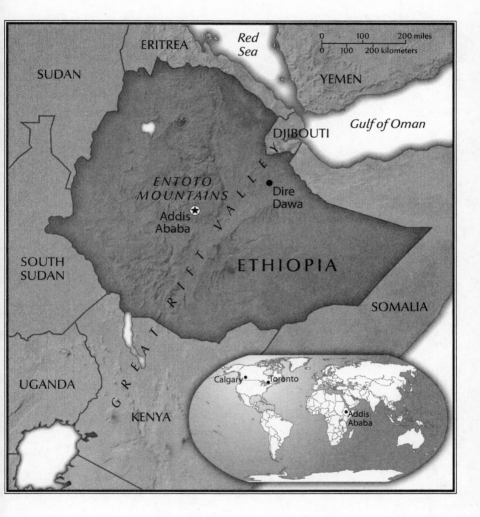

Prologue

"He cannot stay here!"

I jolted to sitting. Blind darkness.

Muscles tensed, breath stopped. Heart bashing through my chest.

Listening. Ready.

Ready for what? No moving shapes. No threat of sneaking sound.

Cold silence.

An empty, black cavern.

A dream, then. A nightmare of being alone.

Just a dream. Rest now. Go back to sleep.

I filled my lungs to capacity, let the air trickle from them like a small leak from a bicycle tire and patted beside me, feeling for Ishi.

A wall of soft fabric, warm from my body. No brother. Where was he?

"He has nowhere to go. He has no one." A man's voice, clear above the freezing room.

"Pfft. You know nothing about him. What were you thinking? Bringing him here?"

"I had to! He was alone. His face covered with blood." His voice, familiar. A name stitched. Ahmed.

13

I was a cornered rat, ears straining, eyes scanning the darkness, ready to bolt. But which way? How to get out?

Movement above. Shuffling feet. The creaking of wood.

"What if the authorities find out?"

"They will not. They know nothing of him."

"What if he is a spy? What if he has come to report on us?"

There must be a door. How had I been brought in?

"Don't be a donkey, you stupid woman. He is a kid. Not a spy."

"How can you be so sure? Informers come in all shapes and in all sizes. And the blood on him. What of that?"

"We have nothing to hide."

"Nothing to hide. Nothing to hide," she parroted. "We are hiding him, aren't we? He cannot stay here!"

There must be a way out. There was always a way out.

My jaw vibrated. Back teeth clattering. It was too cold to think. I drew up my legs and huddled into the furry covering, pulling it tight around my shoulders.

An object skidded above the ceiling. "I'll take him with me to my work. He will come here only to sleep," *the man said.*

"What about my sister? Do you ever think of her?"

The smells of fresh paint and disinfectant. Everything clean. Everything new.

"He will ruin our chances. Ruin everything!"

How dare she speak to him in that tone? Would he hit her?

Thumping overhead, but not violence. The running of small feet. Squeals of children not yet in school, the type of children Gashe liked.

I was below the ground, like a man already dead. But it was a room with a rug below my feet and a comfortable sofa.

There had been stairs going down. I needed to find them.

"And the stink of him," *the woman said.*

"Maybe he is someone. Maybe he can help us."

"Pfft. Now who is the donkey?"

14

I dragged my hand just above the floor. The backpack was still there.

A door opened. A rectangle of daylight. Ahmed stood in silhouette. The stairs now visible. A blinding light strobed as I strained in the glare to hold open my eyes. I snatched the pack and stood tall on the nubby carpet, shoulders back like a warrior. The warm covering slid in a cascade behind me.

"Ah," said Ahmed, coming down the stairs. "I frightened you. Do not fear. You are well?"

"Yes. I am well." The polite response was automatic, even when it was not true. I watched Ahmed and eyed the escape route. If he tried anything, I would stomp on his bare foot. Then, run.

"Good. Good. You will come now," he said. "Eat with my family." Ahmed was wearing a pale blue shirt, buttons down the front, a circle of grease the size of a coin near the hem. His name was sewn over his heart.

This stranger laid his hand on my shoulder and pulled me close, like a brother. He guided me to the stairs.

"You will come with me to work. Until I can think of something," he said.

He showed me the toilet that flushed, pushed the single knob toward the mirror to make water flow.

"Hot," he said, pushing it left. "Cold." He pushed it to the right. "These towels, here. Soap. Everything you need."

I noticed the vessel shaped with a spout, like a small container to water flowers.

Muslim.

I

Addis Ababa, Ethiopia
1991

1

The glow of the melting sun stained the clouds that hung low over the Entoto Mountains, turning all that was familiar into dark silhouette: the gates of the compound with their sharp points of wrought iron, the tall arms of the eucalyptus trees in the garden. Even the chickens looked different in the evening, like demons that moved their heads back and forth on a string.

The guards shouted to each other and rushed to pull the gates inward. Gashe's navy blue Peugeot rolled in. He'd arrived safely, home before curfew, when the gates would be chained and the Special Police would prowl. Night was a dangerous time, full of the unknown. People disappeared after dark, but inside the gates, Ishi and I were safe to race the chickens.

"Go, Chicken Little. Go!" I yelled. My chicken was the best and she was winning. I jumped up and down to encourage her, then crouched to show her the juicy slugs I had collected for her prize. I would win this race and my brother would lose. My belly would be full this night. I would get his portion, plus my own.

"Come. Come," Ishi said, breaking the rules and going behind the chicken to flap frantically at the bird that could not fly. His chicken sat, fluffed her tail feathers and nestled in the dirt.

"I win! I win!" I yelled. I fed Chicken Little the fat worms one by one and patted the soft feathers of her head. Ishi yelled, too.

"No! I win! I win!" he screamed, moving his chicken and lifting a still-warm egg. He held it in the air like the prize it was. "Tonight, I will have this egg for my supper!"

He twirled in a big circle, holding up the chicken's gift as Gashe drove his car into the garden.

Our father did not wave or nod as he moved through our game. He did not toot his horn or notice the prized egg, laid at such an unusual time. He pulled to the side of the house and parked in his line of fancy cars and the ugly pickup he used to drive us to school. We looked his way when he cut the engine, to see if he might be carrying a sack heavy with mangoes or papayas, but today his hands were empty. Ishi and I disappeared like cockroaches into the far reaches of the house. To be seen by Gashe was to invite a reprimand or a slap. We were too old for Gashe now that we spent our days in school, too old to swarm his car in the hope of the first piece of fruit, too old to hold his hand as he wandered through the garden bending to smell flowers and watering already wet plants.

But we were not so old that we had forgotten the feel of his embrace as he laughed and held us close.

Ishi and I hid in the top of the house, in the space with bare rafters where you could see stars through the tin roof at night if they lined up just right. The stars had not come yet and so we waited in this secret room where our cousins from the country would hide and lie quiet when the soldiers came to make them join the army. It was a good place to hide. The soldiers had never found this room.

We rolled on the floor covered in a fine layer of silt and fought for the best place to see the sky, to be the first to see the evening star when it poked its way through the darkness.

"It will be a good night to watch stars," Ishi said. "No moon."

"No moon *yet*," I said. "The moon will rise as big and round as Etheye's belly before another baby comes. And the clouds. Do you not see all the clouds?" I lay close beside my brother. The two of us peered through the biggest hole worn by rain and hail. It was the largest, but still it was only the size of a coin, just big enough to glimpse moon and stars if you moved just right, and if your brother did not get his big head in the way.

"Watch and wait," said Ishi. He stretched full length on his back and folded his arms beneath his head. "Remember, I am the smartest. I am the boy with the egg."

My stomach called at the mention of food. I hoped this night it was three-burn injera with generous amounts of wat, and that Gashe was not so hungry, and that he did not have guests. We listened, as we always did, for the booming sound of Gashe's voice, or the scuttle of servants sent to seek us.

Pulsing light filled the cloud. The *whap-whap-whap* of rotors. The vibration shook our bodies. The helicopter cruised low, the belly of it just visible through the tin roof. It felt as if an earthquake had shaken the world.

"It's on top of us!" I jumped to my feet.

"It's going to land in the garden!" Ishi yelled. We dashed from the secret room, racing to be the first down the cement steps, to be the first to see.

Rat-a-tatt-tatt-tatt. Machine guns. Rapid fire. *Rat-a-tatt-tatt-tatt. Rat-a-tatt-tatt-tatt.*

From the street, maybe? From the top of a compound wall? Whose house? Whose house this time?

Banging oil drums in the street. Rumbling. Motors. *Rat-a-tatt-tatt-tatt*. Loud voices. Commands barked. Screaming from the street. Screaming in our house. Our sisters' high-pitched wails. Etheye calling the little ones to her.

Ishi and I froze in the room where we slept at the bottom of the stairs. He ran to the window, standing on his toes to peer into the dusk, and I followed, our heads as close together as Siamese twins. There was no movement in the garden, just the sounds behind the thick wall that kept us safe. *Rat-a-tatt-tatt-tatt*.

"Can bullets go through walls?" Ishi asked.

"I don't think so," I said. "They're cement. Thick cement."

We moved to the middle of the room just in case.

"Here!" I tugged the edge of a mattress. We flopped it against the window, the tall side nearly to the ceiling. We dragged another and another, until all of the mattresses covered the glass.

Rat-a-tatt-tatt-tatt. Rat-a-tatt-tatt-tatt. The squeal of air released from a balloon. We fell flat on our stomachs like soldiers in a movie.

Boom! A bomb exploded. Its echo traveled from cement wall to cement wall.

Close. The sounds were close.

"What's happening?" asked Ishi.

"I don't know. Maybe someone was on the street past curfew," I said.

"Must be a lot of people," he said.

We wriggled like snakes across the floor, staying low. The groaning now a roar. Heavy machinery crawled on the street. Inside, the warmth of coffee beans roasting, the sound of girls whimpering. We edged the hallway. Another explosion. This one in the distance.

"I want to see," said Ishi.

We slid beneath the layers of curtains, hoping to see what made this noise. We saw only a flock of startled birds through the window grilles.

The window vibrated. We dropped low. The machine guns again. Commands shouted. We inched our eyes above the sill, just enough so that we could see. The clouds shifted to reveal the moon's light. Soldiers with machine guns stood atop our wall.

The guns were not at the house of a neighbor. The guns had come here.

We were surrounded. Guns pointed at our house.

The gate to our compound swung open.

A woman and two men with wild bushy hair held AK-47s, arms extended, slightly bent, gun tips pointed straight ahead. They wore loose ragged clothing the color of dirt, and short pants. Strings of bullets draped an English *X* across their bodies.

"Revolutionaries," whispered Ishi. My mouth fell open in silence. We were as still as mice that smell a hungry cat.

The leader marched across the garden where we played football. The others — the man and the woman — were behind him, turned with their backs to the leader, swiveling from side to side, scanning the yard, the roof, looking for someone to kill. The leader leapt to the veranda. *Bang! Bang, bang. Bang!* He drove the butt of his gun against the front door. Etheye screamed. Through the thin curtain we saw her hands fly to her face. My sisters and my female cousins howled in terror.

"Silence!" Gashe commanded. Our eyes went to him. He stood tall and walked to the door. His gabi swirled like the robe of a king.

Bang! The rifle butt slammed the door again. The intricate cross above the door that had come the long way from Lalibela shattered on the floor.

"*Kafatew!* Open or we shoot!" yelled the man.

I held tight to Ishi's hand. His eyes were as big as the eggs of a chicken.

Gashe clicked the locks one by one. The soldier kicked the door with the sole of his bare foot. The heavy wood crashed against the wall. The leader pushed past Gashe, followed closely by the other two. The rebel spoke rapidly in Tigrigna. I did not know the words, but Gashe listened. His face was serious as he concentrated on the meaning. Gashe nodded.

What did he want? Why was Gashe not killed instantly? This soldier, this rebel, wanted to talk? Yet his words were abrupt. Harsh commands. Not the way people spoke to Gashe.

Gashe scrunched his forehead. The man told a long list of names, some of which I knew, the names of Gashe's father and his father's father. How did he know this?

This man was a relative? This dark man with hair as big as a lion? This man with a machine gun and no shoes?

A smile melted Gashe's worry. He nodded. Once, slowly. The man, the woman and the other soldier relaxed their weapons. Gashe approached the man and kissed him on the cheeks — once, twice, three times.

"Welcome," he said. "You have arrived."

I could not believe this trick my eyes played. Revolution-aries in our house?

Gashe's voice thundered, giving commands to Etheye to make more food. The voice of Etheye ordered servants to work and called to her daughters. Gashe welcomed the filthy people into the best room, asked them to sit on the fine upholstered furniture. Servants scurried to bring basins of water to clean the soldiers' feet. The girls brought small bowls of peanuts and popcorn. Etheye brought the mukecha and zenezena to grind the coffee beans she had been roasting for Gashe's meal. The soldiers watched her light a stick of frankincense and waited silently for the thin trail of smoke to weave toward the ceiling.

I nudged Ishi's arm and nodded at the front door that no one had thought to close. We slipped as smooth and silent as shadows through the garden to the gate. Our guards were gone.

There were four round holes in the pillars of the gate, all lined up, one on top of each other. They were perfect spy holes where we'd sometimes watch beggars fight over the old clothing and rubber tires Gashe left in the street. Ishi took the lowest hole. I took the one above. A tank crawled in front of us, churning the pavement to mush. There were soldiers everywhere in the street, dressed in rags and the spongy Afros that bred lice. Some of the soldiers were women, but they looked as angry as men. They barked orders and moved fast. Dogs howled. The oily black stink of diesel thickened the air. Yelling. Gunshots with bullets traced in red. Fumes of cigarettes mixed with metal. The static of walkie-talkies. Angry faces. The street was alive.

"Tesfaye! Ishi!" Gashe's voice cut through the noise.

We dashed toward the house, though we knew we would be beaten for being outside after dark. We stood before him, hands clasped behind our backs. We braced for the slap, the fierce words. We waited for Gashe to impress the visitors with the obedience of his sons.

The smell of boiling coffee seeped through the air. My stomach shrieked now with hunger, though I knew we would not eat until this cousin and his friends had filled their bellies. Or perhaps this night we would not eat at all. Perhaps the guests would even get Ishi's egg.

Gashe ignored us. He continued to talk with the soldiers, grinning at them as if they were invited guests, as if they were business partners he sought to impress, as if they had not forced their way into our house with guns raised.

The man who was my father's cousin leaned forward on the sofa, elbows resting on his knees, machine gun propped near his leg. The woman was beside him, drawing a dagger beneath her fingernails to clean them. The other soldier was on the floor, head bent, dreadlocks covering his face.

But it was the woman who took my eye. She was tough and beautiful. The darkness of her skin gleamed like polished mahogany. Her hair was as wide as a doorway, the soft shape of her body so clear beneath the bands of bullets that crossed her chest, and when she spoke, I heard not words, but music.

Who was this woman who sat with the men? Who spoke as an equal? Who was this woman who did not serve men?

The cousin pointed one finger. "You-*pse*," he said, then crooked his forefinger toward himself that I should come.

Gashe nodded. I stood before the man, eyes cast down, studying the cracks on his heels and the dirt they still carried. He tilted my face in his hands. Kissed me on both cheeks.

"This one," he said. He gestured with his muscled arm, invited me to sit between him and the beautiful woman, invited me to sit with him in a place of honor.

"Ishi. Go," Gashe said.

My brother ran from the room, I guessed to the secret place above the ceiling, to press his ear against the floor and listen.

2

The rebel leader took me away that night. It was not possible to sleep away from my brothers, in the big room with the mattress raised above the floor and the heavy fringed drapes above my head, even though Gashe's cousin lay beside me, smoothed his hand over my hair and whispered soft words into my ear. I kept my eyes wide through the long night to remember every detail to tell Ishi, about how the room flashed as bright as day from explosions, how the chandelier swung to and fro, making the tinkle of a thousand bells, and the snorting noises the stinky cousin made as he slept.

I perched on his shoulders the next day, the way Gashe used to carry me when I was small. He held my legs tight, even though I curled my feet around the back of his ribs. He swayed back and forth, pretending to be an elephant as we sauntered through the rooms where the Emperor, Haile Selassie, once lived.

Now I was the king and this was my castle.

"Elephant! Down!" I said. He bent his knees slowly and lowered me to the floor. I clambered to the bowl with kolo and grabbed some in my fist. I climbed back onto the shoulders of my skinny elephant with spongy hair.

"Elephant! Up!" I said. He trumpeted and moved his arm before his face as if it were a trunk. The rooms we passed were bigger than our house, bigger than six of our houses all put together, and the pillars so tall a real elephant could pass through.

"You want a snack, Elephant?" I asked.

The head and the trunk moved up and down. It felt like the movement of a ship on waves. I poked bits of roasted grain into his mouth as we passed through a secret tunnel.

The Emperor's throne sat high at one end of the room. Carpets of red and gold littered the floor. There was a high table for dozens of important guests, the top covered with papers and maps and green bits of khat. In the middle was a radio bigger even than Gashe's, the sound on low. Around the table were chairs with curved legs and seats so wide that they would fit the fattest person in the world. But the soldiers in the room were as thin as my elephant who took me from his shoulders and nestled me beside him on the soft blue velvet. I swung my legs as if I was on the branch of a tree and ran my hands along the edge. I liked how the fabric changed from dark to light as I passed my fingers across it, then from light to dark.

My elephant, whose real name was Isaias, talked and talked in a language I did not know. He pushed away my hand when I tickled him behind the ear, but he let me lean against him to watch the small rainbows dance on the walls when sunlight kissed the teardrops of the chandelier that was bigger, even, than me.

I licked the last of the kolo from my palm and chewed it slowly, sucking at the spice and letting the grain roll over my back teeth before I swallowed.

"Can we go now?" I whispered.

My elephant shook his head and cupped his hand over my mouth. I wriggled from the chair to an empty one near him. I was on a ship. I pulled my legs close to my chest. Wild crocodiles with teeth like knives snapped at my legs, trying to sever my feet and make me a street beggar. My ship passed through strange lands where everything was as huge as the Fee Fi Fo Fum giant who threatened to eat boys. With a chair so big, had the Emperor been a giant? Did he steal golden eggs? Did he dine on boys?

No, silly, I reminded myself. He ate injera and wat that smelled of curry. Remember the food left in the great hall? And he had so much clothing that he left it scattered among the potted palms and cement benches in the garden. Or maybe, he had so many children that he dressed them all in the same dull-colored clothes so they would not fight over who got the best shirt. And maybe, to tell them apart, he put on tassels and badges. But where were they, and why had they taken off their clothes? Were the children hiding nearby, waiting to play with me? Or were they sleeping now in the shade of the garden like the men I had seen in the street?

Isaias stood. He crossed his forearms, then flung them open.

"Silence!" he commanded. He leaned to the radio and turned up the volume. The voices inside the box had strange accents, speaking English as if they had clothespins pinching their noses. It was a channel Gashe liked. The BBC.

"The rebels began pushing into the suburbs —"

"Silence!" Isaias screamed again. This time, no one made a sound.

"Rebel tanks moved up to attack the presidential palace and resistance did not last long. The rebels may look a mess, but they've beaten ..."

"Rebels!" shouted Isaias. His voice was angry. "They call us rebels when we save the country from a communist dictator," he said. He made a *pse* sound with every word he spoke in Amharic that made laughter burble inside of me. I bit my lip hard, pressed my hand against my mouth and looked away. Surely he would slap me if I laughed.

The hole between the arm of the chair and the seat was a secret passage. I slid through headfirst, then leapt like a frog across the room to the Emperor's chair. It was like a small room made all of wood with a delicate carved crown sticking from the top. The red cushioned seat was big enough for all of my brothers, and maybe some sisters, to sit on all at once.

My legs stuck out straight ahead on the seat. It was like being God on a cloud high above everyone, where I could see the entire hall. Giant posters of Mengistu, the boss of everyone, lay curled and ripped near the wall. All that remained, tilted on the wall, was a picture of his raised fist. Yellow banners with the red star, the hammer and sickle looked as if they had been trampled by a herd of goats.

I picked up a flag striped with green, yellow and red. It had blue lines in the pattern of a circle, and a yellow star in a red circle. What I liked best was the head of the roaring lion. I wrapped it around me like a cape and ran through the great hall, letting it flutter after me as if I had just won the World Cup for my country.

Isaias pulled the flag from my grip. "No-*pse*!" he said in Amharic. "Not-*pse* this-*pse*! Never-*pse* this-*pse*!" He ripped the flag from my hands, crumpled it and threw it to the floor.

"I want to go home," I said. My eyes floated with tears.

His wife, with the mahogany skin and the voice of a stream bubbling over rocks, lifted me.

"He is just a child," Sabba said. "Leave him!" I clung to

her as if I was a monkey and not a boy already old enough for school.

Isaias shouted. Some of the men around the table walked away with him. All of them had the white flecks on their legs that meant their mothers needed to wipe Vaseline over their skin.

"I want to go home," I repeated. At home was Etheye and brothers to play with.

"Not yet," Sabba said. She set me to my feet but kept hold of my hand. "We have things we must do."

My eyes squinted to slits when we followed Isaias through the giant doors studded with bolts and metal points in the shape of pyramids. The sun boiled the air into little ripples that I could see when I looked closely, just above the concrete. I could smell smoke, but I saw no fires.

Revolutionary soldiers were still there, dressed in rags, squatted with their guns or hugging their weapons as they slept. Isaias spoke to one resting in the shade, in the tone of Gashe when he wanted no questions asked. The soldier sprinted away.

A tank like an enormous turtle with a long nose groaned toward us and stopped. Its gun was pointed to the front, and the head of a man stuck from the top. Isaias scrambled inside. I wanted to be him. Imagine, inside a tank!

He popped out his head and shoulders and waved that I should come. I stretched my leg to the ledge above the track. Sabba pushed me forward when it seemed I would slip on the oily, dirt-covered steel. The metal was warm on my skin when I crawled to the opening to grasp Isaias's outstretched hand, but not so hot that it burned.

The inside was cramped with Isaias and the driver, but I saw circular dials, like the ones in a car but many more, and binoculars to look through, and tiny rectangular windows.

"You see? You like this?" he asked.

"Yes!" I would like it even better if he would let me drive it with the lid closed and at top speed.

Isaias sat me on the edge of the opening and held me around the waist when the tank nudged forward.

We shunted in a long line of tanks and army trucks loaded with soldiers lifting their guns high. People streamed through the streets coming to the heart of Addis as if it was the Celebration of the True Cross. But this number was maybe greater still. People cheered and danced and waved their arms. The joyful noise grew louder as we approached.

"Freedom! You are liberated!" Isaias called through a bull-horn. His words ricocheted off cement walls.

"Freedom-*pse*! Liberated-*pse*!" came back the echoes.

There were drums and loud singing. People held their two fingers up in the sign for peace, while others swayed flags back and forth from balconies.

"Freedom! Freedom!" the people in the streets chanted. They punched the air with their fists. "Freedom! Freedom!"

The bells of the cathedral clanged. The stadium rippled. It was as if all the world was in the streets of Addis, and everyone had gone crazy with happiness. The giant statue of Lenin lay on the ground, as if he had suddenly become tired and fallen onto his side to rest. People crawled all over his head and shoulder and arm. A man standing on Lenin's right ear pumped both arms in the air, causing the flag he held to ruffle like a sheet on a clothesline.

I hoped that Ishi would see me waving my arm on the top of the tank, and that he would be just a little bit jealous.

◆

A few days later, I was at home chasing the football with my best brother.

"I was on top of a tank! I saw everything inside!" I told Ishi.
"Don't tell lies," he said.

"It is the truth! Why would I lie about such a thing?"

Ishi stole the ball from between my feet and kicked it between the two rocks we used to mark the goal.

"Yes!" he said. He threw his arms in the air. Fiyeli bounded across the garden, crushing flowers and kicking up her hooves. A gardener shook his head, then picked up the clods of grass and pressed them back into the ground.

"Look out!" I yelled, but my yell was too late. The goat collided with Ishi and knocked my brother to the ground. Fiyeli flapped her long quick tongue and licked Ishi's forehead, nearly goring me with her stubby horns.

"Get off, Fiyeli! Go!" Ishi pushed on the animal's neck, but the more he struggled, the more the goat wanted to taste his salty sweat. I shoved from the side. Fiyeli took a step back but kept the wide stance of a defender. Ishi rolled away and scooped up our lumpy ball.

The goat stuck out her tongue and screamed, *"Aw! Aw-lubba-lubba!"*

The ball sailed in a low arc when Ishi kicked it. We raced to get it, Fiyeli close on our heels. I snatched the ball with the bottom of my foot. I was Diego Maradona, shifting the ball from side to side and keeping it from my brother.

"You saw me, didn't you? I was the only boy." I dodged the chickens as if they were opponents while Ishi jogged beside me, waiting for a steal. I jumped over the pile of black berries Fiyeli had dropped from her bum.

"I was too busy. And besides, there were so many tanks, it was boring."

I knew he was lying. Tanks and soldiers and guns were never boring. I took a shot at the goal, but the ball curled the wrong way. Ishi took control of it before Fiyeli could.

"There were more soldiers here at this house than I have fingers. More than I have fingers and toes," he said.

"No, there weren't. They were all in the parade, on top of the tanks and in the backs of trucks."

"No, they were here. They slept in our secret room." He turned his back to me to protect the ball. I swiveled my foot around him but wasn't able to get my toes on it. "You should have seen all the food Etheye made. I have never seen so much. Goats and sheep and chickens all at once!" I snatched the ball and moved closer to the goal.

"Well, there's lots of food at the palace, too. Chocolate, even! And licorice wrapped in special paper."

"Etheye made kolo," Ishi said.

"I had kolo, too. I fed some to my elephant."

"Elephants now? You shouldn't tell such lies about the palace or about tanks," he said. "No one will believe you."

"The elephant wasn't a real elephant. It was Isaias." My brother had the ball. He pulled back his leg to punt it with the top of his foot, but I stole it away.

"But I did sit on the Emperor's chair," I said.

"Liar. Everyone knows only the Emperor can sit on the Emperor's chair," he said. "Or maybe Mengistu could. That was his name? After the Emperor went away?"

"But there is no Emperor!" I practiced El Diego's footwork to keep the ball from my brother. "And Mengistu is gone and so are his bad friends. Even their pictures." My kick was true. The ball flew through the invisible net and landed in a bed of flowers. I twirled in a victory dance while Ishi fetched the ball. I could tell he still thought I was lying.

He kicked so hard the ball went to the other end of the garden. The race was on, my brother in the lead. I did not have time to call out. Ishi did not see what I saw. He stepped in Fiyeli's warm poo, slid and crash-landed. He was on the ground, dazed and looking at the sky. I grasped his hand and pulled him back to the game.

"The chair was empty," I explained, "and when no one was looking, I climbed on it. It is made of the softest velvet in the whole world, and it is as wide as a bed. My feet reached only to the edge."

I fetched the ball and nudged it to Ishi to make up for the black smear on his back. He loped with the ball and I followed. Fiyeli sauntered toward us, moving a tangled length of vines back and forth between her soft lips. Gash Hamdala shook his fist at the goat, a rope draped from his other hand. The gardener was not so fond of Fiyeli.

"There were real sweets?" Ishi glanced at me. I snatched the ball and pressed my foot on top to guard it. I drew a crumpled wrapper from my pocket. It was black with white writing.

"See?"

"I want to go to the palace, too," he said. Ishi liked licorice the way I liked chocolate.

I hit the ball with the inside of my foot. Ishi intercepted it.

"We could play football in the great hall!" I said. "No one would even care."

"Could we ride in a tank to get there?"

"Maybe," I said. I kept my back to Ishi and shunted the ball from foot to foot so he couldn't get it. "I could ask Isaias. He is mostly kind, and he knows Amharic, but he speaks in a strange way, like a snake."

"Gashe says he is a great man. Very powerful."

I passed the ball. "How do you know? Gashe would not tell you."

"I have ears, stupid. Two of them. One on each side." He headed toward the goal.

"And Gashe said he is a great man?"

Ishi kicked. Scored again, then turned to me. "He said he will protect us. Because of you."

"Because of me?"

"Yes, he said you have brought honor to the family." Ishi rolled the ball in circles beneath his foot.

"But I have done nothing but play," I said. "And eat sweets."

I shrugged my shoulders and Ishi shrugged his.

3

Gashe did not see us when we snuck past him. His eyes were focused on the red light of the radio as he turned the dial to move between stations, the Voice of America and Deutsche Welle. He tilted his head to the speaker as he worked through the static to bring in the sounds of the BBC for the news broadcast: "Ethiopian Radio says President Mengistu has fled to Zimbabwe. He left his government hard-pressed by rebel forces who advanced on the capital, Addis Ababa, one week ago," the announcer said.

Our older brother, Tezze, put his finger to his lips and waved for us to follow him. We moved quickly from the room where we slept, on our toes, careful not to disturb Etheye from her rapid chopping of vegetables. We made it to the glory of outside without being told to wash windows or Fiyeli.

"Some of the soldiers," whispered Tezze. "They are selling their guns. On the street."

"I wish we had money," said Ishi. He twisted his foot into the soft mud and lifted it slowly, letting it squelch as it sucked at his toes. His eyes grew big and round. "Maybe we could buy one from the soldiers staying here. They look like poor men."

"We are poor men ourselves," said Tezze. "We don't have money."

"What would you do with an AK-47?" I asked. I wiggled my toes, letting the muck squeeze into the space between them, then clenched my toes opened and closed rapidly, trying to squirt the mud into the air.

"It is better than an ordinary rifle. You can shoot while the bad guys are moving, and you can shoot more than one at a time," said Ishi.

"Do you see any bad guys around here?" I extended my hands, palms up. "I think we are safe. That's what Isaias's soldiers are for."

"How much would it even cost?" asked Tezze. I shrugged.

"How do you even get money?" asked Ishi.

Tezze and I both lifted our shoulders and let them drop. "Gashe gets it. In those big sacks he brings."

"I still need an AK. I'd use it to protect you," Ishi said. "You would never have to go to the palace again. You could stay here forever." He held his arms like a rifle and pivoted from side to side. *"Rat-a-tatt-tatt,"* he said, using his finger to shoot at a pigeon.

"We have bigger problems than that," said Tezze. He picked up the ratty football and shoved the rags back in. Ishi and I pulled up some grass and stuffed that in, too, to make it rounder. "If we kick this, it is going to fall apart even worse."

"We could just use a rock," said Ishi. He picked up a curved stone about half as big as a football.

"Too heavy. And think of the bruises," said Tezze.

"What if we tell the girls we want to play house, and make them sew it," I said.

"They will never believe it," said Tezze.

Our heads turned as one to the sounds of commotion on the street. We ran to the gates to spy through the holes.

Hundreds of people were walking all together and chanting, "One Ethiopia! One Ethiopia!"

"What's happening?" I asked.

"I don't know. We need to see better," said Tezze. "Come on!"

Ishi climbed on Tezze's shoulders and onto the wooden beam that ran near the top of the wall that overlooked the street. I followed. Tezze grabbed the steel hook where animals were slaughtered and swung up beside us. The three of us watched the crowd grow bigger and bigger, as if it was pulling everyone up from the streets.

"They look mad," I said. "Not like the day of the parade at all."

"What does your friend Isaias say of this?" asked Tezze.

"I don't know. He's in London. To talk peace, he said."

"This does not look like peace," said Ishi.

"Come on, let's go." Tezze stretched his leg to the top of the wall.

"Into the street? Gashe will kill us if he finds out," I said. I felt dizzy so high above the ground with nothing to hold. And Gashe, when he was angry? Who knew what he would do? It would be better to stay safe.

"So, don't tell him." Tezze leapt from the wall and disappeared.

"We can't let him go alone," said Ishi. He stepped cautiously along the beam to where it joined the wall just above the guard house. "Come on!"

It was a long way down, but I couldn't let my brothers see my fear. I landed upright on the pavement, but my shins ached as if someone had smashed them with a stick.

"We should have gone back for shoes," I said.

"No time," said Tezze. "They have already moved on. Hold hands. And hurry!"

We ran to catch up with the rolling mass of people.

More and more people joined as we flowed up the hill, as hot and steamy and airless as lava going backwards. Even the groups of men who stood in small circles all day arguing about politics and football left their favorite spots on the street to join the pressing rush.

"We should go back," I said. The pavement burned my feet, and we were getting too far from home. The beating from our older sisters would be fierce.

In the distance I saw the two cement lions that topped the Imperial Palace where Isaias liked to talk to his friends.

"It's too far. If we go back now, no one will know," I shouted. I dragged on Ishi's arm, pulling him toward home. But Tezze's pull was stronger.

Car and truck horns honked. The drivers shouted and waved their fists out side windows. There were so many people flooding the streets that the cars were forced to stop. I saw a driver push open his door, leave his car and join the mob.

"One Ethiopia! Keep Eritrea!" People yelled and shook their raised fists as they moved up the hill. Tanks rolled in from the sides.

"We shouldn't be here. Let's go," I said. The crowd moved us farther and farther from home. I yanked hard on Ishi's hand and leaned back like an anchor. If he came, Tezze would have to come, too.

"One country. One nation. One Ethiopia!"

"I don't know what to do!" yelled Ishi. He looked like a stick man being pulled in opposite directions. Tezze was solid. His eyes were huge when he turned to me.

"Look at the tanks!" he said. "Can you believe how many different kinds?" Belching clouds of black diesel, the machines crawled toward the crowd, the churning sound of them drowned by the protestors. The greasy tanks coated in dirt were covered with soldiers holding weapons.

"We have to go!" I said. Ishi dragged on Tezze's one arm, and I on the other, but our brother didn't budge.

"I'm scared," I yelled.

"Me, too," said Ishi.

"Don't be such babies," said Tezze. "You need your —"

Rat-a-tatt-tatt. Rat-a-tatt-tatt.

Insane screaming. People swirled all around us, pushing every which way. I glanced at the soldiers. Their weapons were pointed upward. They weren't shooting at the crowd, just firing warning shots. The pack pushed backward, pressing on us, then swelled forward, taking us with it.

"Now! We must go!" I yelled into Tezze's face. Should I slap him? Shake him the way our older sisters sometimes shook us?

Ishi kicked him in the bum, so hard that Tezze stumbled forward. We used the momentum to change direction and to pull him toward home. Running and pushing, we ran straight into the face of another crowd, so thick it blotted out everything but the tallest buildings. People covered the pavement and the neat cut bricks. They trampled the grass and crushed the purple flowers. They yelled and raised their fists.

"One Ethiopia!" they screamed. "One Ethiopia!"

Above the mob, the United States flag flapped on a tall pole beside the Ethiopian one.

The United States flag? There was only one flag in Addis with the stars and stripes of America. The American embassy. It couldn't be.

I was good with directions. I looked for landmarks. I watched the position of the sun the way Ababa had taught me. I never got lost.

But I had led my brothers entirely in the wrong direction — north, instead of south.

More tanks appeared. More soldiers. *Rat-a-tatt-tatt. Rat-a-tatt-tatt.* More shots in the air. We couldn't get through. The crowd surged closer to the soldiers and engulfed us.

"One Ethiopia!" they screamed. "We will not be ruled by scum like you." We were near enough to see men spit toward the soldiers. "You are worthless," they said, and curled their lips in disgust. The men dug up paving stones and hurled them at the soldiers.

It made no sense. Weren't the soldiers the good guys? *Rat-a-tatt-tatt.* Advancing tanks moaned and spat pavement. Exhaust choked off my breath. A hail of bricks and stones landed on the tanks. A soldier toppled. Another dropped his gun and grabbed his shoulder. The crowd cheered.

Rat-a-tatt-tatt. Rat-a-tatt-tatt. Rat-a-tatt-tatt. Rat-a-tatt-tatt. All around us. More shots.

This time, not in the air.

The mob screamed and pulled away in all directions at once, the way water will when it meets a drop of oil.

The shooting stopped and there was silence.

Then gradually, as if we were in a slow-motion movie, the crowd retreated, still quiet, all eyes on the soldiers with machine guns pointed again to the sky. People dragged the bleeding protesters behind them, the limp bodies trailing long dark streaks on the pavement.

My hands, my arms, my legs trembled beyond control, as if they didn't belong to me. Tears washed my face. Everything was all wrong. I ran and squirmed and shoved between people, not caring if I stepped on feet or knocked people off balance. I ran without looking back.

I had to get home. To safety.

I collapsed like a heap of rags outside our gate, curled into a ball and rocked back and forth, boiling hot, then shivering, crying and howling until my throat ached itself raw.

Where were Ishi and Tezze? I should have looked for them. Why didn't I wait? How could I be so selfish?

A guard carried me like a baby inside the cramped gate house. My blistered feet bled and my heart felt as if it might stop beating. I had left my brothers who could not run as fast or as far as I could. How could I have left Ishi, who I loved as much as Etheye, and who wanted to buy a gun to protect me?

"What is going on? Why were you outside?" the guard demanded. He and the other guard leaned close to me. Their breath was hot and smelled of garlic.

"Don't tell Gashe," I pleaded. "Don't tell."

I was afraid of what Gashe would do to me, but even more, I was afraid of what he would do to Etheye. He would hold her responsible for what we had done.

The guard's hand stung my face when he hit me, and my tears spilled again, like those of a girl.

"What have you been doing?" he yelled. "What game is this?"

I had no answer. What if my brothers were trampled? What if the soldiers began firing again? Ishi would never have left me, no matter what. Why did I leave him? How could I have done this?

The second slap was worse than the first. And when he shook me until my brain came loose inside my head, I was grateful. It was a just and fateful punishment for my disloyalty.

4

Ishi was a part of me, like an arm or a leg. We were together in everything. We were interchangeable, my brother and me. Our age was the same. We wore the same clothes and played the same games. We ate from the same plate. We slept snuggled together on the same mattress, talking to each other even as we slept.

But we were not twins. I was three weeks older, and we were born of different mothers.

The first time I saw him, Ishi crept slowly from the cab of Gashe's pickup, as if he was afraid.

"Come," Gashe said. He led him by the hand to where my brothers, sisters and I had stopped playing football to stare at him. He hid behind Gashe, but slowly, very slowly, leaned his head and shoulders to the side to peek at us. His eyes, as round and afraid as a lemur's, took up most of his bony face. He gazed all around the garden, at the trees and the grass and the flowers and at us, as if he could not trust his eyes, as if he were in a dream.

He examined us, first as a big group, then with his eyes searching each of ours, from one to the other as if he might run and hide if we moved too quickly. And so we stayed still.

When his eyes found mine, they stopped searching.

"This is Ishi. A cousin. A brother now," Gashe said. He often brought older cousins in the back of his pickup to work as servants and to go to school. But never before someone so much like me.

Ishi was smaller than I was and much skinnier, except for his belly. His stomach was as round as a ripe pumpkin, and I saw the plump button of his belly poking out like a small stubby nose through a gap in the front of his shirt. He was dressed in grubby rags, and I could see his bum through the holes worn in his shorts. He was barefoot like us, but his feet looked hard and tough, as if he had the bottom of sandals glued to his feet.

He looked like a beggar from the street with wild dirty hair and yellowed teeth that did not fall in a straight pattern.

But when our eyes met, they locked and held like two pieces of a jigsaw puzzle.

I took his hand from Gashe's. Ishi's skin was rough, and his fingernails were broken and dirty.

"I am Tesfaye," I said. "Let's play."

It was as if Ishi and I had grown together in the same womb, but he knew nothing of the rules of football. We had to teach him how to score and when to cheer.

I never left his side. I stayed with him even while Etheye cleaned him in the big basin, outside by the water tower. She patted the edge of the tub and told him to climb in.

He shook his head.

"Ayi. Ayi," he said, then scurried behind me, scrunching up his shoulders so he would appear even smaller.

No one liked baths, but even I could tell he needed one.

"It's only a bath," I said. He pointed his arm and his filthy finger straight at Etheye. His big eyeballs looked as if they would pop from his head and roll on the ground.

"Very too much." He spoke Amharic, but he made many mistakes. *"Ayi. Ayi."* He clutched my upper arms to use me as a shield and turned me to face Etheye.

"Come. Come," Etheye said, her voice soft and slow. She trailed her hand back and forth in the water. "It be nice and warm."

Ishi squeezed my arms so tight I thought they would snap. He pulled me a step backwards. Etheye sighed.

"Take off your clothes," she said to me. "Show him about a bath."

The water was silky warm from the heat of the sun. Etheye poured water from a cup onto my head.

"See how nice," she said. I smiled as if it was pleasant, but it wasn't. She had gotten a lot of water in my eyes. I got out to shake myself dry, but still, Ishi would not get in.

"Take his hand," said Etheye. "Both of you, get in together."

"There isn't room," I complained, and whoever heard of two baths in one day? The hardness of Etheye's eyes ordered me to climb in and make room.

He gripped my hands tightly when we sank into the water and didn't let go.

"Only before. Small bits water," Ishi said. "Water for thirsting."

Etheye didn't touch me, but she scrubbed him hard, all over, with lots of soap, until it seemed his skin would wear out. She clipped his nails, and she cut off all of his hair, the way a farmer will shear a sheep. The clothes she brought were the clothes I usually wore. They hung on his body like the garments of a stick man used to scare birds away from coffee cherries.

Dressed in my clothes, with short hair, he looked exactly like me, except smaller. Even our skin was the same clean shade of brown. I showed him how he looked in Gashe's tall mirror. His smile, with all those crooked teeth, told me he thought the same thing, and that it made him happy.

I could not believe my luck, that Gashe had found the missing part of me.

We were lured from our reflections by the scent of roasting spices. Etheye placed the plate of injera topped with diced vegetables and shiro on the floor for us.

"*Bihlahh!*" she said, but I needed no encouragement. I ripped off a large piece, scooped wat and shoved it in my mouth before my sisters came to push us away.

"Take some. Take some," I told Ishi, moving my hand in small circles and gesturing to the round platter piled with food. "Eat! Hurry."

He approached cautiously, though he looked most hungry. He gazed at me, eyes large, the way a boy looks before he will get a beating. He dipped just two fingers in the wat, then scuttled away.

"Take the best parts," I said. "Before the others come." I stuffed my mouth with food, so much that it jammed my throat when I swallowed. I grabbed my neck to hold it together. Surely it would split in two. I coughed, but the knob of food did not move. My eyes filled with tears. I wheezed and rubbed my neck to help it work. But Ishi did not move to grab food or to help me. He sat curled in the corner with his legs pressed to his chest and a look of fright on his face.

I swallowed as a snake will, feeling the lump of food bulge through the pipe to my stomach and land at the bottom with a thump. My throat felt as if it had been scraped with a shovel.

"Come. You must eat," I croaked when my breath returned. Ishi remained still. I scooped dollops of each of the toppings, except for the gomen which I did not like, and scrabbled beside my new brother. I held the food to his mouth and when he opened, I fed him. He ate slowly, rubbing the taste over his lips. I grabbed more food — a whole roll of injera — as my older sisters came in, talking loudly and pushing me away. Although my stomach still rumbled with hunger, I ate nothing more. I fed what I had taken, a bite at a time, to Ishi.

◆

Now, sitting alone before two guards near the gate, I had betrayed him. I had left him in the street with an angry mob, with soldiers and machine guns. I had saved only myself.

The guards argued among themselves, then one slapped me again.

"Speak!" he demanded, but what did I have to say?

The circle of the sun hovered over the edge of the horizon. Etheye would notice her sons were missing if we didn't come to eat, and she would cry with worry and wring her hands, wondering what to do. The guards shoved me from the gatehouse. I hobbled on blistered feet toward the aroma of roasting meat, but the smell made me feel sick.

Meat meant Gashe was here.

I glimpsed the bottoms of Gashe's feet in the room where he and Etheye slept. I knew he knelt in humility, hands pressed together in prayer. My head hung low. I knew how quickly he could change, from penitent sinner to raging bull, like the snapping of fingers. I should tell him what I had done. I should confess.

Egzi-Abeher, save us. Save my brothers. I will do anything.

But I must not disturb Gashe's prayers. The cold floor soothed the torn bottoms of my traitor's feet as I slunk to the room I shared with my brothers.

How would I tell Gashe what I had done? How could I live with such shame?

"There you are! Finally," said Ishi. He slid across the floor and bumped my shoulder with his as soon as I stepped through the doorway of our sleeping room. "We were worried that Gashe was beating you."

"You're here? How?" I could not believe my eyes. Ishi and Tezze here? Safe?

"It was a great idea you had, keeping the guards busy," said Tezze.

"We came right through the gate," said Ishi. "Past where you were talking to the guards and pretending to cry."

"They never saw a thing!" said Tezze.

"You're here? You are really here?" I asked. This was the happiest day of my life.

Etheye noticed the dirt and the cuts on our feet as soon as she saw us.

"What you be doing?" she asked.

"Nothing," I said. She twisted the skin on the inner part of my thigh until I yelped.

"Tell me," she said. She lifted my foot, then Ishi's, then Tezze's, looking at the crust of dirt that was up past our ankles. "This be no dirt of the garden. This be filth of the street."

"It was my fault," said Ishi. Everyone turned to look at him. "The football," he said. "It was broken."

"And so, a broken football slices the feet of my sons?" asked Etheye.

"I said to use a rock," he said. "It was hard and it did not roll well. It was not a good idea."

"Yes, that is true," I agreed. "He did say use a rock." Ishi was brilliant. We were not lying at all.

"And I said it was a poor idea," said Tezze.

"My sons have brains of chickens," said Etheye. She shook her head. "Eat, and then you soak those feet, and I put on coffee grounds."

The oil she put in the water stung like a nest of wasps, but still, it felt good to be all together with six feet shoved into a bucket of water so hot that we had to begin by putting in only our biggest toes. It was easy to believe our lie, that our feet had been cut by kicking rocks, and that we had not heard or seen all of the things we had heard and seen that afternoon. That there were no soldiers, no tanks, no blood.

I looked at Ishi to erase the images. I would never leave my brother again. Not ever. Not for any reason. Even a tank could not drag me from him. They would have to shoot me, and I would have to be all the way dead.

5

I did not recognize the revolutionary Isaias when he returned. Only a single week had passed since the peace talks in London, but it was as if he was a different man. His hair was cut as short as Gashe's, and he wore the dress of a Western businessman — a coat with broad shoulders, lapels down the front and matching pants. His shirt was white, buttoned to the throat, and he wore a blue patterned necktie. At first I thought he was a friend of Gashe who had come to talk politics, or a well-dressed student looking for sponsorship to study overseas.

"Ah, Tesfaye," said Gashe when he saw me. "Come. Come." He beckoned that I should join them.

A roll of khat was on the low table in front of them, and near it a bowl of melted honey. The air smelled of the coffee Etheye poured for them in small cups. Besides Gashe and Isaias were the two elders who gave advice to Gashe on all things large and small. All of them had one cheek swollen with khat.

I stood by the table, not sure what I was supposed to do. Why had I come into the house at just this time? I should be happy to see Isaias, but I wasn't. I dipped my head respectfully to stare at the floor and to hide the ungrateful confusion I felt. Was this well-dressed Isaias here to take me away?

"I am happy to see you," Isaias said. He lifted my chin and looked into my eyes. "I have brought you something. All the way from London."

I hoped the surprise was Nike high-tops. The soles of my sneakers were loose and flapping in a way that made them embarrassing to wear. But such an extravagant gift? Not possible. Not even Gashe could afford Nike. I hoped for chocolate, enough to share.

Isaias lifted a white plastic bag with English writing that was beside his chair. It bulged in a way that suggested it might be Nike sneakers that would make me jump as high as Michael Jordan.

"Come," he said. "For you."

Inside was something better. Smooth and perfectly round. Black and white, stitched with pentagons, and stamped with the Umbro symbol.

A real football! I rubbed my hands all over it, traced the straight lines with my finger and examined the logo. This wasn't a cheap ball made in China. This was a true football, the kind they used in the World Cup.

"You like it?" he asked. His smile spread like sunshine after the rain.

I had no words. I had never received such a gift. I nodded up and down and up and down like an imbecile. My smile would never come off. A football! How soon could I try it? What was expected of me now? How long must I stand there? My hands wanted to drop the ball and my foot ached to kick it. How far would it go? Would it bounce?

"Well, why do you wait?" asked Gashe.

"I may go?"

Gashe smiled, too, a slow gracious smile. He nodded as if he had given the gift himself.

The ball rolled so easily that we had to sprint to keep up with it, and when I kicked it, it flew through the air like a missile, just the way it did on television.

"Does this mean you will have to go away again?" asked Ishi as we jogged side by side, trying to claim the ball.

"I don't think so," I said. "Isaias is different now. More like Gashe." I didn't ever want to go away, even if it was to the palace.

Everyone played in that crazy match — all the girls, the guards, the servants. Everyone wanted to be the one to catch the splendid ball with their feet and dribble it and kick it and feel it float through the air. Gashe played. And Isaias, who took off the coat of his fine suit. Etheye stood at the house to clap and cheer, but soon joined the wild game, her strong legs running up and down the garden faster than anyone. When the adults got tired and lost their breath, Isaias took my hand.

"It is time," he said.

I glanced at Gashe, who nodded. A satisfied smile lifted the edges of his lips, as if everything was going as he had planned.

I tucked the ball under my arm. My eyes and Ishi's locked on each other as I walked beside Isaias to the car that waited, my head turning to keep his gaze. Ishi's mouth drooped on either side. No grin with the hole in the middle where two teeth had fallen out. No tongue poking through the gap. He looked as worried and afraid as the day he had come to live with us. He took a few steps toward me, trailing, and then stopped. His eyes said what my mind thought. If only I could stay …

"Stop!" I said, when Isaias opened the door of the car. "My sneakers. I must get them." I ran back to the veranda and stuffed my feet in worn-out shoes that smelled nearly as rotten as a squat toilet. I put the ball where my shoes had been, to hold my place.

"*Ante*, what's the matter? So quiet?" Isaias reached across the car and touched my shoulder.

His accent didn't make me want to laugh. I didn't say anything. It was not possible to speak. I stared out the window and let the scene blur out of focus. I wished he would turn around the car and take me home, to the place where I belonged.

6

My wish came true by the time the season filled with clean smells and the music of afternoon rain reached its end. I missed sliding barefoot in the gray slicks of mud with my brothers. I missed the pitter-patter on the tin roof that sang us to sleep at night. I missed everything about home. Even the scrubbing of the too many windows in our house. Even the evil older sisters who struck us with brooms and sticks. I even missed Gashe.

The palace had been a too-quiet and too-perfect world with nothing to do.

Unlike Tezze and Ishi, I was glad for the coming of the New Year when it was the law again that children could return to school. It was then that Isaias, now an important man with a Mercedes and more than one suit of clothing, returned me to my family. I was at home for the entire thirteenth month before the New Year, when everyone received new clothes and new sneakers to begin the next grade in school.

My lunch was the only thing in my backpack on the first day. No heavy books yet that would sag a boy's shoulders and almost make him fall over backward.

Gashe was behind the wheel of the pickup, and beside him an elder advisor perched on the edge of the seat, arms extended, body stiff with fear, even though the engine was not yet running.

Ishi and I were the first to arrive. We took the best seats, the ones closest to the cab, where the wind would be less. We kept our legs wide open to take up as much room as possible. The rest of the kids and the servants who were still of an age for school streamed from the house and piled on the wooden benches with us.

The dirty bundles of rags between cement walls and road had begun to come alive. The beggars called to Gashe as we waited to pull onto the street.

"*Sile Mariam. Sile Gabriel,*" they cried. "Gashe, by your mercy."

"Praise Allah, the Almighty," said others.

On this day, he scattered coins through the open window. The beggars swooped to gather them and to bow to Gashe, some with palms pressed together as if in prayer.

"God answers our prayers," they called, faces raised to the Heavens.

The streets teemed with the noise of people and cars and animals. People lined up at windows to buy things. A boy pulled a restless donkey by a rope. Men with white beards played dominoes beneath awnings. Small pockets of younger men gathered to discuss politics and football. Orange and yellow buses decorated with the symbol of a lion picked up people and zoomed from the edges of the road. Drivers yelled from blue-and-white taxi vans looking for fares. There were bright yellow taxis with dark windows that carried important government officials. Horns honked. Drivers stuck their arms from open windows to shake their fists at other drivers.

It was a regular day on the streets of Addis.

"Stop squirming!" my sister demanded, but it was impossible not to squirm when someone grabbed your ear or wiggled his fingers in your ribs.

"I can't see! Move your ugly head, *dedebi*." Another sister cuffed Ishi in the head. I jabbed her hard with my elbow.

Bells clanged from the tower of the cathedral. Soon prayers would be recited through loudspeakers on its corners: "Our Father, Who art in Heaven, hallowed be Thy name ..." Hundreds of beggars had their arms shoved through the railing already, palms up, hoping for alms or for food. Those without arms rocked back and forth or bent forward with their faces pressed to the cement, a small container near their heads to collect coins. Others held their blind children, tugging on the clothes of passersby.

I was glad to drive past it all.

Brick and stone walls pasted with paper notices lined either side of the road that led to my school. Kids walked in groups down the center of the street, talking and laughing, and sometimes chasing a football. I wished we could walk to school or that Gashe would drop Tezze and me some distance from the gates so no one would see the embarrassing old pickup. Or better, I wished Gashe would buy an SUV.

We rolled through the iron gate, past the guard house and past the big tree to my school — one of the best schools in Addis. Here, everything was ordered and clean.

It was unnatural for a boy to say he liked to go to school, to sit all day at a desk and learn, and so, even with my brothers, I kept my opinions to myself. But I liked the way the desks were lined up in rows, the smell of the pages of textbooks and the crisp sound when they turned in a quiet room. Writing things down and solving problems, being the first to know the answer, knowing what to expect and what was expected, having rules that never changed. All of these things made school the ideal place.

Ishi, the girls and the servants raised the palms of their hands to us as Gashe eased around the fountain, through the gate and into the gnarled mess of traffic. Tezze and I joined the lines of our classmates ready to go inside when the doors opened.

The first day it was exciting to see our friends and meet our teacher. The second day was exciting. But already, by the third day, even the best of students remembered how dreary and boring and confining school could be and began to count the days until the next Holy Day. It was hard to concentrate when sunshine beckoned. Why were the two months off during the winter rains? We should be off now, to hunt salamanders, create ant wars and spend the day chasing a football. Who made up these rules that made children study during the best time of the year?

The teacher's long ruler slammed on my desk, the wind of it brushing my face like the air rushing beneath the wing of a bird.

"What is nine times seven?" the teacher barked.

"Sixty-three," I said.

"Correct!" he said, but he did not look happy that I knew the answer. It was fortunate, at times like these, that I was so lucky in school.

◆

Time passed, with one day piled on top of the other. Not so many things changed. I wore out four pairs of the Made in China sneakers that Etheye liked to buy. My ankles had shot again from the bottoms of the jeans I shared with Ishi, but the metal button at the waist still closed.

I did not return to the palace, and I saw Isaias only following arguments between him and Sabba. He came to us then, to sleep in the room with my brothers and me, and to debate late into the night with Gashe, their voices rising and falling.

Sometimes my brothers and I sat quietly, just out of sight, to listen. But mostly it was uninteresting talk of politics.

7

"We want Tom and Jerry," I said.

Well past dark, rain drummed on the roof of the house, spilled over the edges and cascaded in great waves against the windows. The sky rumbled and flashed. Etheye sat in the center of the sofa, a shallow basket of popped corn cradled between her thighs. The younger kids moved in and out like birds, nipping at the kernels and running away. Our sisters nestled close beside Etheye, the servants on the floor. All of them bent toward the television. All of them had tears streaking their cheeks.

"We want Tom and Jerry," I repeated.

"Shhh," said Etheye and the girls all at once. Their eyes were suctioned to the television. I was upside down on the sofa, with my head hanging close to the floor.

"This is so-o-o-o boring," I said. My sister shoved me with the side of her leg.

"It be romance," Etheye said. "Shhh … this be the good part."

"Shut your eyes! Close your ears!" yelled the girls. I covered my face with my hands but opened my fingers a crack so I could see. A man and a woman mashed their lips together. The girls cried.

"Romance is just boring kissing. This show is too long," I said. My sister Layla knocked my legs from the back of the sofa.

"Go away!" she said.

"Why do the girls always get to the pick the shows?" Ishi complained. "It's not fair. All they ever pick is kissing."

"We want Tom and Jerry. We want cartoons!" our brothers yelled. They jumped around the sofa in a wild dance. They squealed when Tezze, Ishi and I dropped on all fours to chase them.

"Quiet!" Etheye said. She shifted to the edge of the sofa and turned up the volume.

My smallest brother, Kato, jumped on my back. He rolled off when I reared up, then chased after me for another ride.

"Me! Me! Me!" the little kids yelled, fighting to get on our backs.

"Shut up!" yelled the girls. We pretended deafness.

We tickled the ribs of our little brothers and sisters until they shrieked and curled up like slugs touched by salt. We dragged them by the legs and spun them in circles until they giggled with dizziness.

Etheye raised the volume again. It was so loud, we had to yell.

"Tickle me! Spin me!" hollered the little ones. "We want a ride!"

"It's my turn!"

No one heard the door open. No one heard Gashe walk in, but we felt the chill of him when he strode across the room. He left a trail of raindrops all the way from the front door.

Everyone froze, just like Tom and Jerry when the VCR was turned off in the middle of a scene.

He snapped off the TV. The room was silent. He stood, glaring. Rain dripped from his hair to his shoulders. His hands clenched into fists. Unclenched. Clenched. Unclenched. The servants rushed from the room like cockroaches exposed to light.

"Honored husband!" Etheye leapt to her feet. Popcorn shot from the basket and spewed onto the floor. "We not expect you coming at this late hour."

"What is the meaning of this?" His voice was sharp.

"It be just television," she said. "A silly show."

"There is no discipline here! What are you teaching with this?"

"Come," she said. "I make food." Gashe did not follow. He stood between the television and the sofa, dripping half on the carpet and half on the patterned wood. He stared at us one by one, his eyes a threat, and one by one we dropped our heads.

We had done wrong and we had been caught.

Ishi was the first of the children to move. He grabbed a rag, then fell to his knees near Gashe, patting the water that had splattered on the floor.

Soft melodies of the masinko drifted from Gashe's room, accented by the clinking of cups being gathered on a tray.

"Clean this!" Gashe commanded. The girls moved quickly, heads down. They scooped spilled popcorn into the hammocks they made with their skirts. Kato stuck the basket on his head and jumped around, wiggling his bum. Gashe ripped it from his head.

"Not a toy!" he said. Kato burst into tears. Gashe stomped — not to his quiet room where he liked to eat, but to the exterior cooking room. I carried Kato.

"Shhh. Shhh," I whispered as we herded all the kids into our room. We knew not to make a sound.

"What is wrong with you? You are useless!" Gashe screamed at Etheye.

His loud voice took every speck of air from the house, making it so I could hardly breathe. Tezze, Ishi and the girls gathered the kids close, cuddling the smallest ones in their laps. I shook my head at Kato and held my finger to my lips.

"Tesfaye!" Ishi whispered as I slipped from the room.

Etheye scurried, shoulders hunched, cowering as she poked the coals and fed twigs to the tiny flame. Rain needled a quick drumbeat on the tin roof, then flooded the edge with a curtain of water.

"I sorry! So sorry!" she said. The handle of the injera pan scraped from the hook on the outside wall where the rain cut a groove into the dirt.

"I give you everything!" he roared. "And you cannot cook a simple meal? You cannot discipline children?"

She put the flat pan over the fire. Dribbled water over it to see if it was hot enough.

"It be quick." She glanced up at him. "Be calm."

His face exploded. "How dare you tell me what to do? You useless dog. You donkey."

She scuttled to the corner, arm up to protect her head. She watched him, then darted inside to grab his stool and place it where he liked to sit. Her movements were small, quick and frantic. The water bounced and sizzled on the scalding pan. She stood, but kept her body bent in subservience. She touched his elbow. With the other hand she indicated the seat with the leather worn in the shape of his body.

"Come. Sit." Her soft voice blended with the music from the CD player. He remained stiff and standing in the doorway. She squeezed past, crouched before the fire. Steam rose from the hot pan. I saw her arm tremble as she poured the injera batter.

"Dedebi!" he yelled. He lashed with his hand, flinging

her off balance. She righted herself, back into a squat. Eyes swimming in tears, she continued where she'd left off, drawing the batter around the pan, circles within circles.

"Useless!" he screamed. He kicked. She fell to the floor. Scrambled back up. "I should get rid of you. Send you to the gutter where you belong."

A scorched smell. Smoke rose from the edge of the pan. The sizzling metal slid from her grasp, clattered and spun on the floor. Batter flung in slow motion. The burnt edge of the injera crumbled. Black flecks flew like ash in a breeze.

He struck her head. She lifted her arm, palm up, to ward off another blow.

"You would waste food now?"

"I do better," she said. Her voice was thin. She crawled on the floor, sweeping up the charred injera with her hand, wiping the spilled batter with the edge of her skirt.

My heart smashed so loud I could hear it. I wanted to run in and save Etheye. I wanted to punch Gashe. To knock him to the floor and kick him.

But, standing just to the right of the doorway, watching, I could not move. It was as if I was seeing a terrible program on the television.

"I do better. I do better," she repeated. He kicked over the bowl of batter. It spilled like a thick river of pale brown.

"You will do better," he sneered. His spit landed near her foot. "*Mogne*. The only reason I let you stay ... the only reason is that you make sons."

Now! Go now, Tesfaye. Do not delay! Hit him! Make him pay. Do not let him do this.

But I did nothing. Nothing but watch my mother cringe and mewl like an animal that knows the whip. Nothing but watch my father's power.

I wished he would die.

8

Deep in my heart, I wanted to stand up to Gashe. I saw myself avenging my mother's suffering, slapping him, pushing him away, punching him, beating him with a stick.

"Hypocrite!" I would yell with each strike. "Useless. Hypocrite! Preaching freedom on the street corner, yet beating Etheye, treating her as a slave!"

I would punch his face and make it swell. I'd turn that light skin to purple bruises. "Useless!" And when he'd had enough, when he lay curled like a worm, whimpering in his own blood, I would feed him his own words. I would scream, "The only reason we keep you, the only reason we let you stay, is that you provide for us."

But my courage was lacking. I feared his anger and what he could do. I did not want to be the one who was beaten. I did not want to be the one thrown to the street, living in the dump, starving and sweltering beneath a scrap of tin. I did not want this and I could not risk it. I knew I could not survive on my own.

The only way to survive under the rule of Gashe was to be perfect, to make no mistakes. If I proved my excellence, Gashe would be proud and happy. And if he was pleased with my obedience and academic perfection, he would be content, and he would change. He would stop raging out of control when we least expected it, he would not threaten Etheye and my sisters, and there would be peace in our family. Remaining polite and unquestioning on the outside was the best way to protect everyone.

My loyalty and devotion I saved for Etheye.

"I hate him," I said out loud. Etheye's face had lost its swelling and the bruise had faded to a sickly yellow. "What he does to us. What he does to you!"

"Do not hate," she said. I passed her a dripping shirt. She twisted it tight. A stream of water trickled to the grass. She snapped it in the air to take out the wrinkles and clipped it to the middle line. The two lines behind us were already full of clothes of all sizes that hung limp or flapped in the wind like flags, depending on their dryness.

"But I do! I hate him and I hate his power over us." What I did not say was that I hated my fear. I hated how I was afraid to stand up to him.

"Honor him. Show him respect," she said. A long skirt pushed against her back, encircling her like a bridal veil.

"But I do not respect him. How can I respect someone who treats us as he does?"

"He treats us well," she said.

"How can you say that? He beats you. He calls you names you do not deserve."

"Maybe so," she said. "But he gives everything. The food you eat. These clothes. All my children go to school — good schools, even the girls. You must show gratitude."

Could she not see what was wrong? Could she not see how he talked of freedom and revolution and the power of democracy, but that she was a slave?

"But the girls go to such inferior schools, just like servants," I argued.

"Exactly. Even Gashe's servants learn to read and write and count."

"But anyone can do those things, even small children." Untrue words had escaped my lips. I knew I had hurt the mother I so loved.

"I cannot do such things," she said.

"I could teach you! It is so easy, Etheye!"

"I be having no need for this learning. My children to have better lives."

She stood with her arms in the air, holding Gashe's shirt. She looked at me with the patient eyes of a cow.

"If I be a village wife, you have no hope for the future." She pegged the shirt in place. "Be grateful. Always grateful. You understand?"

"Yes, but ..."

"It be the end of this talk," she said.

But I had not gotten to the main part of my argument that proved Gashe's mean-spiritedness, reminding her how he had kidnapped her for marriage, how he had thrown my oldest sister to the street when she disobeyed.

"I still hate him," I muttered. "I still wish he would die."

Etheye slapped my face with her wet hand. She spat three times on the ground. My cheek sizzled.

"Never! Never say such a thing! Never *think* of such a thing." Her eyes bulged, as did the trail of veins in her forehead.

How could she defend him? He hit her. He called her donkey and *mogne* and useless.

"Think of us without his protection," she said.

She snatched the empty basket. The netting of her dress swished furiously with each step she took toward the girls who sang together as they rubbed clothes and soap on washboards.

The little ones smashed their open palms on the water, giggling when the droplets splashed them.

I touched my hand to my cheek where it seared. What *would* happen if Gashe was gone? It would be better, wouldn't it? Was it not always better when he was away?

9

The gold medal, on a wide ribbon around Etheye's neck, gleamed in the soft light of Gashe's private room the year I was in seventh grade. I had placed its heavy weight over her head in the same way the headmaster had placed it over mine. True, there was no great ceremony before all of the students of the school, but I awarded it just as solemnly.

"In honor of the best mother," I said, then kissed her once on each cheek, and then a second time on the first cheek.

"Best mother," she repeated, then spat three times to ward off evil spirits.

"Not for me," she said. She lifted the medal from her chest. "This be your prize. You study for it."

I stopped her hand. "No, Etheye. For you," I insisted. I had earned it easily for drawing gray boxes, then painting the lower half with cone-shaped trees and a twisted blue river. Etheye did everything for us but received nothing.

She tilted the heavy disc and looked at the inscription. "What it says?"

I pretended to study the words. "It says, *For the best mother in the world, who I love with all of my heart.*"

"Best son," she said. She ran her hand along my cheek. "Clever son." She spat twice.

Gashe wore his best shirt, the one with the delicate embroidery at the collar, usually saved to impress business partners. He sat near me on a simple three-legged stool, so close that our knees almost touched.

Etheye bowed as she placed the injera on the mesob. There were mounds of bite-sized pieces of meat and pureed vegetables, some of which I did not know, arranged all around the edges, reminding me of the mountains that surrounded Addis. It was more food than I had ever seen on a single plate. More even than when I lived at the palace with Isaias. Etheye also offered milk and curdled cheese. My gratitude was great that this was not a day of fasting.

"Esteemed and wise husband," she said. "Honored son." She backed away from us, head bent like a servant, but I caught her grin. She was happy to serve me.

"Eat!" Gashe gestured.

I tore off a small piece, scooped up some kai wat, waited for him to do the same.

It was me, finally, and not Tezze, who shared his meal. Today I was the important one invited to eat meat.

"You are too modest," Gashe said. "Have more." I popped the first bite into my mouth, chewing carefully, remembering to cover my mouth as I ate. Next I tried tere sega usually served only to the most special guests. It tasted of blood. I nearly gagged on the raw meat. How could I swallow something so awful? I needed to spit it out.

"You don't like it?" my father laughed. I shook my head. What could I do? This would hurt Etheye's feelings, to say I did not like the food she prepared.

Gashe leaned close and whispered, "Just swallow quickly. Then it will be over." He dipped a piece of injera in the wat flavored with berbere and held it out to me. "Here, this will help."

The spice seared my tongue. My eyes watered like a crying baby. I could feel the flame lick all the way down my throat and to my stomach.

Perfect! Just the way I liked it. The third burn would be worth it. I reached for more.

Such luxury, to eat without sisters pushing me out of the way.

Mixed with the smells of roasting spices was the earthy smell of smoldering cow dung and the sweetness of eucalyptus. My sisters and my servant cousins hummed and sang as they cooked, the melody rising and falling in waves, punctuated by the swish and pop of coffee beans that Etheye stirred in the corner.

"This prize is a great honor," Gashe said, taking food for himself. "An international prize. For my son. It will bring recognition."

I nodded. What should I say? What was the right thing?

"Thank you, Gashe, for saying this," I said. Could I have more food? I waited to be offered more.

"Take as much as you like," he said, as if reading my thoughts.

My lips burst into an inferno and the insides of my eardrums tickled from the spices. The more it burned, the more I wanted to eat. Tears trickled from the edges of my eyes. Etheye was the best cook.

"Here, take yogurt," he said. "It will cool things down so you can eat more."

Ishi would not believe how kind and generous Gashe was, how much food, and that I could eat until I was full.

This was the best day of my life. My stomach was heavy like the Indian Buddha's when Etheye lifted the jebena high above the cups. There was coffee, thick with warm milk, butter and sugar, even for me.

"With you, I am well pleased," said Gashe. His praise was like the radiance of the sun after days of rain. His pride was my pride.

He drained his third cup, then put it down. "But this is no way to make a living. You will not be an artist. You know this, yes?"

I did not know that. But being an artist did not matter. What I wanted was to be an international footballer like El Diego. That would be the best way to achieve fame and riches.

"You must study hard. Learn everything," he said. "Education is the only way to rise in the world. To gain status. Education is the only way to change a country."

I did not want to change a country. I wanted to play football, and when I was not practicing with the international team, I wanted to draw pictures and perhaps to build a sculpture.

"For this purpose of studying, I am giving you your own room. Just for you," Gashe said. He rose taller in his seat and puffed out his chest like a rooster strutting.

"But we have no extra rooms," I protested. Why would he give me my own room? No one had their own room. Only him.

"In the servants' quarters. You will study there and you will sleep there. It is the best way. To have solitude and time to think," he said.

I was being punished for doing well? For making him proud? Why would he take me from my brothers?

"It is being readied now. A fresh mattress, even. New paint on the walls. All the cracks fixed. Tonight you will go there." He clapped a hand on my shoulder and squeezed.

"We are alike," he said. "The two of us, cut from the same cloth."

The burn of the food in my stomach was no longer comfortable.

Me? Like Gashe? Never. I was not like him and I did not want ever to be like him with fancy clothes, a false smile and a concern only for making himself look good.

The room that was now to be my sleeping quarters was down a passage just a few doors from the room where Etheye kept her goat and chickens. It was the same size as the animal room, and the walls were made of the same concrete blocks. Three walls were painted yellow. The one with the small window was painted the blue of a summer sky. One mattress stuffed tightly and smelling of fresh cotton was in the corner, draped by a cowhide with no signs of wear. The mattress was too hard. The room was too quiet and too empty.

How could I sleep without Ishi? Without the stinky farts and dream talk of my younger brothers? How would I know what was going on if I did not sleep with them?

I stared at the ceiling and *Aw-lubba-lubbaed* like Fiyeli — first the sounds she made at milking time, then the bawling when her kid was taken. I scrunched the cowhide and pretended it was Ishi. But it was impossible to get warm or comfortable. I curled on my side like a newborn baby. I lay flat on my back, then on my stomach. I turned finally on my side and stared at the wall.

Why would Gashe punish me like this?

A cool hand touched my forehead.

"You be lonely?" Etheye whispered. I nodded.

She crawled beneath the hide with me, leaving all of her clothes on, but holding me as if I was much younger. The medal I had given her pressed hard and cool against my back.

"This be a great honor," she said. "Who knows of a boy with his own room? Only the Emperor had this, I think."

"I don't want to be alone. I hate it!"

"Gashe be pleased." She stroked my hair. "We must please him."

"Why? Why must we please him?"

"Because he gives everything. He gives us life," she said. I had left the curtains and the window open to hear the chirping of crickets, and so it would feel less like a prison cell. I leaned on one arm and turned to look at Etheye

"He doesn't give us life. God gives us life."

"God, Gashe, same thing." She shrugged.

"No, it is not the same. He is just a man."

"Ah, yes, but a man of influence, a man of power."

"But it's wrong. What he does. How he treats you. He yells. He hits people. He understands no one," I said.

"Not so. Learn from Gashe and you live well." I did not understand Etheye and her stubborn loyalty to a husband who mistreated her.

I drifted to sleep in Etheye's arms, but when I woke during the night, she was gone. I slipped through the house like a thief and onto the mattress where I fit best, with Ishi.

10

Gashe was wrong. We were not alike. There was not a single thing about us the same. He was light-skinned; I was darker. He was tall and graceful; I was prone to tripping over my feet. He spent his days on street corners giving speeches; I preferred to be at home with my brothers. He was violent; I was peaceful. He was a hypocrite; I was honest.

How could this be my father? How could we be so different, yet share the same flesh and blood?

I stared through the glass of the car window as we passed street after street of crumbling buildings with peeling paint and lifeless clothing draped on ropes, window to window.

"Bring down the window," he said, his voice generous. A breeze shifted the air in the vehicle.

Gashe beamed. "Better? Yes?" he asked.

"Yes," I said. The change in air was welcome, but even more welcome would be if I was not in the vehicle with him. Why did he insist now that I accompany him everywhere?

Our progress was slowed when the street filled with goats and sheep and cows and people on their way to the Mercato. Beggars and cripples with their stumps tied with the rubber from old tires pressed against the car trying to get close to Gashe.

How was it that so many healthy-looking people were without hands? Without legs?

Gashe reached his arm out the window and smiled as we crept along the crowded street. His was not a wide friendly smile but a smaller one that did not cause his lips to part. This expression said, "Look at me. Honor my greatness." He grasped hands with people he did not know, wished them God's blessing and received it in return. It was as if he was a prince, and they his loyal subjects.

From time to time he reached for the spot between us where he kept birr of small denominations. He pressed the coins into hands and scattered them in the street the way Etheye scattered feed for the chickens. The diseased and the crippled scrambled to pick them up, their heads bobbing like birds as they bowed and gave thanks to Gashe, to Allah and to God.

I hated this display of his wealth and power. It was wrong that he had so much, and these people so little.

"Gashe! Look out!" I yelled. He was not paying proper attention to the road and the obstacles on it. What if the wheels of his car crushed a person? What was wrong with him? Did he not care?

"Stop!" I screamed. "There! Close to the wheel. Do not drive!" A young man with no legs was on his bum near the tire. Using his arms to lift his torso, he twisted and tipped into the crowd to move from harm's way.

I cringed with embarrassment. To be so healthy. To have a car. To have two arms and two legs.

Hands and arms in all shades of brown pushed in when we stopped, palms up or clasped together as if in prayer. "Gashe. Gashe," they panted, the smell of their breath like an unwashed gutter. The man without legs had dragged himself to the side, but barely. If he had had legs, they would have been destroyed.

I reached for Gashe's coins, stretched as far as possible out the window, and with my arm dangling loose tossed a coin to the hand of the young crippled man. He bowed his head to give me honor. I watched the man as Gashe wove his Peugeot through the crowd, watched him stranded on the side of the road while the others trailed us like a swarm of flies smelling blood.

"You see," Gashe said, "how good it is to give? You feel better now, yes?"

If I scattered all of his money in the street, I would not feel better, but I did not say these words out loud.

I said, "Yes, Gashe. But what you give, is it enough?"

"It is enough to live another day," he said.

Perhaps there had been a mistake. It *was* possible that he was not my father, was it not? Could it be that, like Ishi, I was a nephew or a cousin? Brought from the country for school?

Or perhaps I was no blood relation at all, an orphan snatched from the gutter. Could this be the reason Gashe and I shared nothing in common? I smiled at this thought, that the self-centered businessman beside me was a distant relative or a stranger. It made absolute sense.

"Ah, I see it now," he said. "The look that tells me you understand. The best way to ensure loyalty is to give."

It was clear he could not read my thoughts. I remained silent. Let him think what he would. We shared no blood of father and son and that made me happy.

We passed incomplete houses with steel rods sticking from the top like rows of antennae. Paint bubbled and flaked like dry skin from some houses, while others were painted only as high as a man could reach. A flimsy curtain danced through an open window. Elders sat in chairs nearly as broken as they were. Their heads turned to follow the car as we passed.

But if Gashe was not my relative, how was I related to Ishi? It was not possible for two boys to look so much alike, to be two halves of the same whole, and not share the same blood. Could it be that we were true brothers? That it was the mother we shared?

I focused on my hands folded in my lap.

Not possible. Ishi and I were born just three weeks apart. We could not share the same mother.

Cousins, then, related through Etheye's blood, not Gashe's. Was Ishi not the most like Etheye with his love of animals and plants? Did he not share her humble ways?

Gashe slowed to allow a donkey to pass. It pulled a cart heaped with a tangle of long sticks that bobbed so low they nearly touched the road. Inside the car, the soothing strings of a cello, "The Music of Europe's Greatest Composers."

For certain, Etheye was my mother. She told me often of my birth, how I was so small that I gave her no pain. She said it was for this reason that she loved me best of all.

Etheye was my mother, so she couldn't be Ishi's. But one of her sisters. Surely he was the son of a sister. A cousin of Etheye's line.

I glanced at Gashe. My eyes caught his hand on the steering wheel, manicured fingernails that shone pink with good health. He had the lean, delicate and graceful fingers of an artist. Between his index and his middle fingers was a peculiar bowing.

I knew this trait. Why had I not noticed before?

His hands looked exactly like the hands woven together in my lap. My hands and his were identical. It was as if his pale hands had been dipped in brown dye and grafted onto my body. How could this be?

The similarity of our hands was precisely the same as how Ishi and I looked so much alike. It could happen only if we shared the same blood. Only if Gashe were the father, and I the son.

It was as if God was laughing at me, as if he had drawn my fate to become as pompous and controlling as Gashe, who hummed to the sounds of famous composers as he drove his expensive car.

But why, if I wanted to be so different than him, did I crave his approval? Why did I excel at school and do everything he asked without question? Why did I not stand up to him? It was not love I felt, nor respect. It was duty, and it was fear of what would happen if he learned my true thoughts.

Gashe slammed the brake and leaned on the horn. My body flung forward like a doll. The other driver threw his arm from the window and raised his fist, middle finger extended, but it was Gashe who had avoided the crash.

"Everything is fine?" Gashe asked as he touched the accelerator.

I settled back into my comfortable seat.

"Everything is fine," I said.

11

Something had changed, but I did not know what. Gashe still spent more nights away than he did at the house, and when he was at home, the air was strung with electric wires of tension. He still spoke in commands, demanded silence and mostly ignored everyone but the smallest children. But more and more often he sat head to head with my older brother, Tezze, teaching him the ways of business.

We all still went to school every day. Etheye's belly grew again with another child. The seasons faded, one to the other. It was as if nothing had changed, and yet it was as if everything had changed so slowly that you couldn't tell it was happening.

When finally I noticed, in the year I was in eighth grade, it felt as if I had awakened from a long sleep, as if only now did I see the world as it truly was.

It remained dangerous to be out after dark. Special Forces and curfews ruled the night. The same curfew but different police. Different police, and yet familiar in their ways. Ready to shoot or to slash with a baton and ask questions later for those who lacked proper connections or money for a bribe. It was best to leave the walls of our compound only to go to school. This suited me, for what else did I need that was beyond the heavy gates spiked with wrought-iron?

Ishi and Gashe had been right about Isaias. He became a powerful man, but more and more, I sensed that his politics and the politics of Gashe differed. No longer was Isaias a revolutionary fighting for democracy. He had become part of the government. He still spoke of democracy, but he no longer desired it.

And with his power, he turned his back on the Amhara roots he shared with Gashe and sought to hide them.

I was bent over my science homework, working from the light that came through the window, completing a detailed diagram of an ant.

Gashe came to my door. He was dressed in his best clothes. "You will come with me. Now," he said.

I did not want to leave. I wanted to finish what I was doing, but I did not protest, nor did I ask where we would go. I put down my pencil. The drawing must wait.

Gashe strolled to his newest Peugeot, a pearly white 504 that sparkled when sunlight hit it. It had square headlights and inside, bucket seats made of leather, shiny wood grain on the console and electric windows.

I got in beside him as if it was something I did every day, but my brothers and I had only before peered through the windows. I kept my hands on my lap, afraid to leave finger-prints on the gleaming surfaces.

The guards pulled open the gates. The beggars swarmed the car like ants to a drop of honey. We moved through the streets in the familiar pattern. Fast, then brake. Fast, then brake. Fast, fast. Brake. Swerve.

Still, we had not spoken. I wanted to ask where we were going and why he had chosen me, but I was afraid of a rep-rimand. Better to look out the window and to enjoy the sights. He pushed a cassette into the dash when he stopped to let a shepherd wearing a drab headdress straggle his flock across the street. The car filled with soft music.

Ahead was a military truck with metal ribs and a canvas covering. Crowded in the back were ordinary people. Armed soldiers stood on the bumper and on the step by the cab, watchful and menacing. One of them thumped the butt of his rifle on the roof of the truck. It rolled ahead, gushing black smoke.

I did not understand the changes that were happening just beyond our compound gates, and Gashe did not explain. Could these be criminals? And if so, how could there be so many?

"It is political," my teacher had said. "It is of no consequence to you. It is not something to be discussed."

But it was of consequence to me. How could a sighted person turn a blind eye?

"Be a child. Enjoy your freedom. Do not think too much. Do not see. You will grow up soon enough, and then you will wish you were a child," the teacher told us.

But he was wrong. Being a child was not freedom. It was having decisions made for you, like today, when I wanted to work on my diagram, and Gashe made me come with him. To be a child was to pursue the dreams of the father. I wanted to make my own decisions, but as the son of Gashe, I knew that would never happen.

When he switched off the car, we were in a part of the city I did not recognize. He passed me a heavy cardboard carton he had taken from the trunk.

"You will give out these," he said. "To anyone who looks as if he can read."

Inside were half-size papers covered in writing and folded in half. He took another box from the trunk, a wooden one, which he upturned on the side of the road. He stood on it and began to speak.

"One man," he began. "One man standing alone." He stood slightly above everyone else, his rich voice drawing people to him. When a small crowd had gathered, he repeated his words. "One man, standing alone, is like the flicker of a single candle. A small flame, easy to extinguish." He paused. "But a thousand men standing together, a thousand men, their flames are a conflagration, a light that cannot be put out. Their light can light another and another. One candle can light the world."

The men assembled near the street corner nodded and murmured agreement as Gashe continued to speak. His voice was strong and sure. His conviction so deep and powerful that for a minute, even I believed him.

"Will you hold a candle? Will you work for an Ethiopia where all are equal? Where tribes are of no consequence? Where anyone can prosper without thought of race, religion or tribe?"

But how could he speak so? How could he talk of change and freedom when, within his own family, there was none? How could he speak of choice when he forced us to his will? When my sister now lived in a shanty because she disobeyed him and chose her own husband? How could he call for change?

His voice grew quiet. The men pressed closer.

"We know people are disappearing. Who will be next?" Gashe asked. He extended his arm to the crowd. Men looked uncomfortable. They cast down their eyes and shuffled their feet. Gashe laid his hand on his chest and asked quietly, "Will it be me? Will it be my son here?" He stretched his arm to identify me, displaying me as a valuable object.

Inside I shrank from the open gazes of the men, but

outside I stood as I knew he wanted, tall and proud, unsmiling, like a statue.

His hypocrisy sickened me. Neither he nor I were in danger because of his status as an esteemed businessman and because we lived under the protection of Isaias.

I stood on the edge of the crowd, watching.

And yet …

He made these men believe. How did he do that? How was it that when he spoke on the street corner, even I believed?

"There are those who say they will stand behind you, protect your back. But these men with elegant words are cowards, not supporters. They will use you as a human shield to protect and advance themselves.

"Do not trust these men.

"The ones to trust are the timid ones who go about their business every day. These good, quiet men who toil in the heat for their bread are the beating heart of Ethiopia. They stand for what is right. They demonstrate their support with courage and action."

I remembered, then. I was to hand out the papers. It was an easy job. Everyone wanted one.

"No matter what happens. No matter the time of day," said Gashe. "No matter the circumstances. Remember this. Seek those who gain no profit. For we are the people, the bricks and mortar that will build one Ethiopia. Strong and proud. Free and equal."

Gashe was quiet on the way home. It was as if his thoughts, like mine, were elsewhere. People gathered easily to hear him, almost as if he had been expected, which led me to wonder what he was doing and why. Would true democracy not be bad for someone like Gashe? He already had a comfortable life. He was well connected. He knew the people in power. He had nothing to gain by change. Why would he care?

I met up with Ishi in the goat room where he was scraping out old hay and laying down fresh. Lately, he was working more and more with Fiyeli and her new goat friends, letting Etheye have more time to make the cheese and spiced butter Gashe liked. We were hauling away the dirty straw in a cart when I told him about Gashe and his speech.

"Well, what did they say?" Ishi asked.

"They didn't say anything. They cheered a bit, but mostly they just listened."

"Not the people, dummy, the papers. What was written on them?"

I shrugged and pushed the heavy cart while he pulled. "I don't know. Just a bunch of writing. I didn't read them."

"You are such a dope. I can't believe you," he said.

12

Gashe ordered the heavy curtains shut and the house silent as he adjusted the dial to the European stations. The reception was best late at night when the young ones slept.

"Tell no one what you hear, you understand?" he said. "Do not discuss it at school or with your teachers or with your friends. Trust no one."

Tezze, Ishi and I knew that listening to any stations not sponsored by the government was as illegal as it was for people to gather. Even two could be called an assembly by the police. Two friends joking on the street could be suspicious behavior.

And so everyone kept to himself. Each family cloistered behind walls. Silent as monks, but afraid. Anything could happen anytime without notice, and no one would speak up for fear of what might befall him. The fear was greatest for those with Amhara or Oromo blood filling their veins. Amhara was Gashe's tribe.

Radio Ethiopia and the headlines of Gashe's newspapers reported the protection of citizens through the purging of terrorists. Dissidents and insurgents were detained for re-education. But my brothers and I noticed only the

Special Police had weapons. They carried AK-47s and heavy sticks we heard were filled with lead.

"Be hit on the head with one of those sticks and your skull would crack," said Tezze. He dribbled the football between his feet, then nudged it to Ishi. The three of us were in the back garden gathered in a circle. "You might die. Or worse, you might not know who you were or where you belonged, information of great importance should the police decide to question you."

"With their boots," said Ishi. He shot the ball to me with the inside of his foot.

"You've seen them when you are with Gashe?" I asked Tezze. "Near the university? How they swarm in and grab anyone?"

My brother nodded. "And stuff them in the back of a truck," he said.

I hopped back and forth, lifting the ball and shunting it from side to side.

"Where do they take them?" asked Ishi. He wedged his foot between my legs and stole the ball.

Tezze and I shrugged.

"The prison?" I suggested. Ishi popped the ball back to me.

"But with so many prisoners ... It doesn't make sense," said Ishi. "Where would they put them all?"

"Maybe they let them go after a while," I said. I released the ball to Tezze. That answer did not feel right, but neither Tezze nor Ishi offered a better guess.

"Or they don't," said Tezze. He tripped me and ran off with the ball. Ishi and I chased him and fought for the wobbly ball held together with thin wire and layers of tape, but our hearts were not with the game. Our thoughts were on the things happening around us that we did not understand, no matter how closely we watched Gashe or how often we strained to overhear conversations with his advisors.

We stretched on the ground and looked to the fast-moving clouds. The coolness of shaded grass refreshed the backs of our legs and arms. I plucked the green strands and tossed a handful in the air.

"Why do they always go after the students?" I asked.

"You heard? The university is to be shut down," said Tezze. "The schools, too. All schools. Christian and Muslim."

"No school?" said Ishi. I could hear the joy in his voice.

"I saw it in the national newspaper," said Tezze. "No classes tomorrow. Or any day after that."

◆

Our fear became normal. It became a way of living, to not think about what might happen next. Tezze was head to head with Gashe most evenings, learning techniques for accounting and investments. Ishi tended the animals, and I helped with Etheye's growing business, filling small containers with fresh milk and passing them to neighbors through the gate. We played football and fought over injera. We studied at home. We went to sleep.

For us, nothing changed. At least, not at first.

Gashe arrived by sunset on most nights, and when he did not appear for a few days, no one worried. Gashe was no one, a simple businessman.

"If we remain within our walls. If we remain silent, it is as if we have given them our permission to do as they please," he explained as we drove through unfamiliar streets.

A military vehicle was ahead, parked to the side of the road. Near it were two armed soldiers dressed in army fatigues and wearing reflective sunglasses. A soldier stepped in front of the car ahead of us. Stance wide, face grim, both hands on the gun, tip pointed down but at the ready.

The Lada stopped. It had a dent in the rear fender and was missing the passenger-side mirror.

An officer leaned on the driver's side, left hand on the roof, right one at his hip near a holstered gun. He peered through the open window, looked around. He checked papers and slipped the birr hidden within the folds of the documents into his front pocket. He nodded, shouted, "Clear," and slapped the roof. The Lada rolled forward.

Gashe lifted his hand briefly, showing his palm as we approached the checkpoint. The soldier waved through the gleaming Peugeot.

"Have you ever been stopped, Gashe?"

"No." He shook his head and glanced at me. "They will not stop me."

"Why?"

"They know who I am. They know this car."

But if they knew the car and they knew who was in it, would it not be a target?

I did not speak this fear. If Gashe said we were safe, we were safe. Still, I wished I was at home helping Tezze with the accounting, or milking the goats with Ishi.

Or, better yet, I wished I was at school filling my head with knowledge, getting simple answers to all of my questions.

I needed to know one thing.

"Is it dangerous, Gashe, what you are doing?"

"It is dangerous to cross the street," he said.

"But what if someone hears what you say?"

"I want people to hear what I say." We drove for a time in silence.

"What if someone reports you?"

"The buildings have ears. The streets have mouths. It is certain I have been reported," he said.

"What does that mean?"

"It means I must follow the path God has set."

"But the danger ..." I gulped, not wanting to say the next words.

"It is more dangerous not to speak," he said. He reached across the space between us, then, and gripped my shoulder. "Do not fear. I have connections. Partners in business. The students I have sponsored. Their families. I am safe. You are safe."

"But, Gashe, aren't you breaking the law?"

"If we will not stand for our country, who will? There must be change. There must be democracy."

"But Ethiopia *is* a democratic republic, isn't it?"

"It is what they tell the world. But tell me this, what true democracy has only one party? What democracy, where people have the right to choose, wins a one hundred percent majority? Can you tell me that?"

We were leaving the city behind, moving into new territory.

"I don't like what you are doing."

"And so, you would make me a coward?"

"There must be another way," I said.

"I have fought silently my whole life, Tesfaye. I have seen a monarchy, communism and countless revolutions promising change. Nothing has changed in my lifetime.

"We will fight, not with guns and grenades, but with knowledge. We will make the outside world care as much for Ethiopia as it did during the years of the Great Famine."

The meetings were illegal. I knew that. We all knew the laws that prohibited gatherings, but sometimes, Gashe explained, you had to think of who was making the laws. If corrupt people were making laws to suit themselves and you broke those laws by doing what was right …

"We must get together and we must discuss," he said. "The edire is our only way to share information."

He said the meetings of the elders were too important not to attend. Holding them in Addis was too perilous, and so it was decided to hold them in the smaller cities outside of the capital, where they would be less likely to raise suspicion.

My breath was shallow the day we drove farther from Addis than I had ever been and rolled beneath the tall gate that framed the entrance to Dire Dawa. But I was excited to be part of something daring. I was also sure that if Gashe was arrested, Isaias would set him free.

13

It was near to sunset when I kicked my sneakers into the air —
one, then the other — letting them skew the neat rows of my
brothers' and sisters' shoes on the veranda, and not bothering
to straighten them. The cold marble refreshed my steaming
feet. I was out of breath, tired, but still fired with the excitement that came from flying through the streets of Addis in the
back of a pickup, like a wild bandit on the run. I was a valiant
rebel who could defy the rules and elude the police. It was a
powerful feeling that caused my heart to pump hard and my
chest to swell. I could hardly wait to tell Ishi of the excitement
he had missed by tending to his beloved Fiyeli and the garden.

No one was outside. The house was in darkness, not a
single light from lamp or lantern. And no noise from inside.
The door handle needed oil, as did the hinges that screeched
when I swung open the door.

Etheye rushed at me.

"Praise be to God!" she said. She squeezed my upper arms
and kissed on each cheek. "Praise God! My son, you be
safe!"

Her eyes were crazed with terror. Her grip like the talons
of a hawk.

"Gashe is taken!" she said. "You must leave. You be next!"

She turned me to face the door and reached for the handle.

"What are you saying?"

"They arrested everyone. At the meeting. All of them. Go!"

"But I wasn't at the meeting. I was just giving out papers."

"Why you do this? How you be involved?" Tears flooded her face as she banged her hand flat on my chest. "Why?"

Why was Etheye acting in this irrational way? I had not attended meetings or spoken on street corners. I was a kid, a student at the Cathedral School, a protected son without a thought of politics in his head. Etheye was mistaken.

"Forgive me for being late. I was with my new friends." My new, older friends from the university. I was the youngest son at the edire.

"You sons," Gashe had said, looking up from the lists he had made of names and home villages. "You will take those boxes of papers back to the city and distribute them." The papers on the floor in front of him looked like the ones I had given out after his speeches. Normal paper. Cut in half. The words in Amharic.

"Divide into sections. Stay together in small groups, but do not be seen," he warned.

We were glad to be released from the shuttered house, stuffy with the breath of far too many people. They came, parched and dusty, from all parts of the country, to tell of missing husbands, children in jail and lives of fear.

"My husband, he be a good man. He be taken. Now, how my children live?" a woman wailed.

"My son, tied to a tree. Killed with a bullet in the head."

"All the young men, herded like cattle. Taken. On the night of the second moon."

We ran, all of us sons, for the pickup, the older boys fighting over who would sit in the cab. Another boy and I sat in the back. We didn't pass the papers one to each person as I had on the street corner. We grabbed handfuls from the box, leapt from the bed of the truck and shoved them at the first people we saw. I tucked one in my pocket for Ishi. Back on the pickup, we sped away. To bus stations, the Mercato, dropping them into the open windows of taxis. Anywhere! Someone had the idea to leave the open box in the back. The colored pages fluttered like leaves torn from their branches during a storm.

No one knew who we were. We were nameless, faceless boys. None of us had taken the time even to read what was written on the pages.

"Everything is fine. I have done nothing wrong," I told Etheye. She shoved me toward the door.

"They know who be there. At the edire. They make a list." I had been there only a short time.

"But how?"

She scurried around the room with the rapid, nervous movements of an animal seeking escape from a trap.

"Your friends be in danger, too. Do not delay! Get! Out of here, before the police come." She ran to the window, lifting the edge of the curtains to peer outside.

"Isaias," I said. The first name on my lips. My beloved elephant. He was the government. He would protect us. "Call him!"

Etheye's agitated movements stopped as if I had thrown a bucket of cold water at her. Her eyes were steady for a moment.

"He be gone, too," she whispered. "Even Isaias who be only half Amhara. Like you. You *must* go!"

Isaias was gone?

Not possible.

Etheye snatched the telephone on the first ring. I had to check my room and Gashe's. Make sure there were no papers to incriminate him.

"Yes. Yes," she said, then hung up.

Etheye seized my arm when I tried to move past. Her eyes drilled into mine. "The brother of Gashe be coming. He take you."

"Take me? Where?"

Etheye scurried to the window. "Praise God that Kofi arrives before the police."

The telephone trilled. We both startled. She spoke swiftly in a low tone. Her eyes were sad and worried when she turned to me.

"Obadiah be gone. Daniel be gone. Moza be picked up."

How did she know the names of my new friends from the university?

"This cannot be right. There must be a mistake," I said. "We were together."

The buzzer rang from the gate.

"He be here! Go! Go now!" Her eyes were as crazed as an animal whose throat has not been cut all the way through.

"Etheye ..." I said.

"Go!" She pushed me out the door.

Kofi's car was outside the gate. Engine running. A tall man with muscled arms unfolded from the back door of the sedan. I crawled in beside a man in the traditional dress of an elder. He was slumped against the door, his eyes bugged out, forehead sweating. His cheek bulged on one side. A thin line of green spit drooled down his chin. His hands fidgeted, and he muttered unintelligibly.

My uncle glanced in the rear-view mirror. He peeled away as soon as the door shut, the tires squealing on the pavement the way they did in American movies.

He did not say *Selam,* and neither did I. Kofi leaned into the steering wheel, his knuckles tight. I had never seen him like this. He was always dignified and proper.

The big-shouldered man beside me had the sharp smell of sweat. His eyes scanned the streets, as did mine. He spoke so fast his words blended almost to nonsense as he told Kofi which roads to take, where police might be stationed, who would accept bribes. My uncle shot through the streets, tipping us this way and that, paying no attention to signs that said Slow or Stop. There were few vehicles on the road at this time of day, mostly mini-bus taxis all driving fast, trying to get to where they were going before the sun vanished into darkness. Special Forces police trucks waited at intersections, not moving, not chasing anyone. Just grim-faced men in uniform, arms folded over their chests, the lower half of them leaning on vehicles. Waiting.

A fourth man was in the front passenger seat next to Kofi. Like the stinking man beside me, he also had big arms and blurted directions. Rapidly, like an exchange of gunfire from automatic weapons, they argued loudly over the best route.

Kofi veered abruptly onto a rutted street without pavement and without streetlights. He dimmed his headlights as night took hold. Clouds of dust rolled behind and beside us as Kofi sped like a madman, swerving to avoid other vehicles and gaping potholes.

I sighed deeply when we stopped. I hadn't realized I had been holding my breath.

The guard beside me opened his door even before my uncle cut the engine.

"Come!" he said and beckoned to me. Kofi got out, too.

I recognized nothing. The three of us walked to a cement building that appeared by its size to be a warehouse. There were two large doors at its center, a small door on one end, and a tiny window, high up, laced with barbed wire.

Goats and sheep bleated softly near one side of the building where they seemed to be feeding. Frogs chirped in the cool air. A goat with an ear that flopped over one eye trotted toward me and nuzzled my leg with short horns. I patted the top of its head, then followed Kofi through the wide wooden doors.

Open sacks of grain, their tops rolled down as they were in the Mercato, sat in one corner. Behind them were stacked piles of bulging cloth bags stitched closed. A worker with an old scar on his forehead and a sightless eye made little clouds of dust with the broom he passed over the floor. He bowed slightly before us. Our shoes, I noticed, left tracks of clean, the opposite of the mud that sometimes made Etheye yell when we didn't remove our sneakers.

"You will stay here," Kofi told me. "It is the house of a cousin."

I nodded as if I had a choice. We passed through another door into a storeroom with a very tall ceiling that was filled along its edges with more sacks of grain. Some of the bags were stamped with a red banner that said *Canada* and showed a small flag of that country. The men in the storeroom glanced up, nodded to my uncle and returned to their tasks. Some were seated on the floor playing cards. Some rubbed oily rags over guns. Some slept on sacks. None of them wore shoes.

Kofi used a silver key on a ring to unlock a thick steel door. Inside was a house alive with children, all younger than me and all of them with shaved heads. They stared at me in sudden silence, as if they had never seen a boy before. Kofi spoke to the cousin's wife, then dropped his hand heavily on my shoulder.

"You will be safe here for now. Until I think of something else. You understand?" he asked. "No one will look for you here."

The woman showed me where I would sleep. It was the main room, but there was no upholstered sofa, chairs or low tables. Just stained mattresses outlining the floor. She led me to another door that released an overpowering stench of human excrement when she opened it. She pulled a string that dangled from the ceiling. A bare bulb glared. Truly, not a toilet, just a hole cut in the cement floor. Visible waste that did not drain. Flies buzzed in the air and crawled on the walls. Nowhere to wash.

I hoped Kofi thought of a new plan quickly.

All of the children piled and squirmed onto the mattresses, jumping around and rolling and showing off. The mattress crunched when I sat on the edge. Bits of straw poked through my jeans. Rather than sleep beneath the cowhide, I lay on top fully clothed — jeans, jacket and shirt — and studied the thick cobwebs that draped from the ceiling. A small girl, with the same smoky eyes of her mother, rubbed her hands over my hair, kissed my face and, before I could protest, snuggled beside me.

◆

I itched like a dog with fleas the next morning. Had I really slept? My neck felt like a giant, raw welt, as did the tender skin behind my ears and at my ankles. I tore at my skin, but nothing would stop the itch. Bedbugs had had a feeding frenzy with me as their meal. I was glad Ishi was not here to laugh at how I must look.

I was roused more fully by the smells of cooking. The woman brought a platter piled with eggs, bread and rounds of fried potatoes.

"For you," she said. "Come." She spoke to me in Amharic, but her accent made it sound like a different language.

I sat on a low stool as Gashe did when he ate. One by one, the children gathered to sit at my feet and watch. It was difficult to enjoy the meal with so many eyes following every movement of my hand to my mouth. I held out the platter to offer some to the children. They snatched it with small greedy fingers, stuffing the food into their mouths with the speed of hungry salamanders.

"No! No! No!" their mother yelled, shooing the children. "For him. Only for him! Be gone! Be gone!"

But would these children eat? Or was it the same as it was at home, that Gashe and his guests ate first, and we had what was left?

"I have had enough," I said. I rubbed my stomach to show it was full. "The rest, it can be for them."

"Nonsense," she said. "You eat. You too thin."

But not, I noticed, as thin as Kofi's cousin's wife, who had a row of horizontal bones visible across her chest, and arms that looked like those of a skeleton.

"Too much," I said.

She grinned at the compliment.

"Your mother," she said, "what food she cooks?"

"Injera," I said. "Stews filled with spices. And eggs. Scrambled, like this." Should I tell her I had never before had eggs for the morning meal? Should I tell her they were a rare and precious treat?

She nodded. "She makes this food well?"

"Yes, very good. Etheye is the best cook in all of Ethiopia." The woman's face fell slightly. I had not meant to cause offense. "Exactly as good as what you have made," I added.

My words restored her real smile that showed a gap between two of her front teeth.

When I finished the last of the spiced, sweet tea, she said, "You go. Now. At the mill."

Was I to work, then? Was I to earn the eggs this woman had cooked?

14

The mill was shrouded in a haze of dust even though the large doors were open. Fine powder covered everything — the floor, the walls, the windows high in the roof, and the air tasted of it. The cobwebs that swayed in the slight breeze were heavy with it. Even the workers were sifted with white or reddish brown, depending on what they were grinding.

There were four workstations lined up in a row, where men hefted sacks on their shoulders and poured grain into funnels. Pulled by a wide spinning belt with a twist in the middle, cement discs that looked as wide as I was tall revolved around each other to crush the kernels into flour. The sound from the motors that drove them was deafening, and the reek of diesel was enough to make me wish I had not eaten. I had never thought before of where flour came from, or how it was made.

A man stooped near each motor, watched it closely. One poured grain into the machine, another scooped the ground flour into sacks. The chaff, I noticed, spat out the side of the building. But through all of the noise and dust and putrid smells filtered the rhythmic rise and fall of men's voices in song.

Outside the big front doors was a long line of people in the rough dress of farmers. Some had sacks of grain at their feet. There were oxen with wide horns and braying donkeys hitched to carts piled with grain. Men lounged on sacks or leaned against the front of the building, smoking and waiting to load or carry purchases. Voices raised and arms moved in a flurry as customers bartered and argued over prices.

What was I doing here? What was I supposed to do?

"They tell you where you go. Tomorrow," the wife of Kofi's cousin had told me.

I picked up a broom leaning in a corner and began the futile work of sweeping the mill floor, moving the broom to the rhythm of the men's voices.

"No! No! No!" A man scrambled to me and snatched the broom from my hand. The white powder in his hair made him look prematurely old. "My work!" he said.

"I would like to help," I said. "I have nothing to do." He shook his head.

"No help!" He moved the bristles back and forth in swift motions that raised low clouds of dust, and he looked at me with fear.

Then I understood. He thought I would take away his job.

Outside, I discovered I was not in the country as I had expected, but still in the city. There was no wall or gate. Most of the buildings had low flat roofs with cylindrical metal tanks on top to collect rainwater, and like the house part of the mill, most were made of mud.

The goats I had seen the night before munched from a pile of husks of wheat and teff. Others rummaged near the base of scraggly trees in the yard. One nibbled the ear of another, while a goat with soft eyes and a slight, friendly-looking smile tilted its head to look at me.

I thought of Ishi. I stroked its ears when the goat pressed its head against my hand, then wiggled its lips to nibble the edge of my jean jacket.

The bald-headed children ran in the yard with a burlap sack, trying to fill it with air. I took a step toward them, but the cousin's wife dropped her basket and ran to me.

"No here!" she said. She lifted her arms to cover my shoulders, swirled her dress around me, and pushed me toward the building. "No be see!"

"Nobesee?" I asked. She shook her head and glanced over both shoulders.

"Go! In!" She motioned with the back of her hands. I entered the building and when I looked back, she was again busy with her work.

Nobesee. Do not be seen.

I stayed, then, in the back room among the bulging sacks of grain and flour. The men who worked at the mill, I learned, were former soldiers released from their posts when the government changed. But they told me that here, at the home of Kofi's cousin, I would be safe. They told me they kept their weapons, the useful AK-47s, that they were not just dumb workers who bowed before customers, ground their grain and carried the sacks to the waiting vehicles or carts.

"We protect you," an elder worker told me, his voice quiet and solemn. He had a wide puckered scar that ran from his temple to his nose. "Never worry."

"Do you have bullets?" I whispered, for I knew that while guns were plenty, bullets were scarce.

The ex-soldier nodded. Smoke from his cigarette drifted from his nose and from his mouth when he spoke.

"Do not worry," he said.

I found the old soldier again the next day. The mill was closed. The machines quiet. No clouds of dust made it hard to breathe. The only sounds were of men talking in groups and, nearby, slapping down playing cards.

The scarred soldier sat on the floor, his back supported by a bag of grain. He watched the gray smoke from his cigarette drift to the ceiling as if it was incense. I sat beside him. His chest was nearly as thin as mine, but his shoulders and arms were thick and rounded by muscle.

"Why don't you leave? Why not return home?" I asked.

"To go back to the village? That solves nothing," he said.

"But to go back to farming. You could raise food for your family."

"How to farm with no seed? When you plant, but must give the harvest to the landlord? That be a slave. To labor with no hope of change."

"But here you have nothing. You sleep on sacks of grain."

"Here, Uncle lets us stay. We work for him, yes. We make money with the strength of our bodies. But, we no be slaves. You see, him." He nodded his chin toward the man who moved slowly and slept often. "He no work hard. It be a choice to move slow, to sleep, rather than to work. Uncle no make us work. It be a choice."

"I don't understand." But I thought of the cousins who hid in our secret room so they wouldn't be taken for the army. Without Gashe's protection, what choice had they?

Had these men who worked now at the mill been forced to be soldiers?

"No one get to Uncle. No one get to you," he said. He tapped the end of his cigarette to extinguish it and put the butt in his pocket. "Nothing to happen in this place. We protect it."

15

The tomorrow of the cousin's wife was not the literal tomorrow, but a day in the future. When it finally came, it brought with it Etheye, Kofi, a dark-green four-wheel-drive vehicle called a Nissan Pathfinder, and two strong men.

Etheye's face was covered with nearly as many welts as mine, as if she, too, had fought an army of bedbugs. Her left forearm was encased in a plaster cast. But she glowed with joy as she ran to me like a child with her arms open wide, singing *la-la-la-la-la-la* loudly and calling my name. I felt the same happiness rising in me, like steam from a boiling pot. I rushed to meet her. She had come to take me home.

Etheye held me too long, pressing our bodies together, her cast heavy on my shoulder. Then she kissed me over and over, so many times that I wanted to swat her away and wipe them off.

"My son, my son, my son," she repeated as if it had been years and not days since we had seen each other. She ran her hand all over my hair and my face, then left her palm to linger on my jaw.

I looked past her to see the sport-utility vehicle with the spare cans of gas strapped to the back. Ishi would be so jealous when we drove into the garden. I would remember every detail of my stay at the mill and the journey. I would tell my brothers about it slowly, drawing out each piece of the story.

Etheye stroked my jaw with her thumb, then took both of my hands in hers.

"You have need to go. To go far away." Her voice was so quiet, it took my attention. I looked at her closely, not understanding. She was here, wasn't she, to take me home?

"You go to my father. In the country. Where it be safe." She spoke the words clearly, but her eyes said something else. Her eyes were shot with blood that I had not noticed before, and they spoke still of fear. She lifted her broken arm to my face again and caressed my cheek with the back of her fingers.

"There are soldiers," I whispered. "Here."

"Here? They be here?" She backed away. Her eyebrows pressed together like two caterpillars.

"No. No," I said, shaking my head. "Good soldiers. Ones who protect me."

She dipped her head. She sighed deeply, as if gathering strength. When she looked up, she said, "Gashe be not returned."

How selfish I was. I had thought only of my longing to return home. Not once had I thought of Gashe.

"Still gone?" I asked, although I knew what "still gone" meant. Gashe might never return.

"They tell me nothing," she said. How quickly I had forgotten that night. How quickly I had forgotten her fear.

"I try," she said. "To ask the proper questions at the prison."

"Did they come for me?" I asked. She nodded but said nothing more.

The bruises and cuts on her face, her broken arm — these were my fault, from the night the police searched for me. Had they barged in the way the revolutionaries had years ago? But the Special Police were not seeking food and shelter. Had they beaten her with fists, with sticks, or with boots and batons?

"Etheye, what happened?"

She shook her head. "It be nothing."

"Tell me." I needed to know. She closed her eyes and shook her head. I laced my fingers with hers. "You say, 'Tesfaye, you are my mountain.' You must tell me this."

She glanced at me, then shifted her gaze past my shoulder.

"They come," she said. "They took apart the house. Top to bottom. They find the secret room beneath the roof. They find writings in your room."

"Your arm," I said. She lifted the cast in the air, as if to show me it didn't hurt.

What did they do to her as they demanded answers? Is that when they broke her arm? Or hit her face?

"Ishi and Tezze come to fight them. They jump on the backs and punch."

No! Ishi looked so much like me.

"They took Ishi?" My voice was small.

Etheye shook her head.

"The police, he points it the gun at my head. We stay so still. I tell him, 'Tesfaye he go in the morning. With my husband.'

"'Where?' he ask.

"'You think my husband tell me his business?'"

Etheye took a slow breath. I held mine tight.

"And then I say, '*You* know where they be! *You* took them!'

"'Take another son!' he yell. 'Take both!'

"I scream, 'Look at this house! You think my husband no have connections?'"

"And then?" I asked.

"And then they sneer with ugly faces. 'We come back,'

one said. But they no come back."

"And so? Everything is okay?" What a stupid question. My mother's face was bruised. Her arm was in a cast. What else was she not telling me?

"They want only you," she said. "They have a list. Even, it be on the TV."

My mother's broken body was not because of Gashe. It was because of me thinking I was important handing out papers. How stupid I had been. It was as if I had beaten her with my own hands.

Now she wanted me to go away.

But with Gashe gone, there was no one to give her status and no one to provide for our family. These were the responsibilities, now, of her sons. Tezze, Ishi and I were the oldest boys.

"I cannot leave you," I said.

"It be a short time until they forget you. Until they hunt someone else," she said.

Etheye turned from me suddenly, as if she had run out of time, and ordered the ex-soldiers to move packages from the trunk of Uncle's car to the Pathfinder. I saw cardboard cartons filled with plastic bottles of water, cans of Coca-Cola, and a market basket with clothes.

"This be for him," she told the driver. "Only him. You understand?"

Coca? For me? A whole box?

Drinking soda, driving in a SUV, tricking the police, running away from the bad guys. I was like an American movie star.

Etheye's voice was firm as she commanded the men. She could look after herself, and if she couldn't, she could rely on Tezze and Ishi, the servants and my uncles. She did not need me. Not really. She was cunning. She knew what to do.

And it was only for a short time that I would be gone.

I had never been to Ababa's village, and while part of me feared for my stubborn mother, I could hardly wait to climb in the special vehicle and slam the door. Loading the supplies and saying goodbye took far too long. Why did we need to take so much? When he came to us, Ababa arrived with only what he could carry in one hand.

I stepped from the running board into the front seat with the driver. He had no neck, just a thick column of muscle that attached his head to his body. Another man of similar body type was seated directly behind me. An automatic rifle was on the seat beside him. Both men had revolvers at their belts.

The vehicle lurched into gear and the driver rammed his foot on the accelerator, shooting a spray of dirt from the tires that smudged the image of my mother standing beside Kofi and waving with her good arm. I would be back soon.

The driver was a lunatic who sped much too fast for the road. He leaned into the steering wheel, his biceps bulging as he swerved to the left and the right to avoid potholes and farmers with bony animals. I felt like a table-tennis ball, jostling to and fro in the front seat, sometimes with my whole body lifting into the air. I clung to the edge of the bucket seat, braced myself with one hand on the dash and stared out the front window. The driver pulled the SUV onto the wrong side of the road to navigate a sharp curve. A loaded truck hurtled toward us. Its horn blared. I latched onto the handgrip and prepared to die. Our driver yanked the wheel. He veered onto the proper side of the road at the last second, so close that I couldn't believe we hadn't collided.

My head followed the flash of the heavy truck. Out the back window, I glimpsed a jet rising in the sky. The airport was east, which meant we were headed west.

The driver floored the accelerator when the pavement

ended, bouncing us on a warped and twisted path. Dust billowed in a cloud around us. The windshield wipers flapped frantically to clear the powdery dirt. The cargo in the back slid from side to side as the vehicle rocked so hard I thought it would flip. I learned quickly not to leave my tongue anywhere near my teeth, and not, for one second, to loosen my grip.

There was no arguing over the best route, or guards or bribes as there had been when my uncle drove me to safety the night of the edire. No one spoke. No one seemed to breathe.

We sped through an empty countryside, barren but for the umbrellas of the oda, clusters of scraggly bushes, and dry grass that shifted in the wind. We passed people walking on the road carrying bundles of sticks on their backs, shepherds with their dirty flocks, and cowherds with scrawny cows. It was only then that the driver slowed to keep from hitting anyone or burying them in the flying grit.

As the hours passed, the landscape transformed from vast moonscape to bush. My head drifted to my chest as the blackness of night fell, and from time to time I startled from my restless sleep. I must stay awake. I must help watch the road. But my eyes were uncooperative, growing heavy and begging to close for just a minute.

A loud smash. I jerked awake, my eyes wide in the darkness cut only by the beam of our headlights. The windshield dented inward, cracks spreading in a concentric spider web.

"Shiftas!" shouted the driver. The man in the backseat grabbed the rifle and snapped off the safety. Outside, men yelled. A flurry of stones pounded the side panels and slid across the windshield. I ducked when one crashed against my window. The driver stooped to see through the damaged glass and hauled the Pathfinder off the road. The headlights caught the startled faces of men leaping from our reckless path. I was sure we would crush the men, or that their bodies would fly across the hood, but I was too scared to scream. I hung on and didn't breathe. We jolted and twisted over the rocky ground, then fishtailed violently through a swampy area.

I might make it to Ababa's village, but I would be dead when I got there.

"What did they want?" I asked when our speed leveled off and I could breathe again.

"Anything they can get," he said. "Petrol. Food. Money. You."

"Me?"

"For ransom," he said. "It's not every day they see a SUV."

"They know we have some thing or someone important," said the guard in the backseat. He kept the gun in his hand, still pointed at the side window. The other hand was on the armrest of the door, ready to drop the window.

"Hang on!" the driver said. He tore through the night, until I heard a loud thump.

The back left side of the Pathfinder dropped.

"*Sagara!*" yelled the driver. He slammed the steering wheel with the heel of his hand.

"Shiftas?" I asked. My timid question croaked in a most embarrassing way. The taste of metal coated the back of my tongue, and spit pooled in my mouth.

"Flat tire! Shit!" He scrambled from the seat, as did the backseat passenger. He took the automatic rifle with him. I blinked from the sudden rush of light when they lifted the hatch. Cool air breathed into the vehicle as they shunted the boxes and fished out tools. I got out, too, and offered to hold the flashlight while the driver jacked up the SUV. The guard turned his back to us, holding his weapon in position and scanning the darkness. I squinted into the night.

What did he see? All I saw were stars high in the sky and the smiling sliver of the bright moon.

The driver worked faster than a machine, cranking, releasing the spare, lifting the vehicle, swapping the tire, tightening the bolts, lowering it, re-tightening. He threw the old tire in the back, tossed in the crates and slammed the door.

"Let's go!" he said. I piled in the front seat.

"I'll drive," said the guard. He tossed the AK to the driver, who caught it mid-air.

The driving was less frantic, and we encountered no more bandits, but now and again the headlights caught the shine of animals' eyes moving in the darkness.

The Pathfinder jerked to a halt just past sunrise, pitting my forehead against the dash. The vehicle pointed straight down. A river with steep banks was below.

"You will never make it," said the man in the back. The man at the wheel did not answer. He gunned the accelerator. I shot my hands against the dash and stiffened my legs against the floor. We careened toward the water. The Pathfinder's engine roared, then sputtered when we plowed into the churning water.

"I told you! I told you!" the man in the backseat yelled, thrusting his arms into the air. "Why do you never listen? You should have let me drive!"

"Get out!" the driver said. The rear door opened. "You, too," he said to me. "We stop here."

The muddy water sucked at my legs and pulled them downstream. I clung to the door as I sloshed through the river to the front of the vehicle. The first driver loaded the food and water bottles into the guard's arms. He swung the basket over his shoulder, like a woman going to market, then took half the load. They hoisted the boxes onto their heads and waded through water that swirled in circles and deepened as high as our waists.

16

The mud path from the river was narrow but well packed, as if trampled by many feet. But unlike mine, in shoes with a Velcro strap that squished water with every step, I suspected the feet that had gone before were bare. I should have been tired, but I was strangely awake, glad to walk for hours and to carry nothing as we followed the dirt trail. It was humid and damp, but not lush jungle as I expected. The grasses were green and the huge trees with soft trunks were plentiful and of a kind I did not know. I recognized the long wide leaves of banana trees but little else. The trill of birds I could not identify filled the moist air, and sometimes I caught the rapid movement of small animals in the undergrowth. In the spaces without trees, I could see forever, rolled out in front of me in muted shades of yellow and brown, complemented by a sky of transparent blue.

How different things looked on foot and away from the city, how richly beautiful was the landscape of my country.

I smelled the village before I saw it. The familiar aroma of smoldering eucalyptus and dried cow dung, the scent that meant Etheye was cooking, mixed with roasting meat. Saliva poured into my mouth, and my stomach rumbled its warning of hunger.

When had I last eaten?

The wood smoke and the soft notes of singing brought us to a clearing with an assembly of round mud huts with grass roofs. A thin stream of smoke drifted from the top of each one. A rooster with a wobbling wattle pecked the roof of the largest hut, which was set slightly apart from the others. There were animals everywhere — cows, goats, sheep and chickens that grazed and foraged without curiosity about intruders. Two women squatted near a cooking fire burning meat on a long-handled stick. Others I could see in the distance, slapping clothes on rocks near a murky river and draping the shirts, dresses and pants over low bushes. Children of all different sizes yelled and ran to kick a wad of leaves. They abandoned their game when they saw us and rushed to greet us, the girls like birds in bright-patterned dresses, the boys in sandals made from scraps of leather or old tires.

They swarmed like mosquitos, touching my hair, my clothes, my arms and hands. They pointed at my feet and laughed, as if my sneakers were funny, and they exclaimed over my watch that glinted in the sunlight. I bent to show them, but the numbers were incomplete and fading; the battery was failing. After they'd had a good look and they kissed me all over, they grasped my arms, several on each side. Chattering all at once, and too quickly for me to understand, they pulled me into the village. The guards followed, carrying my food on their shoulders.

Some of the village women had black lines inked along the front of their necks — straight, horizontal lines, zigzag lines, or a combination of both. The women looked up from their washing and cooking, their glances as curious as those of the children, but they did not stop their work.

The hut of Etheye's father was the one set a little apart. He was dressed in tribal clothes, a long tunic of cotton gauze and pants held up by a drawstring. His smile when he saw me showed all the teeth he had left. He kissed me on the cheeks, praised God for bringing me here and spat on the ground the way Etheye so often did. He held me at arm's length to examine me, turning my shoulders to the right and to left, and indicating that I should turn around so he could see all of me.

He looked just as tall and just as dark, but somehow softer here, more relaxed, more wise than he did when he came to stay with us in the city. In Addis he sometimes looked ridiculous, how he sat on the front edge of the seat, clinging with his fingernails to the dash of Gashe's car, as if it was a terrifying thing to move through the city so fast. But here in the country, he did not look frightened or stupid. He looked thoughtful and dignified as he greeted me and invited me to sit.

"What brings you?" he asked in Gurage. He spoke slowly and clearly.

"Kofi, Gashe's brother, sent me," I said in Amharic. I wished I could speak his language, at least as well as I could understand it, but the sounds and the twists of the tongue eluded me, no matter how hard I tried.

"Ah." He nodded sagely. "I see."

Inside, the hut was dark and hung with animal hides. The air was thick with the odors of cows and goats, their feed and their dung. It was like the room in the servants' quarters where Etheye kept her goats and chickens but worse. Much worse. The invisible stink choked me like smoke. I wasn't sure how long I could sit there in silence with Ababa.

The insides of my stomach pressed on themselves, squeezing, squeezing. I stumbled from the hut, bent over, sweating and gasping for air. Vomit burned my throat, but when I swallowed and gulped air, the contents of my stomach receded. A girl brought water in a gourd, but I shook my head. I wanted it so much, but Etheye had warned me about drinking the water here or eating village food.

"You be sick," she said. "Very sick. And die fast of loose poop."

Where had they put my bottles of water and cans of Coca? I worked my mouth to make as much spit as possible to rinse away the awful taste of vomit.

Ababa came outside. He seemed to be trying to suppress a smile.

"Why don't you keep the animals outside?" I blurted. "They should be outside!"

Ababa threw back his head to laugh in the way we laughed at our country cousins who knew nothing.

"The cows are my wealth," he said. "Why would I feed my wealth to the jackals?"

And so it came to be that I slept on the straw with the animals and with the ticks and spiders that lived there. The smell gagged me and I worried all through the night that one of them would step on me and break me or perhaps worse, that one of them would spray me with urine or empty its bowels on my face. And the sounds of the night kept me awake, the shifting of the cattle and their lowing, the crunching of hungry goats, and the calling of hyenas in the distance.

How they laughed at me, far from home, living in a mud hut.

◆

Village life had the incessant rhythm of the women's songs. Everyone kept busy washing clothes, boiling food, collecting water in clay pots, slashing huge plants with machetes, tending to animals or to babies. It was a pattern of life that seemed to have no end. Elders squatted on the ground to talk and tell stories, drink coffee, sing and pray. They spat on me when I ventured too close. Only the very youngest children understood fun. Like me, they loved to chase anything that rolled, and to keep it from the others.

With legs nearly as long as they were tall, I had the advantage with distance, but they were swifter and more cunning with their feet, stealing the ball and burbling with glee, and calling to be ready for a pass.

But even the youngest of children had animals to tend. I followed them like a towering, orphaned goat as they herded cows to the feeding grounds. They gathered sticks for cooking fires and sometimes helped the women dig roots. They hooted and pushed away my hands when I tried to help.

Only I was useless, with no skills to offer. What good was the ability to read and write and to calculate numbers in the village?

When I trailed after the women, they tried to carry me across streams as if I was an infant child, worried I might lose my balance and land in the water with my foolish shoes. But to go barefoot? Sharp stones, thorns and prickles tore at my city feet. I couldn't wait to go home.

I walked to the hilltop behind the village to see the large round hut topped with a cross that served as a church. It was also the best place to see what lay beyond the village.

I explored the slow-moving river upstream and downstream, surprised that the women fetched water for cooking and washed clothes in a river where cattle drank less than a half-day's walk away. Across the river were open fields where oxen dragged plows and turned dirt to prepare for the planting time. What would they grow here? Teff? Nug?

Wheat? I didn't know, nor could I ask. I had discovered my knowledge of Gurage was as limited as my ability to speak it. Ababa was the only one I understood, and he was kept too busy with prayers and elders and animals. Everyone else spoke Gurage so fast that it blended like the garbled melody of a song that made no sense. By the time I picked out a word I knew, they had used a hundred more words I did not know.

Back at the village, the women chattered as they used the hard shells of gourds to scrape and scoop the dirt near the base of a magnificent tree with a wide trunk. They dug for hours until the ground beneath it was hollowed like a deep bowl, exposing gray roots thicker than my arm that protected a heavy pot wrapped in giant leaves. A woman used a machete to hack at the roots, cutting out the bulbous tumors that another woman chopped into pieces and added to the pot of stew that bubbled over the low fire.

When she put down the machete, I moved closer to see what was inside the leaf-wrapped pot that had been buried. She shucked the dried leaves and released a metal band. Inside was a stink so powerful and so rank it had to be poisonous. Yellow or green or black — a rotting, fermented smell that sent me stumbling away from the raucous laughter of the women.

It was as if I was an imbecile who could do nothing right — unless you counted giving people a reason to laugh.

How had Ishi survived this life? Perhaps he was correct. Perhaps he was stronger and tougher than me.

There were many plants and trees I did not recognize, and more birds than I had ever seen or heard before. I worried snakes might slither near my feet or dangle from trees ready to strike. Or that vicious animals might stalk me. I kept alert to sound and movement, and noticed that sometimes a girl trailed me at a quiet distance. Still, I jerked back in horror the day I found a hare hanging from a tree, a thin wire looped around its foot.

The breeze was slight, the hare newly dead. It made me think of Gashe, how he liked to say that when spiders unite they can tie up a lion. I had always pictured the lion in a spiders' net hanging from a tree. I had also wondered how many spiders, exactly, it would take. Thousands? Millions? And how long would the spiders have to work? Could it be possible?

All things are possible. I heard Gashe's words in my head as distinctly as if he was standing beside me, laying a hand on my shoulder. But I was alone on this path I walked.

Where was Gashe now? What had they done to him? I turned from the hare, the image too awful. I ducked low and pushed leaves and branches from my way as I edged the muddy river. Why was it so wrong what he did? Why couldn't he have left things alone?

I remembered the papers that had gotten me in trouble, how they swirled and blew from the back of the pickup. I remembered how happy I had felt that night, and how free.

I rubbed my back pocket, then slid my fingers inside. Holes had worn through at the folds of the leaflet I had saved for Ishi, but the words were clear: *Let us be strong. Let us be one people.*

As I returned the paper to my pocket, I felt the girl's eyes on me. I hadn't sensed her today. It was the girl with the curious eyes who had a thin line tattooed below her bottom lip that ran straight to her chin. She had brought me water on my first day in the village. Whenever I caught her looking, she dipped her head and glanced away, but not before I saw her lips curve upwards.

Why did she follow me? Was it to make sure I didn't get lost?

As with every other day, I ignored her. But I slowed my pace. I hoped she would catch up and want to come beside me.

I would like to talk to her, but what was I supposed to say?

On the days I saw her busy with the endless work of women, I repeated Gurage words while I explored outside the village, trying to work my tongue around the unusual sounds. I practiced separate words, and some things I might say to the girl: "The moon tonight is pretty. Ah, I see that you are making food. What are you cooking? Your eyes shine like stars. The pattern of that basket you weave makes me think of a rainbow. What kind of seeds are you sorting?" Everything I thought of saying sounded stupid, and with my accent and handicapped tongue I would seem even stupider, and she would laugh at me, and it would be a great embarrassment. So mostly I pretended that I didn't notice her.

In the evening, the only light was that of the stars and the moon. I lay on the cool earth, arms crossed behind my head, and listened to the night sounds of bats, crickets, frogs and distant hyenas. I stared at the face in the moon, directly where its forehead would be. I wondered if Ishi was doing the same thing. I concentrated my powers to send Ishi a message with my mind.

My message was this: What is the best thing to say to a cute girl? I waited for a long time, until all of the stars glittered in the sky — many more than we could see in Addis — but Ishi did not answer. I wished I had paid more attention to my sisters' romance movies. How did you get a girl to like you that way? What were the proper things to say?

Some younger children came and lay beside me, all in a row, all lying in the dirt exactly as I was.

I pointed at the moon. *"Chereka,"* I said in Amharic.

"Hay hay," they laughed. *"Candra."* They giggled when I repeated the Gurage word. Then we pointed at the stars and exchanged those words.

All of a sudden, the kids jumped up. They grabbed my hands and pulled me to the middle of the village where everyone was gathered around a large fire to share the food the women had made.

Although I knew the insult, I shook my head each time they invited me to eat. I didn't want to die in the manner Etheye said I would if I ate their food, so instead I sat a little apart, drank fizzy Coca from a can and ate the injera that Etheye had packed for me.

I snuck closer after the meal, when they told stories by the light and warmth of the fire. Babies curled in their mothers' arms, some latched on their mothers' breasts. Older children sat close together, some of them propped back to back. Their faces glowed eerily from the shadows cast by the flickering and snapping light. The adults laughed loudly in a way that spread even to the smallest of children.

I watched the storyteller's expressions, and those of the listeners. I wished I knew the places to rock back, laugh and slap my leg.

This was also the time they cleaned their feet. I was glad to have eaten little.

The smell of rot was overpowering, like the stink of eggs forgotten in the sun. They scraped with twigs at the black fungus that grew between their toes. This night, a man near me eased a worm from the place between his smallest toe and the next one, calmly pulling it where it had crawled through his skin. Bile rose in my throat, but still I watched, fascinated at his skill. If he broke it, would two worms grow?

There were exclamations and pointing when he lifted it high to show everyone, as if this was a great prize and not an embarrassment that wriggled from his fingertips. His grin was glorious as he flung the worm into the fire.

Singing, clapping and the patter of drums followed the stories, and soon the women's colorful dresses swayed to the music. And then, when the flames died down and Ababa's final prayer was said, I fed Gashe's leaflet to the red coals. I watched the paper ignite, flame its brilliance, then turn to ash.

◆

The days passed slowly, one after the other, each one the same. The flow of the river had lessened, and the moon had shrunk its face by half. All that was left of Etheye's injera was a piece the size of my palm. I nibbled it slowly around the edges, savoring each tiny bite and thinking of Etheye, how she mixed the batter and poured it with such care in a circle from the outside in, and how it bubbled on top to a pitted finish. How many times had I watched her do it? How many times had I wished I were a girl so I could hold the bowl high and make it pour? Why always the same way? From outside in? Why not start in the middle?

The tasty bits of wat had been gone for days. Tomorrow I would be out of food completely. What would happen next? Would I be forced to eat the villagers' stinky concoctions? How long would it take before I died?

Maybe I should save what was left. But no, I had gnawed the injera to a morsel, not worth saving.

How would it be to perish from hunger? Slow and painful.

Dying of hunger would be like Abiy Tsome. Fifty-five days without meat, milk, cheese, yogurt or eggs. Nearly two months with nothing good to eat. How famished we were for something delicious by the time Fasika came, and how we acted like locusts who set upon food without tasting.

Starving would be a fast without end.

Perhaps death by loose bowels would be better.

I put the last bite in my mouth, chewing, chewing, chewing, as thoroughly as a cow, trying to make it last. I longed to go home. I wanted to sleep on a soft mattress with Ishi and to be away from the stink of animals, the greasy burnt meat and the incessant praying of Ababa. I would not miss these things.

The moon, though. The moon I would miss. It was so bright here in the country, like a spotlight straight from the Heavens, so large when it was full that I could see dimples in its face. I knew this was the same moon Ishi and I spied through the rusted slots in the roof, I knew it, yet here it was even more beautiful, more peaceful.

And the stars. Who knew there could be so many in the black hood of the sky? I could hardly wait to tell Ishi I understood now why he watched the night sky, and I knew he could hardly wait to hear of my journey, and to tell me all that had happened in my absence. Telling him would make this strange dream I lived real. And living it in memory would be better, I was sure, than living it in real life.

17

Etheye came the very next day, as if she knew that I had run out of food. Kofi brought her. A stranger came also, but in a second vehicle. I wished they had brought Ishi.

The stranger was dressed in solid black pants and shirt, and he wore the Roman collar of a Catholic priest. His name was Solomon.

"It is he who will take you," Kofi said.

"Uncle, if it pleases you? He will take me home? To Addis?" I could hardly wait to get home. Running water. A toilet that flushed. Fresh clothes. People who spoke the same language and understood me, even during the times I did not speak. No ticks. No bedbugs. No cows sleeping in the same room. No stinking feet. No foot worms.

"No," Kofi said. His face was stern, like Gashe's when he was not pleased.

"No?"

Etheye took my hand. Her cast, I noticed, was ragged along the edges, and she bore no scars or bruising on her face.

"He will take you away. Out of the country," Kofi said.

"Out of the country?"

Why was Kofi trying to get rid of me? I had done nothing but deliver meaningless papers. I had simply driven through the city having fun with my friends. I had been an obedient son.

"Until," he said. He scanned the village, then let his eyes rest on me. "Until all of this blows over. It will be so." He dismissed further questions with a movement of his hand. I watched him step past the cooking fire to the river, back straight, head high, exactly like Gashe.

I could not leave Ethiopia. Like others at the Cathedral School, I would leave only to go to university, and then I would return immediately to help Gashe and to take care of Etheye and my sisters. That was the plan. I was not old enough for university. It was not my time to leave. What Kofi said was not possible.

I felt the heat of my mother's body and the movement of her dress as she came near and took my hand.

"Etheye ..." I said.

"It be for the best," she said.

"How? How can it be for the best? I cannot leave!"

"You *must* leave. You understand?" Her look was direct and unwavering. "Here, you no survive."

"What if I stay here? In the village? With Ababa? It is safe."

"It not be safe always. They find you. Sooner or later."

"But, Etheye ..."

"They have ways. They know things. Sabba ..." Her voice trailed off. She looked down, then raised her face to me and spoke with authority. "You must go. It be better to be a poor slave in the world than to be having no life here."

A slave? I was going somewhere to be a slave? To Egypt, then.

"I can't."

"You can," she said. "You will." She cupped her hands around my face. We were both the same height, I noticed.

We were both lean and strong. The curve of the baby had begun to round her stomach, like the waxing of the moon. She gazed into my eyes and spoke as if I was a small child.

"It be the *only* way you to survive," she said. I wanted to ask news of the others, about my friends Obadiah and Moza and Daniel, but I was too afraid of what she might say.

"But how? Where will I go?"

"No worry about how. Kofi make it happen with his friend. You go," she said.

Kofi had made things happen before — hiding in the mill, the village, now this. To be transported, to live as a slave … I could not. I had skills of the mind, not the body.

But to live? Wasn't that the most important thing?

Yet my life drained away, seeped from my head, down through my body and out my feet. My life pooled on the soil and sank into the earth of my homeland.

A chilling breeze shook the leaves of trees and caught the sunlight like the discs of a tambourine. Etheye's long skirt swirled around her legs. I glimpsed her feet, the second toe longer than the first. The wind rippled the sides of my favorite T-shirt, the lucky shirt with the grinning face of a monkey on the front.

My lucky shirt had not saved me. My life ended, standing with my mother in a village of mud huts.

"When?" I asked. I couldn't look at her. Instead, I looked in the distance, to Kofi and his Catholic friend, talking by the river.

"Today. Now," Etheye said. Her voice held the sorrow I felt in my heart.

"Now?"

I saw Ababa then, coming down the hill from the village church where he often went to pray. He held a long stick upright in his hand, but he did not lean on it. He lifted it with each step as a shepherd will when he walks with his sheep. He stopped in front of me, opened his arms wide, and with his deep voice resonant, he called everyone together. Slowly, everyone left their tasks and circled around. He explained that I would be going on a journey, and he asked for God's blessing. It was no coincidence that he faced me to the east, the direction of Christ's second coming.

"Blessed Almighty God, we give You thanks. We adore and glorify You. O Lord have mercy on us," he said. Everyone but Ababa pressed their palms together, fingertips up. He lifted his arms and face toward the sky. I dipped my head.

Ababa prayed to God and to the Blessed Virgin that I would remain safe. The others joined him to intone the Mariam prayer: "Hail, O Mary, full of grace. The Lord is with Thee ..."

We stood then, in silence, Ababa's hands still in the air as I felt the villagers' energy and prayerfulness enter me in a way I had never experienced. Why had Gashe kept me from church as I grew older? With his thumb, Ababa made the sign of the cross on my forehead. When he released his hands, everyone, including me, made the sign of the cross. "In the name of the Father, of the Son and of the Holy Spirit, One God."

My grandfather took my face in both his hands, kissed me once on each cheek, then once again on the first cheek. Then he pressed his lips against mine — a lovers' kiss, like in the movie *Titanic*. And when he did, he forced a great wad of saliva from his mouth to mine.

My eyes flew open. My eyebrows hit my hairline. A gag rose in my throat, and although I did not know this custom, I knew the offense I would cause if I spat his spit in the dust.

Etheye stood behind and to the right of Ababa. Hers was a broad, knowing smirk, and her eyes danced. She had known this would happen, yet she had not warned me.

Ababa's spittle pooled in my mouth, mixing with my own disgust. Everyone stared at me. Not moving.

Then I heard Gashe's voice in my head, the day I had foolishly taken tere sega. *Just swallow quickly. Then it will be over,* he had said.

Obedient son, I swallowed. I couldn't wait to get out of there, to wash my mouth with big gulps of Coca.

Everyone came to kiss and hug me, nod, grin and offer Etheye's style of spit blessings for my safety. Kofi and Solomon moved toward the vehicles, heads close, voices low. They stopped beside the car and shook hands. Solomon got into the driver's seat. Kofi went to his vehicle. Etheye held my hand and stroked my face.

She kissed me on both cheeks, the forehead and my chin, then pulled me close and held me as if she would never let go.

"You be safe, my heart," she whispered. Her eyes pooled.

A fist swelled in my throat. A man must be strong and brave. A man must not cry.

She pulled back and looked into my eyes. "You a clever boy, a strong son. I never forget about you. Never. You be my soul," she said. She squeezed my hands. "You must live."

And she spat on the ground.

Three times. To ensure good fortune.

18

The backseat of Solomon's car was covered with cardboard boxes, bright blue where they weren't worn at the corners, and heavy enough that they squished the upholstery. Suitcases were piled on top, also old. The kind with soft sides, zippers and belts around the middle.

"I will keep you safe," he said after a time, but he didn't have the thick neck and shoulders of the men who had kept me safe before. He looked more like a teacher than a guard, and I had noticed no gun.

"Do not fear," he said. But how would he protect me from bandits if they came again? Or soldiers? Or police?

He spoke Amharic, but he did not speak well. He groped for words and often used the wrong ones. How much did he understand? Solomon was a Ugandan name, but neither did he look Ugandan. Near his hairline was an unusual ridge of black that looked like a stain of ink.

At the outside edges of his eyes were the crinkles of an elder, but he had no strands of white in his hair, and he moved in the village with the health and assurance of a younger man. I sensed something about him that was false, but I could not discern what it was.

Solomon gripped the steering wheel with both hands and focused on keeping to the path I had walked a few weeks earlier with the guards who had carried bottled water and boxes of Coca on their shoulders. Giant leaves and branches scraped both sides of the vehicle. Solomon's jaw was clenched, and the bones of his knuckles showed through his skin.

"Where are we going?" I asked.

"Away," he said.

"But where? Etheye said, 'out of the country.' To which country will we go?"

He took his eyes from the trail briefly and glanced at me. "I cannot tell you this. Trust me. I take care of you. You understand?"

"No, I don't understand. I would like to know, at least, where I am going." I did not like giving my trust to a stranger and not knowing what would happen next.

"There is danger," he said. "Too much danger in knowledge."

And so, again, I would be kept in the dark as my life was decided for me. You will not be an artist. You will no longer share a room with your brothers. You will finish top of your class. You will not ask questions. You will do as I say. You will obey, obey, obey! Each command like the lash of a whip in Gashe's hand.

The river, when we came to it, was no longer full and swirling in wild rage. I leaned out the window to watch how the water splashed as we drove across easily, soaking, this time, only the tires.

"I have water. Clean water. For you to wash before pray," Solomon said. He took his left hand from the wheel and pointed out his side window. "East. We can stop when it is time. Just tell me. It is fine."

He was Catholic, but he knew the Orthodox traditions. Should I tell him I was a bad Christian? That my belief was weak? That I hated to pray?

"It is not necessary to stop," I said. He sighed, a sound of great relief, and relaxed his hold on the wheel.

"That is good. The biggest danger is now. In this country," he explained, his voice a strange staccato. "It is safer across the border. We be there soon."

If east was on the left, we were pointed south, toward Kenya. We continued mostly in silence. Me thinking of Ishi and how perfect it would be if he were with me. If the two of us were going, it would be a great adventure. We would make our own futures and not be told what to do, and when we were rich enough, we would come back and get Etheye so that she would not be under the thumb of Gashe.

But that was not right.

She would no longer be under his thumb, anyway. Gashe had not returned from the edire. He had vanished as if he had never been born.

Music drummed from the radio, a beat that got faster and faster. My sisters would like dancing to this music, shaking their shoulders and their bums wilder and wilder, keeping up to the beat until they collapsed in a heap of giggles. The eerie, echoing peal of a news bulletin pierced the song. Solomon switched off the radio and accelerated.

"We caught in Ethiopia, we go in the jail," he said.

He did not need to explain what that would mean to both of us. My brothers and I had heard stories. People who went to jail rarely came out in one piece. Others "disappeared." What, exactly, would happen to someone like me whose name was on a list?

Solomon was correct. Ethiopia was not safe.

Hours and hours passed with little conversation as the

endless gray road stretched through an emptiness I could never have imagined. Solomon looked at me once in a while, as if he wanted to say something but didn't have the words. I had nothing to say as he took me farther from home. It was better not to think about it, to just stare at the dotted white lines that separated the road, one side from the other.

And yet my mind wandered to what was at the end of that road, across the border in Kenya. A sprawling refugee camp filled with thousands upon thousands of people adrift and homeless. Living in plastic tents. Crowded, Muslims and Christians together. Pushed in with Somalis and Eritreans, our cruel and bitter enemies of decades-long wars. How could I stand such a sad makeshift life of waiting and waiting, maybe until I was an old man, praying for a future that might never come? ·

Would I find anyone like me? Could I find other Amhara to help? Or would I find only enemies I could never trust?

Solomon lifted the flap of his leather bag and passed me a bottle of water. I twisted the cap and took a swallow.

How would I live? I knew nothing of survival.

Or, had I been sold already into slavery?

My life had been so easy, so good. I had a family and a home, a good school, the best teachers in Addis. I was the son of a respected businessman. The only thing expected of me was to do well in school. There were too many rules, too many high expectations, but maybe the rules had been not so bad.

I would go back, then. I would ask Solomon to turn around. Maybe Gashe had come home after all. Maybe everything could go back to the way it was.

I turned in my seat to speak to the driver, but he spoke first.

"You are ..." Solomon said. The front tire crashed into a rut when he looked at me. It bounced out and he wrenched the wheel to keep the car on the road. "You are," he paused again. "You are not safe here. You are one telephone call away from death. You know this?"

His simple, blunt words felt like a kick to the stomach. I knew what he said was true. I knew, but still I wanted to stay.

"When we leave, you will be safe, okay? To find you, they would have to hunt. They will not do that." Solomon glanced at his watch, and after he did, he pressed the accelerator to go even faster. The car vibrated so much that the suitcases on the backseat slid to the floor, knocking over one of the boxes. The lid slipped off as I caught the carton and pushed it back. The box was crammed with papers in manila folders. "If someone hunted you, it would be ... to make a statement. They have your father. I do not think they come for you. They lose interest, okay?" he asked.

How was it that what I had done was so wrong? How was it that my name – a good student, a good son — was on a list of those to be arrested?

Solomon checked his watch often, and whenever he did, I checked my digital Casio with the built-in calculator, forgetting each time that the battery was dead. But what did it matter? I didn't even know where I was going.

"You are hungry? I have the food," he said. I shook my head. "I brought the proper food. That you like."

"Ayi," I said.

I would never be hungry again. I would never have happiness. How could you have happiness when you were leaving the country of your ancestors? When your mother got smaller and smaller, until you could no longer see her? How could you ever be hungry, not knowing when you would laugh again with your brothers or run with them chasing a football? I had not even said goodbye to my brothers.

What would happen to my family? What *was* happening to my family while I bounced around on the road to nowhere?

Solomon interrupted my thoughts. "More people will come. Together. With you and me," he said. He moved his hand back and forth between us, then pointed his fingers down and wiggled them as if they were legs walking. "Going across."

"We will all go together. A lot of people," I said to show him I understood. He nodded enthusiastically and grinned. He repeated my words the way I had repeated the Gurage words the children in Ababa's village had taught me.

We slowed when we passed through the gates of a place that reminded me of the edire at Dire Dawa, a mud street and a string of colorful single-story buildings all joined together. Solomon stopped in front of a place with turquoise paint that was patched roughly with plain cement. The cinnamon aroma of morning tea enticed us inside to a room moist with steam and crowded with tables where people shoved food between their lips and didn't cover their mouths to chew.

"We eat here," said Solomon. He shooed flies from the table and motioned that I should sit.

"I am not hungry," I said. This was not a lie. Who could eat here in these conditions? If I had not eaten in a year, I could not eat in this place. A woman brought kitfo for Solomon and a scalding chai for me. I tasted it slowly, covering the cup with my hand between sips and waving at insects with the other.

Through the open door I saw a battered pickup park beside Solomon's car. The driver nodded a slight greeting to Solomon when he came inside, and lowered his eyes, but he did not speak. He scraped a chair over the ceramic tiles, joined a table of men and called for a berele of tej.

No one but the server otherwise acknowledged or spoke to us, which was fine with me. I liked the feeling of anonymity.

Being with Solomon was so different than being in public with Gashe, who always needed the fawning attention of others.

I was glad to leave the flies, the babble of languages and the oppressive heat of the restaurant when Solomon scooped the last of the meat into his mouth. I helped him shift the suitcases from the car to the back of the pickup beside us.

"Stay with me," he said, his voice quiet and his eyes looking into mine. "Close, always. I keep you safe. I promise."

Half of the restaurant poured into the bed of the pickup. They shoved the luggage out of the way and crowded onto the rough wooden benches and onto the floor. Only Solomon and I sat in the cab. It was as if we were going to school, except I was in the front for a change. I always wanted to have the best seat, but it didn't feel right to have so much room when the others had so little. I kept glancing back, thinking I should ask Solomon to stop so I could switch places, or at least tell him to slow down. He was traveling much too fast for this road and much too reckless for someone with a load of people in the back. The women and children slid to the floor and clutched the legs of the men as if they were the trunks of trees. The men leaned forward and gripped the edge of the wooden benches to keep themselves from bouncing out.

When the windshield wipers began to scrape at the afternoon rain, two men bent their heads and balanced the biggest suitcase on their shoulders. The others huddled beneath the makeshift roof that did little to protect them.

"We should stop. I can go in the back," I said. "The women and the little children, they can come in here. It would be better."

Solomon shook his head. *"Ayi."* He tapped his watch. "No time. Soon."

We stopped in the downpour near a neon green bus pitted with dents and missing a front fender. Solomon instructed each person to carry a suitcase or a bag that the tallest men pushed onto the top rack of the bus. The inside was already sweltering and crowded, almost every seat taken. I stood about midway down the aisle and latched onto the back of a seat, hoping I could keep my balance as the bus rattled over the rough pavement.

Children squealed when they flew into the air when we hit ruts, and more than once someone tumbled into the aisle or smashed his head against the window. The driver leaned over the steering wheel of the hurtling bus and rubbed his forearm on the cracked windshield to wipe the fog from the inside. The wipers flailed wildly but could not keep the windshield clear. It hardly made any difference when one flew off entirely. The small side windows screeched, metal on metal, when men reached up to open them and release some of the steam. It felt good to breathe fresh air, but the rain streamed in on one side, soaked those nearest the window and sloshed from side to side on the floor.

"Close the window!"

"No, keep it open!"

"We will die without air. There are too many of us." People yelled and argued "open" or "closed," mostly, I noticed, depending on where they were positioned. At least no one was still sitting in the back of the truck where their skin would be shriveling like that of a dried fig.

The road curved to reveal small houses of poor quality built close to the edges of the road. The chatter in the bus dulled as we drove through the village. Made mostly of rotting wooden slabs and tarpaulins propped up with sticks, the houses had sloping roofs of corrugated tin, lined along the edges with buckets to catch the rainwater. People walked all along the road in an unhurried way, oblivious, it seemed, to the downpour. Some carried jugs or baskets on their heads. One boy balanced a long tube on his shoulder. They scattered to either side when the driver leaned on the horn.

I squatted in the aisle to rest my legs, but I didn't like the feeling of not seeing where I was going. I was glad when I stood up, that others ahead of me had sat on the floor, giving me a better view. The rain, by now, had let up.

Just ahead, the road split in two. In the center was an area with gigantic trees and a cement building with blue-painted bars on the windows. Leading up to it was a row of signs: *Kenya Police, Moyale Border Control, Police Post. Department of Immigration. Moyale Station, Offices, Campsites.*

Police dressed in army camouflage stood on guard, AK-47s at the ready. Closer to the building, uniformed officers tipped precariously on cheap plastic chairs, the officers' legs propped against the trunk of a tree, their weapons nearby. They smoked their cigarettes sheltered from the accumulated rain that still dripped from the outer branches. They glanced at the bus, but they did not move.

The bus stopped. Solomon seemed to grow taller.

"Stay calm. Wait here," he announced in Amharic and in Oromo. He brushed my arm when he reached overhead to pull down his satchel. He looked into my eyes and wordlessly told me everything would be fine, which did not explain why my mouth was dry and my heart was beating so fast.

You are one phone call away from dying, he had said.

Was it a warning? Or a threat? Was it here that he would make that call? Had he brought me to the border to show my intention to escape?

The center-hinged door of the bus sucked open. Solomon got off. He walked slowly and with confidence. Was he go-

COLD WHITE SUN

ing, now, to accept his reward? He spoke to the men at the table, who pointed to the door of the concrete building. A baby cried. I saw the flash of a breast as a woman suckled the child. We waited, each of us seeming to hold his breath. Had he delivered all of us?

I watched the door where Solomon had vanished, and I watched the rain drip, drip, drip, drip from the widespread canopy of the trees. The soldier with the AK-47 sauntered to the side of the bus, as if the combat boots he wore were filled with lead. He craned his neck and examined the bus.

If he entered, should I duck? Hide beneath a seat? He lifted the automatic gun to his shoulder. Angled it up toward the roof.

What if he started shooting? What if he riddled the side of the bus with his bullets? Glass would spray everywhere, everyone would scream, there would be blood, people would die. How would I help them? What would I do?

The soldier walked a slow circuit around the bus, studying the roof. Inside, no one moved. Even the children seemed to know not to speak or whine. Behind me an old man wheezed, his breath coming in short labored breaths. The driver scraped a match. The fleeting scent of sulfur. The smoke from a lit cigarette drifted lazily down the aisle like the seep of poison gas.

The soldier left my line of vision. Where was he now? Directly behind the bus?

If he found someone, would he open fire? Just on the roof? Or inside the bus, too? Would he kill us all if he found one illegal migrant?

What if he found me? I had no papers, no identity card. Would he drag me from the bus? Or shoot me where I stood? Would he gore me first with his bayonet?

137

Do not worry, Solomon said. *I take care of all the things.*

But I did worry. Solomon could barely speak Amharic. How could he explain?

The weight of the soldier landed on the back bumper. A strangled scream, from me. He rattled and yanked the handle of the emergency exit. Watching the handle twist, I stepped back and toppled over the people cringing on the floor. The women shrieked, too, and some began to cry.

The soldier appeared on the other side. I could no longer breathe. Would he come through the front? Where was Solomon? What was taking him so long? Could this soldier read the list of names on the television broadcast? Did he know I was on the bus? What if he killed everyone because of me?

The soldier relaxed his weapon. He returned to stand beneath the shelter of the trees, but that did not lessen my fear. How would I escape? The back door was locked. Through the front? I kept my eyes fixed on the soldier and on the men in the background, ready if anyone moved. But what would I do? What *could* I do?

Solomon emerged from the building. He nodded and gave a small wave of the hand to the men at the table. He came on board, looking pleased. He held his finger to his lips for silence. The driver turned the key. *Ra-ra-ra-ra. Ra-ra-ra-ra.*

The engine was without life. The driver puffed smoke from his cigarette and tried again. *Ra-ra-ra-ra. Ra-ra-ra-ra.*

Nothing.

Not a breath exhaled. *Ra-ra-ra-ra.* The emptiness of metal on metal. The mean-faced soldier gripped his weapon at waist level and eyed the driver. *Ra-ra-ra-ra.*

The engine ground to life. It sputtered and shot a stream of black smoke. We chugged across the border. Into Kenya. We exhaled as one.

19

I did not ask how I had crossed into Kenya without identity papers. Kofi must have paid well, enough for a generous bribe.

We left the others behind with the bus and switched vehicles again. This time just the two of us in a low Toyota pickup, the heavy suitcases laid flat in the back.

How far would Solomon take me? I hoped Gashe's brother had paid well so this quiet man would stay with me. My biggest worry was the refugee camp. Is that where I would be purchased to live the life of a slave?

Solomon was calm and his movements unhurried, as if the job of sneaking people into Kenya was routine. How, I wondered, did a person get the job of a smuggler? How many people had he taken? I assumed he was good at his job and that he had never been caught. I could trust him? He was a good man, wasn't he? A Catholic priest, yes, but one, I noticed, who did not pray with the sign of the cross before he ate.

The bumpy road riddled with potholes smoothed. Solomon broke the silence that so often fell between us.

"Tell me," he said, "some thing, about your school."

"I am a student at the Cathedral School," I said. I heard the pride of Gashe in my voice. "It is an excellent school. Very expensive."

"I know this one. How you like it to learn from the Catholics?"

Was this a test? It was better than some schools. The teachers were well trained but believed too much in discipline.

"The teachers at my school have knowledge and wisdom," I said. A diplomatic answer, and one that was true.

"Your best subject?"

"Football!" I said.

Solomon nodded. He seemed pleased. "A defender? Or one who attacks?"

"Defense." We fell into silence, both of us watching the road. "My brother? Ishi? He is the best forward. One day, he says he will go to the World Cup."

"And you? You think this is so?"

"It is a possibility," I said. "His aim is always true." Solomon nodded briefly, as if considering.

"It is, some of the times, better to do the work and not to draw attention," he said. "You understand? The background, going without notice?"

Solomon was the opposite of Gashe, who believed in adulation and power and influence. If Gashe was more like Solomon, perhaps I would be at home now, kicking a knot of rags in a game of football with my brothers, and not in Kenya, barreling down the road with a stranger dressed as a Catholic priest.

"Yes, I understand this," I said. I agreed with Solomon. Although I did well in school, I liked to stand out only to please Gashe. If I did well enough, if I brought him enough recognition, he was happy and calm.

Solomon was more cautious on this side of the border. He kept both hands on the wheel and watched the road — always, it seemed, scanning ahead. The road became even worse than it had been on the Ethiopian side. It deteriorated into a slimy soup that washed the hood with muck, and that the wipers smeared across the windshield. I pressed my face nearly against the glass to peer through the sludge, ready to call out if I saw an obstacle.

We skidded and my head walloped backwards. Solomon braked suddenly. My forehead smashed on the dash just as we rammed into a deep hole filled with water. Waves splashed from the wheels of the vehicle, and my teeth banged together so hard I thought they must all be broken.

"Hold on!" He yanked the wheel to the left and sped up to pass the craters, pulling back to the right just as a truck coated with mud and loaded with cattle blasted toward us.

"Look out!" I screamed.

Driving on this road was terrifying, but I worried even more about where the road led, and what would happen when we stopped.

"Will you stay with me? At the refugee camp?" I asked. He couldn't leave me, could he?

"No," he said. He stood on the brake and veered right, taking us off the road. An oil tanker was in our lane, bearing down on us. It breezed past, horn blaring. It gave us a flood of muck as thanks. Solomon stopped to allow the wipers to catch up.

"I will be on my own?" I hated the smallness and the high pitch of my voice.

"No, no, no," he said. He waved his hand from side to side, then turned to me and laid his hand on mine. "I promise to keep you safe. No camp. You stay with me."

"Where will we go?"

"To a place safe. Soon."

Another vehicle came at us. Head on.

"Solomon!" I screamed. He pulled from the road to let it pass. Both of us panted with fear. "What is wrong? Why are the trucks trying to kill us?"

"I forget this," he said. He went back on the road, now in the left lane.

"What are you doing?" Surely, I would die this day.

"Kenya. Drive left," he said.

Long after we left Moyale, we saw a man standing beside a truck with a heavy metal frame on the back. One tire was off. The driver waved and waved, signaling with both arms for us to stop. Solomon sped past.

"That man? He needs help. Why didn't you stop?" A Catholic priest — *Do unto others as you would have others do unto you* — and he didn't stop?

"Shiftas," he said.

"Shiftas? He wasn't a bandit. His truck was broken."

"An old trick," said Solomon. "Very old. They make you sad. You stop. They rob you, maybe beating you up, steal your car."

"Truthfully? They would do that?"

Solomon nodded. "Yes," he said. "They do that. Trust no one."

◆

I memorized the name. Francis Marin. Place of birth: Kampala, Uganda. Date of birth: March 9, 1986. The photograph on the passport was mine, a picture without expression, taken in the house where Solomon had brought me.

The house was empty except for a woman of Etheye's age, and a girl dressed in the style of India, who looked a bit younger than me. Inside the suitcases were all the things we needed — blankets, pots, dishes and soap.

"We travel as family," Solomon explained. "Mother, father, son, daughter. I be with you always. I no leave you."

"Where will we go?" asked the woman.

"It is better — more safer — if you not know," he said.

"When?" she asked.

"I tell you when the time comes to leaving this place. I make arrangements, and then we go."

My brain was trying to catch up. "We're not staying here?"

"No," he said. "It is safe here, but not safe more enough."

The cellular telephone on his belt trilled. He flipped it open, walked from the room and spoke rapidly in a language I did not recognize.

The woman, the girl and I sat in silence, looked down at the floor and waited for him to return.

"You must practice these informations I gives it to you. The names, the birthdates and birthplaces. Be ready. You must be ready, when you asked. You understand?"

Francis Marin. March 9, 1986. Kampala, Uganda.

"Forget real names. Do not even tell each other. Be these persons I give you. Understand?" He pointed at each of us in turn. "Namuddu. Francis. Maria."

Francis Marin. March 9, 1986. Kampala, Uganda. Mother is Namuddu, sister is Maria, father is Solomon.

"I speak for you. I tell the authorities we have a trip to make holiday with family. Understand?" We nodded.

"What if we make a mistake?" the woman asked.

"You not make the mistake. You *cannot* make the mistake. You be arrested in jail. They send you back. Make mistake and you kill all the ones of us."

Francis Marin. March 9, 1986. Kampala, Uganda. Mother is Namuddu, sister is Maria, father is Solomon.

"Understand?" We all nodded. "Also, do not make the noise. Do not open curtains or go away from house for any kind of reason. Never. Dangerous. Very dangerous. I bring it all the things you need. Food. Clothing. You need it some things, you tell me."

"What will we do while we wait?" the woman asked.

"You practice your identifications. You must know the other people's ones like you know your own. You must answer to these names ... ah ... when ... an authority say it to call you, when you not expecting to hear these names.

"They play the tricks. We must be ready. We be a family. We must know it each other. It is the only way." The smuggler pulled a ring of keys from his pocket. "Tomorrow I return, give it to you the test." He locked the door when he left.

Could I forget who I was? And where I came from? To forget your life, was that possible? Who could do that?

20

It was time to leave. The tension of hiding had passed into boredom, repeating names, ages, birthplaces, family history and reason for travel. Solomon came each day — always, it seemed, with the cellular phone pressed against his ear.

"Speak to no one," Solomon instructed before we left the house. "Let me do it, the talking. I tell them you not speaking the language. Understood?"

Each of us, in our own language, said we understood. Solomon was well dressed with newly polished shoes, but I noticed he was not wearing his Catholic collar. He had a plain gold ring on the second to smallest finger of his left hand.

I carried the backpack with both straps over one shoulder, hoping everyone on the bus would notice the DC logo stitched on the front. Solomon had given it to me. To Maria he had given an expensive pink backpack, and to Namuddu a leather handbag with a large purple flower sewn on the front. Inside my backpack was a T-shirt with a Quiksilver symbol, a football magazine, and food he said I could eat anytime I wanted. I wished it also had a Sony Discman with foamy headphones, but I remembered instead to be grateful for what I had. Still, Francis Marin would look so cool with headphones *and* a backpack.

Signs for international airlines hung from the roof of a huge building where the bus pulled to a stop. Solomon told us to get off.

The airport? We were going on an airplane? It was as if all of my dreams were suddenly coming true. Cool clothes and a cool backpack, adventure, an airplane. I paid attention to every detail inside the airplane so I could tell Ishi — the comfort of the seats with a bump built in to rest my head and how they tilted back, and about the little window with rounded edges. He would like the woman who showed us about using gas masks as we rolled along the pavement and told us how to get out if the plane crashed.

No one was putting on a mask. When did we put these on? Was there bad pollution where we were going?

I glanced at Solomon. He smiled slightly and consulted his watch.

The engines roared like massive fans. I imagined I was the pilot easing the throttle all the way forward. The airplane shuddered so hard it felt like it might come apart. Faster and faster, we sped down the runway, forcing the back of my head against the seat.

And then a miracle happened. We lifted off the ground, with me inside the plane. Outside the window was a perfect three-dimensional map: Streets and tiny houses, cars and buses that looked like moving toys.

"Look! Look! Everything so small!" I yelled, but I didn't move my head a centimeter to let Solomon see.

Beside me, I heard a small chuckle. I gripped the edges of the window with my fingertips, wishing I could stick out my head to see better. The world became tinier and tinier as we rose higher and higher. Wisps of clouds beneath us made shadows on the ground as Kenya blended into a mass of colors, exactly like a topographical map in a school atlas.

I would tell Ishi how my feet went numb with cold, and how my body shivered from the wind that blew from the roof.

Solomon tapped my arm.

"Something to drink?" he asked.

The woman who had shown us the gas masks and the exits stood in the aisle holding a cart with a carafe, juice and soft drinks in cans. I glanced at Solomon. Did it cost something? I had a bottle of water in my backpack that he said I could have any time. Was I allowed to have something more?

Solomon twisted a latch and a small table released from the seat ahead of him. The woman put a steaming cup of coffee in the indented circle and looked at me.

"You would like something?" she asked. I had noticed a familiar red and white can on the top of her cart.

"Coca?" I asked.

"Coca-Cola," the smuggler interpreted. I unhooked my tray. The woman reached in front of Solomon, passed me first a square of soft paper stamped with the airline logo, then a plastic cup filled with fizzing Coca. She also gave us each a small bag of cookies. I was glad to see that Solomon did not have to pay. I was also glad that she had given me *two* things. The cookies I would save for Ishi.

◆

We smoothed through the security checkpoints. Solomon smiled, motioned with his hand to indicate his family and gave the forged passports and travel visas to the agent. Francis Marin was too excited to be nervous. He grinned like an imbecile. He had been on an airplane!

"First time," Solomon nodded with his head to me and chuckled.

The agent did not smile. He slammed a heavy stamp on each document and passed them back to Solomon.

The air outside was moist on my face, even though it was not raining. A private car picked us up, Solomon in the front with the driver, the rest of us in the back. It was a big city with signs in Arabic and English. The driver left us at another empty house. Solomon had a key.

"Where are we?" asked the girl.

"It is better that you do not know," said Solomon. His voice was gentle. Did he know the girl had cried each night we stayed in Kenya?

"That was very well," he said. He passed us each a paper with a new name, new birthdate and birthplace. "We repeat it the process with this new informations. Forgetting the old ones, as if you never heard them. Yes? You understand?"

"We're not going to stay here?" I asked.

"No, we must continue going in this way. The bigger the distance, the more safe for everyone."

How much farther could I go than days of driving and an airplane ride? The farther we went from home, the longer and harder it would be to get back.

"Okay?" asked Solomon, but he did not expect an answer. "It will be as before. You stay here. No going to the outside. I bring everything. No one to know you are being here. Practice it your new names, over and over, until you are forgetting the other names. Understand? All of our histories must match."

It was the same as before. The woman cooked eggs and bread and made tea for everyone. I was careful to keep my jeans clean, and alternately wore the Quiksilver shirt and the monkey shirt. Solomon took new pictures, came with new passports and birth certificates, and we practiced. It was like being a prisoner. No books, no pencils, no paper, no television, no talking to each other, except to practice each other's names. I began to like washing my shirt in the basin. At least it was something to do.

Solomon came every day to bring things, usually food. He put on a stern face and pretended he was an immigration official, testing our knowledge.

"Good. We do it same as before. A Muslim family this time. I speak. You do nothing. Be ready for the trick." He gave scarves to the woman and the girl and taught them how to drape them over their hair, forehead and neck.

I put up my hand as if I was in school.

"Will not the authorities notice our different tribes, our different nationalities?" I asked.

"No be to worry," he said. "We go to a place of white peoples. To them, we look all the same," he said.

Another take-off and landing. Flying high above puffy cotton clouds. Another city, this one at night, filled with so many streetlights they looked like low stars. And when we traveled from the airport, I noticed no military trucks, armed soldiers, or checkpoints along the road. Instead the streets were filled with moving cars and buses even though darkness meant it was well past curfew.

A new house. A new identity. Ethiopia was fading from me with each move. How would I find my way home? And when would we stop? How far was far enough to evade the Special Police, their batons and their machine guns?

"Not yet," Solomon said. "We continue. No fear. I be with you all stepping of the way."

Kofi must have paid him a great deal of money. Was Gashe's brother also looking after Etheye?

Her face had been so filled with worry. Would it make her happy to know I was so far away? Or would it make her sad for a lost son?

Where was she now? How was she living? Was my family still together?

Better not to think these things. Better not to think at all. Better to memorize who I was now, where I lived, and why I was traveling. Better to forget everything in the past.

21

I wanted daylight more than anything, to go outside and kick a football, to feel the sun on my face, or the rain, or the wind. Anything but the cloying and cramped feeling of living all of the time inside with the silent woman and the girl who sobbed.

"Do not open. No one must know you are here." Solomon pulled the curtains shut. The same warning each time he came.

But what would it hurt? Just one look out the window of this place. Where were we? When would we stop moving? I hated Solomon's evasive answer: "It is better not to know."

Everything moved too quickly when we were outside, too slowly when we were locked in. I had lost track of the days. How long had it been since I left Ababa's village? Weeks? A month? Two months?

"Stay together," Solomon instructed at the last airport. No checking of passports this time, no questions from authorities, but the flight had been long enough for us to eat hot noodles with cheese while looking down at the clouds.

Where were we? Why wasn't there a sign?

"Move. Quickly," said Solomon.

People wove in and out and around, in a pattern as random as the vehicle traffic on the roads that merged at Meskel

Square. The movement a constant dance with no one running into anyone else, like ants rushing to bring food to the queen.

How did people know where to go? How did Solomon?

The noise at the airport was a thrum of sound, loud and constant, with garbled announcements over it all. Solomon brought us to the end of a queue at a kiosk where he bought tickets. People here, taller even than Ethiopians. And so pale. Gashe would love these giant people with straight hair and transparent skin.

"Follow me," Solomon instructed. A moving staircase made of metal, a train that swayed on the tracks, a woman in uniform who checked tickets while single drops of rain smeared the length of the window.

Airplanes, now a train! Ishi would be jealous beyond belief.

Through another huge building, then outside. Not raining, as I thought, but the air so dense with moisture that I drank water with every breath. It felt like Addis when the rains came, but the air was so cold here, it made me shiver inside my jacket and raised small bumps on the skin of my arms, making me look like a freshly plucked chicken.

Black, orange, red and brown umbrellas danced up and down as people walked only on the edges of the road. We moved toward a collection of sleek, narrower trains with antennae that reached to electric wires. Curved tracks. Some trains moving, some stopped.

"Careful," warned Solomon as he directed us toward one. "Pay it close attention."

Solomon bought tickets inside the train. There were not enough seats together. The woman and the girl sat beside each other. Solomon and I separate, but I was beside a window. Glistening streets. Water outside the window. Not an ocean, not a river, but lanes of water lined with cement, like roads. Boats tied along the edges. Cars parked so close to the edge they looked as if they could be pushed into the water. Many bridges. Huge trees with leaves that quivered in the breeze. Colorful houses as tall and thin as the people, all jammed together.

The language? Like English. Too fast to understand.

Solomon nodded to me. "Next stop," he said.

We stood at the door, me in front, Solomon, then the girl and the woman, all of us holding onto an upright pole to keep our balance. Down two steps to the road. Solomon grabbed my arm. A bicycle flew past, then another and another.

Handles wide, like the horns of cow. Riders with good posture, pedaling slowly, but moving fast. All in the same direction. Baskets in the front, bags draped over the back. A wheelbarrow attached to the front of one, with a small child inside.

Solomon took us across the street. Bicycle lane, train tracks, vehicles moving in two columns, right, then left, train tracks. Everything so orderly. No one blowing their horns or shaking their fists.

Solomon's arm shot out to protect us.

"Watch. Bicycles," he said. None were coming. Down a narrow street, past a machine digging its claws through the bricks with an arm that bent like a human elbow, a scoop that moved like a hand on a wrist.

We walked to an open square edged with tall trees and outlined by brick buildings on three sides. To the left a waterway. We turned right, down the street.

"Not far now," said Solomon, but I hoped the walk would last, that I would have time to see where he had brought us, that maybe he had a ball for us to kick on the grass.

Benches edged the grass. Women sat beside wheeled carts covered with fabric. Small children called to their mothers, climbed and hung upside down from a colorful apparatus.

"Quickly now," encouraged Solomon. A steamy shop with rows and rows of electric washing machines, a restaurant with bright-yellow tables.

We followed Solomon to the end of the street and through an alcove that sheltered us from the drizzle. There were three heavy doors painted a glossy dark green. Solomon tugged off a rubber case beside the door, pressed buttons with numbers and retrieved a key.

I looked around while Solomon fit the key in the lock of the nearest door. Trees all of the same size and same type, planted equidistant from each other. Bicycles leaning against each side of them and on racks along the street. A hairless man hunched, sitting on a bench. He wore a long black coat, elbows on his knees, smoke trailing from a cigarette between his fingers.

I turned away quickly when he caught me looking.

The lock did not click open. The man was watching. I could feel his eyes on my back. Solomon pulled out the key, reinserted it. Tried, again, to turn it.

I wanted to grab it from him, shove it in the lock, break the lock if I had to and get inside where it was safe. Hurry, Solomon! Hurry! The girl whimpered. The woman's eyes were large and frightened. Solomon examined the key and ran his finger along the jagged edge.

"You need to jiggle it. Up and down," called the man on the bench. We all turned to his loud, authoritative English voice. He exhaled a long slow breath of smoke.

Solomon nodded. When he turned, I saw a worried crease line his forehead. Solomon joggled the key back and forth in the lock. The man, I noticed, continued to study us. The lock snapped open. We rushed into the hallway crowded shoulder to shoulder and closed the door.

It was dark and airless inside and smelled of must. The only light was from a bare bulb high up on the ceiling.

"Come," Solomon beckoned. "Everything be fine."

Everything did not feel fine. Before us was a steep, narrow wooden staircase. The steps were worn in the middle, like a scuffed and shallow dish. We followed Solomon up to a small landing, the passage so tight I could reach both sides without fully extending my arms, and so steep I was losing my breath. Then, up more stairs. Solomon in front, the woman, the girl, then me. We turned a sharp corner to a hall planked with rough wood. A shelf along the wall displayed dozens of pairs of shoes. Umbrellas dripped a puddle by a door.

Solomon swiveled to face us and held his finger to his lips. It was not necessary. We were too scared in this place to make any noise.

The wood squeaked and moaned. A dog with small sharp teeth barked. The woman gasped. I startled, too, and jumped backwards, causing five shoes to fly from the shelf on the wall. The dog yapped and scraped its claws on the door. I tossed the shoes on the rack. Passed the door quickly. Another turn. More stairs, up and up and up. How many? The smell of damp earth and rot. My heart pounded and I panted.

How far was he taking us?

Another landing, identical to the last, but with no rack of shoes. A railing on the right. I looked down, so high up we were. Everything made of wood. In an earthquake, we would die.

A bristly mat by the door. The lock clunked when Solomon turned the key. All of us inside. All of us breathing heavily and looking at each other with relief.

Safe, at last.

22

It had been days since Solomon pulled the shades on the windows and gave us the usual warnings: Do not open the curtains. Do not go outside. Do not to make any noise. Open the door for no one.

He had not returned as he usually did.

We listened for his key in the lock. I was sure I heard it many times, but when I went to the entryway, the lock was not turning and Solomon was not there.

We listened, too, for anything unusual. But every noise was strange and frightening. The creaking of a wooden floor when someone passed the door outside, a yell, the bark of the dog below us, even the gurgling of a toilet. Our nerves were stretched and tied in knots.

Where was Solomon? What if he had been caught?

I stood to the side of the large window.

What would it hurt to look outside? Just a peek. Just one little peek. No one would know.

I nudged the blind slowly away from the window and held it there, making sure to stay to the side, out of sight.

I was above the trees, looking down into a crown of leaves, the branches in dark contrast. I could see the bricked street and the benches, looking nearly as small as they had when I was in the airplane.

I looked both ways. Nothing moved. The street was deserted.

There was no one to see me. There was no danger.

Letting the blind flap against my back, I pressed the left side of my face against the cool glass and stretched my eyes to where I had seen the waterway on the day we arrived.

Where were we? I scanned the street. There were no signs on shops to give me clues. Everything was plain, all the buildings across and down the street were built with identical brick and identical windows.

It was then that I saw him. Standing very still in the window across from me, slightly to the left, one story up. Bald head. White T-shirt without sleeves.

I ducked to the floor, back pressed against the wall.

What had I done? The man from the street who had told Solomon to jiggle the key. It was him. He had seen me. Clear as day.

Please. Let it be a mistake. Make it not be the same man. I wanted to slide up from the floor and lift the edge of the blind again. To look at him once more. Just a glance. To be sure.

My heart rammed my ribcage as if it were trying to get out. My hands trembled. I could breathe air only in small gasps. Was I dying?

I stared down the long hallway, directly at our only exit. A thick door painted blue. I had to do it. I had to be sure it was him. I had to know the level of danger.

My fake mother padded toward me, her dress swishing from side to side, her feet bare.

"What's wrong?" Her face turned worried when I didn't answer. "Why are you on the floor? Have you heard something?"

I shook my head. I could not look at her. She would know.

A deafening buzz filled the flat. The sound, loud like a swarm of angry bees, came from the door. The woman and I glanced at each other. Our eyes held. Our bodies frozen. The noise stopped. We breathed. *Buzz. Buzz. Buzz.* Over and over. *Buzz. Buzzzz. Buzzzz.*

The girl, rubbing her eyes, came from her room. She squinted at the door, then looked at us with lemur eyes. *Buzzzz. Buzzzz. Buzzzz. Buzzzz.*

We remained as still and silent as prey. Banging on the door now. The side of a fist. Two fists. Loud and insistent, banging, banging. A weaker door would splinter. The voice, a man's, belligerent and angry.

"Open! Open de deur!"

The woman stepped, as if she would answer the call. I gripped the hem of her skirt in a fist and held tight. The girl scurried toward us. She slid in a crouch beside me. My free arm went around her back to hold her close and to lessen my fear.

What had I done?

A woman's voice screeched outside the door. *Thump, thump, thump,* someone running on the steep stairs. A slap. Angry voices, the woman's and the man's. Arguing outside the door.

"Idioot!" The woman's voice. A slap, and then another. *Thump, thump, thump* up the stairs. Quick, light steps. Followed by ones heavier and slower. A door above us slammed. The picture of flowers on the wall tilted. A crash of breaking glass above, water running through the pipes.

Tears came to my eyes for the relief, for the terror being now with someone else. I hung my head and drew my legs to my chest.

I was so weak. How could a man be so weak? The girl rubbed her hand in circles on my back.

"It is fine now," she said. "The bad man has gone."

Water poured from the tap. I heard the *click, click* of the burner igniting, the scrape of the kettle on the flame.

How long could we keep this up? How long could I live like this?

"Have no worry, brother," the girl said.

"It will be over soon," said the woman, as if reading my mind. "Solomon will keep us safe. Then it will be as if none of this happened."

But what of the other man? The bald one who had seen me? Why was he watching us? Why didn't Solomon come and take us away?

Water churned and bubbled on the stove. A piercing, high-pitched whistle. Steam whooshed from the spout.

"I will make tea for all of us. We will drink it together. We are a family, no?"

Honey drizzled from the spoon into my cup. The tea burned my throat, but it took away the other pain, and somehow, drinking tea with the woman and the girl lessened my panic.

A floorboard creaked. The three of us looked, one to the other. The woman reached a hand to each of us and squeezed tight. A key in a lock. We moved to the hall. The bolt turned and snapped. The handle turned. The blue door opened.

Solomon, with hair as black as a village night, stepped through the door.

We ran to him as if he was our real father, and we were too young for school.

II

Toronto, Canada
2001

1

The hinged flaps on the wings adjusted as we drifted toward another landing. Beneath us, no longer clouds or an ocean but a city studded with electric lights strung yellow and white.

The airplane pounded onto the pavement, bouncing and shaking as it flashed down the runway. The engines blasted. The world outside the window blurred. Too fast! The food in my stomach roiled. What if it overflowed? What if I vomited all over the comfortable seat?

Closing my eyes made it worse. I clutched the armrests and stared out the window. We were going too fast.

When we crashed, the belt, would it hold me?

There were eight emergency exits – two in the front, two in the back, four in the center. The nearest emergency exit was in front of me, just over the wing.

"*Egzi-Abeher*, save me!" I cried.

It was one of God's miracles that the Boeing 767-300 slowed down almost to a stop. I panted like an overheated dog and gave thanks to Almighty God.

We rolled beside a plane with the red leaf of Canada on the tail, and a platform with a rectangular metal box scissored up to it. A small truck trailing a train of empty carts swiveled toward our plane, the workers all wearing bright-colored vests made of mesh.

Solomon touched my arm and stood. There was movement all around me as people lined up and rummaged for bags in the overhead bins, but the sound was wrong. The voices seemed to come from underwater, and deep inside my head, something hard pressed on my eardrums.

I followed Solomon off the plane and noticed him take the hand of my pretend mother as we turned up the ramp from the airplane. The girl was beside me when the smuggler smiled and passed our documents to the scowling Chinese official. The uniformed man examined the passport photographs and looked at each of us individually, matching our faces to the pictures. My heart beat so hard, I was sure he could see it thumping beneath my shirt.

Why was he taking so long? Did he know?

He asked Solomon some questions. In English. His voice was far away and muted, as if it were down a long tube.

"My wife's sister, she lives here," Solomon lied. He put his hand lightly on the small of my fake mother's back. She moved closer to him and gazed at him with romantic movie eyes. "She is not well. We have come to assist her."

"All of you?"

"Yes. It has been many years since we have seen her. The children, you know, so big now!" The conversation was difficult to follow, even though I knew some English from school.

"How long will you be in the country?" My heart sped up. Surely it would explode from the pounding. No one had asked us questions at any other border.

"Ten days. The children, you know, must return to their studies," Solomon said. I rehearsed my name, birthdate, birthplace, the names of family members, my school, the sick aunt, and remembered she had surgery for her gall bladder.

"How lucky you are. Two children, so close in age," the official said. He looked at us and at the pictures again. He knew!

He put the passports beneath a scanner. My heart was in overdrive and still gaining speed. My hands trembled. A knife drove through my eardrum.

"Agghh!" I screamed. I cupped my ear with my hand and doubled over. The pain was excruciating. My pretend parents and pretend sister rushed to surround me. Garbled voices full of concern. Hand on my shoulder. Hand on my waist.

"What's happened? Are you all right?" my fake mother asked in Amharic. Her eyebrows pressed together, vertical lines between them. Eyes frantic and worried. She removed my hand from my ear to check for injury and smoothed her thumb gently on the outer part, the way Etheye would.

The knife twisted and then released.

"The pressure," the official said. He twirled his hand in the air. "From the descent." I heard him clearly. He lifted a stamp. Smashed it on the passports. *KaClunk! KaClunk! KaClunk! KaClunk!* He folded the documents and slid them across the counter.

"Welcome to Canada," he said.

He said "Canada." But everyone was Chinese. The clerk had been, the security guards in blue uniforms. All of them smiled at us or nodded and said, "Welcome." Why would Asians welcome me to the frigid country Canada? And if I was in China, why were the signs in English?

Flags were everywhere — the red leaf, the two vertical bars of red on each side — the symbol on bags of grain I had seen at the mill. Canada? North America. A happy place where everyone was rich, but very cold. Ice and igloos. White bears. Fur coats like Russia.

We moved quickly through the airport. Everything was fast. Wide conveyor belts that moved people. People running on them, carrying suitcases and rolling others on small wheels. Cellular phones pressed to ears. Crowds of people moving left and right. Smiling and laughing. So much English coming all at once, and another language I did not recognize. Not Italian. But similar. Spanish?

Solomon told the girl and the woman to pass through an opening.

"Toilets," he said. "We meet again here."

He and I went through a curved passageway that opened to an entire row of basins below a huge mirror. Men stood near a wall, backs to us. Solomon pushed a door on a small enclosure where there was a toilet. Just what I needed.

Everything clean as a cathedral! Men lathered their hands at the basins, but there was no soap, no way to turn on the water. Liquid squirted into Solomon's hand when he held it below a plastic box on the wall. The water turned on by itself when he needed it. I mimicked his actions. The water stopped when I pulled away. I stuck my hands beneath again, and it turned on. Such a miracle! Hot air gushed from the wall to dry our hands.

Ishi would definitely think I was lying.

Solomon stood beside the passageway, his eyes dancing.

"Come," he said.

"This is a *public* toilet?" I asked as we left the room. I looped my arms through the backpack as we crossed the glistening hallway to meet my make-believe sister and mother.

My sneakers squeaked with every step as we strolled through the tall wide hallway, so shiny that the overhead lights reflected on it. There were restaurants and market shops on each side, and a moving staircase. The double doors at the bottom of the stairs opened automatically, sliding into a wall of fogged windows. Beyond them, we were greeted with joy, kisses, hugs and handshakes from a group of Ethiopians I had never seen before.

"Welcome!"

"Ah! Look how you've grown!"

"We are so glad to see you."

"You had a good flight?"

"Come, come. This way! We have a party planned."

They met us and fussed over us as if we were family.

It was as if I had come home.

2

"Come! Come with me!"

He was a young man, displaying all of his teeth, even the crooked ones on the bottom. One of the men from yesterday. Not a man really, but not a boy either. Older than me, but not by much. He showed me the television that had more than one channel and that he said worked all day and all night.

His name?

Ah! Yosef, the father of Jesus.

"Hurry! I have something to show you!" His words in Amharic came fast. "Put on your clothes. Brush your teeth."

I rubbed my eyes. Daylight seeped around the edge of curtains. A thin covering edged with satin blanketed me. A green sofa beneath me.

Where was I? Was this real? Or was this a dream?

Yosef, yes, but who was this impatient Yosef? A cousin? Come from the country to avoid the soldiers?

"Come on!" he said. He yanked the cover from me and pushed the long curtains aside. I was blinded by sudden light. The girl was on the balcony, curled in sleep. I snatched the blanket to conceal my naked body. Yosef was in the cooking area, pulling food from the refrigerator.

I had been at home sleeping beside Ishi, telling him, "Don't worry. We will always be together. Nothing can separate us." There had been the smell of roasted coffee and the spices Etheye liked to use.

Where had all of that gone? How could this dream with Yosef and the girl and the green sofa be so real?

"Go! Go! Wash yourself. Brush your teeth as I showed you. We haven't much time," he said.

The tiny living compartment was in a building so tall it nearly touched the sky. It was built of stacks and stacks of light-filled boxes, one on top of the other. There had been millions of streetlights, a city that wasn't dark even at night. It was the dream again of floating in a movie. The fast car, the belt across my right shoulder and hips so I couldn't run away, the orderly traffic, streetlights that blinked yellow, then red, then green. The celebration with strangers. So many people, more than enough food. Delicious food from home, plenty of doro wat well spiced, boiled eggs and chilled yogurt. A working refrigerator with milk in a skinny rectangular carton with a picture of a cow. Cold milk that tasted like water.

"*Bihlahh!* Eat. Eat more," the women encouraged. No limits. I ate until my stomach was stretched full and round, hardly able to breathe with the weight of it.

Laughter. So much laughter. What had been so funny?

The make-believe mother who had traveled so far with me had gone after the meal, touching my shoulder as she left. "Be well," she said.

The girl had stayed.

Yosef put his face close to mine. His eyes were shining. "Come!" He lifted a backpack into my line of vision. "We haven't much time, but I want to show you."

I swung my legs to the floor that had carpet all to the edges and pulled on the jeans that had been given to me the night before. Yosef pointed to the small room where a roll of soft paper for blowing the nose hung from the wall, and the toilet flushed every time. I pushed the small handle twice, just to watch the water swirl and eddy and be sucked away. Hot water when I turned the tap, or cold, whichever I wanted.

How could people be so rich? How could I dream such miracles?

I squeezed paste on the small brush to clean my teeth as Yosef had shown me. The mint frothed white and overflowed my lips. I looked fierce, like a rabid dog, so I scrunched my nose and growled before I spat. The T-shirt I pulled over my head was the one I had brought from home — the lucky one with the monkey on the front.

The hallway smelled of warm cumin, cardamom and coffee, and behind the row of closed doors, each one painted the same dark brown, came the sounds of Amharic. A circle on the wall lit up when Yosef pressed it. There was the noise of a shunting object, then two metal doors slid to opposite sides to create an opening.

I backed away from the death trap. Yosef took my arm.

"Come! Come! It is quicker than the stairs," he said, pulling me inside the mirrored box.

I braced myself against the walls when it plunged, afraid of the crash that would kill me. Yosef grinned.

"Why so scared?" he teased. "You make it look like you have never been in an elevator."

Who, with a choice, would use such a device? Electricity could stop at any time, or there might be an earthquake. Fear kept the words inside of me.

Yosef watched the lighted numbers above the door count backwards. The landing was smooth. The door slid open. Outside, the street sped with delivery trucks, shiny fast cars and expensive SUVs. Everything so fast, so new. So much to see. Everything spotless and so organized, as if someone had scrubbed the silt from buildings and roads. People walked on raised cement platforms beside the road, the cars in the middle. No dust at all. No stinking gutters for waste. No reek of diesel fumes. There was an emptiness of smell, a vacuum.

There were no animals, no beggars. No dogs lying in the shade ready to tear at my legs. Only one animal, a curly-haired dog tied to a woman who walked alone.

I looked straight up between the towering buildings to a blue sky with wispy clouds. The sun on my face lacked heat. But this was the best dream ever. I hoped never to wake up. The only thing missing was Ishi. Why wasn't he here? He was in all of my dreams.

But everything was so mixed up, the real and the not real. I wished I could make sense of it, put it in the proper order.

"Now you are safe," Solomon had said. *"You are safe here."*

Uniformed Asian guards saying, "Welcome to Canada." Tall buildings of light. Cool air that raised bumps on my skin. Trees without leaves. Not one igloo or bear or expanse of ice, but still, I shivered inside my jean jacket.

Well-dressed people of many nationalities walked with brisk purpose. Gigantic shops closed to the street had windows to display food and clothing. The aroma of coffee drifted from doors that opened.

If not a dream, then a Hollywood movie. It was impossible for my eyes and ears and nose to take in all the sensations. There was too much. Everywhere I looked, all around, in every direction, abundance and something unusual to see.

"Do not worry so much," said Yosef. But what did I have to worry about in this perfect place? Was this Heaven?

We stopped beneath tall trees with scratchy bark. The grass was a mix of yellow and green, clipped short, the same as the garden at home, but I saw no foraging goats. There were patches of flowers, pale purple with yellow centers, and taller ones, bright yellow, that looked like a cup and small plate on a stem.

I sat beside Yosef on a wooden bench, the backpack between us.

"Soon, you will be like me," he said. His eyes were huge and earnest when he said this. "Soon, you will have a job and be able to send money back home."

He had a good job, he told me. "I work in a restaurant. It has many fancy dishes that must be washed in a certain way. I use a machine to wash them!" he said.

A machine? To wash dishes? And who would have use for so many dishes that they would need a machine to clean them? Even in a dirty restaurant.

"And when you get enough money, you can get married! I can't wait to get a wife," said Yosef.

"I don't want a wife," I said. "I want to go to school. To learn more things. To study."

He looked at me as if I was the one who was insane.

"*Everyone* wants a wife," he said. He unzipped the pack and withdrew a pair of stiff boots with wheels.

"Look! Look at these!" He pushed off his sneakers and put his foot into the boot.

Whoever heard of a boot with wheels? Surely this friendly Ethiopian guy had gone crazy. Why would he do this?

He pulled the laces and tied on the boot. First one foot, then the other. He shuffled from the bench, moving his legs as stiffly as pendulums. On the pavement, he fell to his knees. He laughed like a hyena seeking a mate.

Over and over, he did this. I could not understand. Why would he do this thing?

He crawled to the bench like a baby before it can walk.

"Now you," he said. "You try this. It is called skating. Inline skating!"

It was not a wise thing to do. It was like Ishi pretending to be Texas Tom, swinging a rope from the top of our wall, trying to lasso a passing cow. He had landed in a bruised and nearly broken tangle.

Yosef removed the boots and passed them to me. This was madness, but I was too exhausted and too confused to argue.

◆

Yosef and I *both* laughed like hyenas during the coming days as we tried to learn this inline skating. The girl remained on the balcony, preferring to sleep than to risk her life with skates. She left the balcony only to eat, and I noticed she ate little. Her hand moved to her mouth as slowly as if it was made of cement. Her eyes, rimmed with red, dropped toward sleep even as she ate. Still, I thought she should come with us, even if it was just to watch.

She shook her head. "No. I am too tired," she said. "Too heavy."

It was easier to keep our balance on the grass, but then, neither Yosef nor I could make the skates move, even if we pushed the other person. Mostly we ended in a heap. We watched as people swooshed by on the paved path, moving rhythmically and fast on the four slender wheels we could not master.

"How do they do that?" I asked.

"It is because of the hockey," Yosef said. "Canadians, they are born wearing skates. Africans have to learn this."

"The hard way," I said. I lifted the leg of my jeans. I had a huge bruise growing on the side of my calf muscle. Yosef lifted his. He had cuts on both knees, like a little kid who runs too fast.

◆

On my fourth day in Canada, Solomon was at the living compartment when I returned. I was glad to see his familiar face, the way his eyes crinkled at the edges, and to hear his funny, staccato Amharic. Solomon looked happy to see me, too. He embraced me and kissed my cheeks.

"You like it here?" he asked. "Yosef, he treats you well?"

"It is like a dream," I said. "There are so many things. So much of everything." Solomon's hair, I noticed, had turned gray around the temples.

I sat on the edge of the sofa where I slept. The bathroom door was open. The girl was missing from the balcony.

"The girl?" I asked. "She is not here."

"She be gone. Away. She be safe," Solomon said. His face grew serious. He looked much older when he did not smile.

"You must go, too," he said. He did not leave time for me to ask questions. "It be safe here, but not enough safe. Your case be not approved here. You understand?"

"My case?" What was he talking about? What case?

"You be a refugee. Canada protects you from death, but too many people comes here. They not let you to stay," he said.

Not stay? How could they not let me stay? I had come so far. I had a friend here. I was learning inline skating.

"You be going somewhere far and away. For the safety — for the safety of all — the woman, the girl, me, you." He leaned toward me, elbows on knees, hands clasped together, face somber. "I make it the arrangements."

How could I possibly go any farther than I had already gone? Had I not traveled from country to country? From city to city? Had I not crossed an ocean?

Pressure built behind my eyes and in the sockets beneath. He wanted me to leave? Again? I squinted to control the tears that threatened. I would not cry.

"Even without me, no matter the happenings, you be safe in this one country," he continued.

"Then why must I go?"

"So they cannot find me, because of you," he said. "Or find you, because of me."

I listened as if he was Gashe or a respected uncle. Had he not helped me escape the Special Police? Was I not still alive with food in my belly and a place to sleep because of him? Had I not put all of my trust in him?

But I was so tired of the moving, of the running, of all the different people I was supposed to be. All I wanted to do was to sleep, and then to wake up to the sounds of my brothers playing, the annoying Bollywood music my sisters liked so much, and the aroma of chai and sweet buns drifting through the house.

It was time to wake from this dream of a perfect, too-clean world. It was time to tell everyone about it, and how crazy my imagination was.

Solomon had moved to the indoor kitchen and flipped on a light. Cool air seeped from the refrigerator when he brought out the platter piled with layers of injera. He rolled five of the discs, then slid them into a clear bag.

"No one be hurting you. You understand this? Canada be a safe country," he said. He filled more bags with all the different types of wat. His movements were steady and unhurried.

"What if I am caught?"

"It be for that reason that you go away from me," he said. He stacked three KitKats on top of the Ethiopian food and crossed the room. He looked into my eyes, his voice not angry or accusing, but kind. "I leave the country, too, but even if we be catched, there be no ties between us. We not know each other."

I was in a strange country with strange customs and a language I barely understood. He was the only person I had trusted for weeks, and now, he, too, was leaving? He, too, would deny knowledge of me? It was the way the apostle of Jesus denied knowledge of his friend three times before the cock crowed.

"You understand? Even if they bring us to the same room. Even if the police have evidence. I say I not know you. I say that I never see you before in all of my life," he said.

"I will go ... alone? You will not come with me?"

"It be your time to be a man," he said. He squashed a puffy coat into the bottom of the pack he had given me in Kenya, then added bottles of water, a can of Coca-Cola, an apple, two oranges, the KitKats, and the transparent bags filled with injera and wat.

So much food. Why so much?

"How far will I go?"

"You just go. Someone to tell you when you go far enough," he said.

He passed me the pack. It bulged with the food, a roll of paper tissue and the strange clothing Yosef had given me — the cotton tubes for my feet, the scratchy knitted hat that stretched over my head, the gloves for a mechanic, and the gonch to wear beneath my jeans that made Yosef cackle with hilarity when he demonstrated their uselessness.

Why did I need so many pieces of expensive clothing? Where was Solomon sending me? High into the mountains with air thin and cold? To an igloo where the arctic winds blew? Why did I need to go by myself?

And yet part of me was proud of all of these things I had been given, the backpack with the American logo, the high-top basketball shoes that did not seem as if they would fall apart if I used them to kick a ball across a pitch, and the puffy coat. How would it feel to wear it?

I was scared to leave Solomon. The thought of it made it hard to breathe, but I was excited to be an explorer in a strange land. For the first time in my life, I would be alone, to make my own decisions about how to live. This is what it meant to be a man.

I fed my arm through the two straps of the pack, slinging it over one shoulder the way I had seen Canadians do on the street, but the weight made my shoulder ache to hold it this way, so I wore it on both shoulders, like an Ethiopian going to school.

"There maybe comes a time when you need this," Solomon said. He placed one hand on my shoulder, and with the other he gave me a folded piece of paper. It was one I recognized by its size and color and its worn creases.

The certificate of my birth, the one that carried not only my picture, but my real name, the name of my parents, the place and date of my birth, bordered by all of the twists and turns of the Greek meander key. It stood for infinity, the eternal flow of all things. It meant love and devotion, and its corners held the four points of a compass.

I swallowed the rock in my throat and turned so Solomon wouldn't see my face.

Etheye. She had given him this. What was she doing, precisely now, in this minute? What would she tell me to do?

And Gashe? Did he live?

Do not think. You cannot go back. You can change nothing. Go to the future.

"You maybe also need this," Solomon said. From his pocket, he unfolded two bills, colored purple and yellow, like a bruise that has begun to heal. They were the size and shape of birr, with a large number 10 in the corner. He gave one to me. The other he returned to his front pocket.

"It be money. For buying things," he said.

I slid the papers into the back pocket of my stone-washed Levi jeans, stood tall and took a deep breath. The compartment was quiet, the girl and the woman already gone.

Did this room wait now for more refugees? I inhaled deeply and exhaled.

"I am ready," I said.

3

The bus station was as busy as the Mercato before a Holy
Day. There were people everywhere, carrying children,
hoisting duffel bags on their shoulders and dragging wheeled
cases behind them. There was every color and nationality of
people — Asian, African, Indian, North American — and
their voices combined into indistinguishable noise, like loud
static.

Solomon passed me a ticket, explained the bus would
stop often, but that I must remain on it.

"Stay until someone says to you get off," he instructed. He
told me there was a toilet on the bus, as there had been on the
airplane, and reminded me there was food and water in my
pack and money in my pocket. He gripped both my shoulders.

"You be safe," he said. He kissed my cheeks, then made a
small cross on my forehead with his thumb. "May God go
with you."

He put his arms around me, and I around him. Our embrace was brief but strong.

This bus was unlike the buses in Addis where as many
people as possible jammed in, arms and legs touching,
children — and sometimes grown women — sitting on
laps. Here there were many seats lined up, two on each side.

Seats with tall backs and a wide aisle like the airplane that crossed the ocean. A metal rack above the seats was stuffed with coats and packs. More luggage and plastic market bags were piled on the seats nearest the aisle. The seats beside the windows that reached almost to the roof were taken by people reading or staring out the window, though there was nothing to see but the inside of the station. A fat man overflowed his seat. Two children sat hip to hip in the same seat beside their mother.

Would I have to stand?

At the very back, I found an empty seat. A girl with hair as black as a panther, tribal markings, and metal studs in her eyebrows and bottom lip dropped her backpack in the aisle and slumped into the seat beside me.

"What a load of crap this is," she said. "A full load." She dug through her backpack and put Sony headphones over her ears. I could hear the hard beat of the music as it pounded into her head.

I shoved my pack beneath the seat in front of me the way I had learned on the airplane. Was this the right thing to do? The girl moved her head back and forth like a chicken walking in the garden. She kept her worn-out pack on her lap and fished out a magazine.

The bus flew on the wide smooth streets filled with all types of automobiles and trucks of all sizes.

Where were we going? Would it seem stupid to ask the girl? Yes, yes, it would. No one gets on a bus without knowing the destination. There were more cool cars on the streets of this city than I thought existed in the whole world. So many that I could not identify them. I didn't see a single Peugeot like Gashe's.

Plastic crinkled. The smell of open spices at the market. What spices? Cayenne? Peppers? The girl lifted a triangle of food to her mouth. It crunched loudly when she chewed. The sides of my mouth oozed with saliva. I tried not to pay attention to the smell. I tried not to watch the girl.

Her eyes lifted from the magazine, looked at me for a few seconds. Then she tilted the open bag toward me.

"Want some?" Her voice was loud. She shook the bag closer to me. "Go ahead. Have some."

I dipped my thumb and forefinger into the bag to extract a curled, triangular crisp. I nibbled it slowly. Salt, then sweet, the slow burn of hot peppers on the very tip of my tongue. A flicker of tiny, invisible flames lit up the front edge.

Immediately, I wanted another one.

"You ate that like you've never tasted chips before," the girl said. I wished she would speak more quietly. "Like it?"

"Yes." I nodded. What was the English word for "delicious"? "Good. Very good."

"My favorite," she said. "Sweet Chili Heat." She turned the shiny black bag toward me. The picture showed a chip with its edge on fire. She offered me another.

I wanted to talk to the girl, but what could I say? I didn't have enough English words. Why did I always want to talk to girls who didn't speak Amharic?

The markings on her face and neck interested me, as did the rows of white beads wrapped around her wrist and looped around her pointing finger. Why the tattoos? Her skin was lighter even than Gashe's. With skin so pale, she could pass as white. Were they the markings of a slave? But why would a slave have an expensive CD player?

I touched my fingers gently to my eyebrow, then patted my neck to correspond with her tattoos.

"What tribe?" I asked.

"What?" She pulled the headset from the top of her head and hung it around her neck.

181

"The drawings. What tribe?"

She laughed. "You think I'm an Indian?"

"I do not know."

"Well, I'm not. I dye my hair like this. Usually I'm blonde, but I hate blonde. Men always hit on blondes and think they're retards." She sucked the spices from her finger, then her thumb.

"Yes," I said. Was that the right answer? What was blonde? Why did people speak so quickly?

"It's like you're right off the boat." She studied me as if I was the exhibit of our famous prehistoric ancestor, Lucy, whose bones are kept in the National Museum in Addis. "Are you?"

"No," I said. She traveled without an escort. She must be a servant.

She laughed. "Want another chip?"

"I have food," I said. "It is the time to eat?"

"It's a free country. You can eat whenever you want." The girl slouched in her seat, pressing her knees against the chair in front of her, and peered at the magazine.

I pulled apart the top of the clear plastic bag of injera the way Yosef had shown me, then pressed it together. I shook it upside down. No matter how hard I shook it, the food did not fall out. Was there no end to the marvels of Canada? Ishi would believe none of this.

The girl stopped reading. She put the magazine in her lap and watched me.

"Really? You've never seen a Ziploc before? Where are you from, anyway? Mars? Pluto?" she asked.

I smiled. I knew the English names for the planets. "I am Ethiopian," I said.

"That's like where? Africa or something?"

"Yes!" I raised my eyebrows high and nodded vigorously.

"Ethiopia is in the north." I waved my right hand as if I was demonstrating on a map. "East! North and east."

The injera was still soft, not dried out and crispy the way two-day-old injera usually was. I offered the bag to the girl.

"Injera," I said.

"The same to you," she said. I shook the bag the way she had shaken her bag of Sweet Chili Heat. "What do I do? Just take the whole thing?" she asked.

"Like this." I tore a small piece from the roll and chewed. The girl ripped off a piece and chewed slowly.

"Interesting. Rubbery. Kind of like naan, but thinner," she said. "Or maybe a crepe."

I dug into my backpack and opened a bag of wat and showed her how to scoop it with the injera. She tasted slowly, a smile growing on her lips as the spice spread fire on her tongue.

"Oh, my God! Hot!" She fanned her hand in front of her mouth. "Hot!" She rummaged through her pack, swiveled the cap from a water bottle and glugged half. "Oh, oh, what is that?"

"You like?"

Tears streamed down her cheeks. She panted like a dog. "God, that was like the hottest thing I've ever eaten. It was like ... straight habaneros! You eat that? In Ethiopia?"

"More?"

"God, yes!"

We shared a full roll of injera, then the girl returned to her magazine with shiny pictures of angry women wearing almost no clothing. I let my full stomach and the vibration of the bus motor carry me home.

Days and nights, dreams and waking flooded together. Ishi and I fought for the football. Fiyeli chased after us and called *Aw-lubba-lubba*. Etheye whispered in my ear, "You be my favorite. So small. You gave me no pain." Isaias's muscled arm held me on a tank. The bus stopped and started. People shuffled on and off. The soldiers with the wild hair came. Coughing. The smell of cigarettes. Gashe took me with him in his 504.

I woke to light in the bus, but outside, empty darkness. The girl with the Sweet Chili Heat was gone.

Was she real? Had I dreamt her? Ishi stared back at me from the window. An elder with long straggly hair who reeked of cigarette smoke snored beside me, body splayed, his mouth open. I pressed farther into my corner by the window, not wanting to touch him.

When would this confusion end? When would I wake up and know for certain? When could I go home?

4

"Hey, buddy."

The English words came from far away. Muffled. Down a long hollow tube.

Who would speak English here in the market? I turned from the sound. I had to follow Etheye's bright headscarf, not lose sight of her. Ishi and I gripped hands as we cut through the thick haggling crowd, trying to keep up with her.

"Hey! Buddy!"

The English voice shook my shoulder. I blinked into a dream. An elder, pink skinned, haphazard white hair, bushy eyebrows.

I recoiled. The eyes of a wolf wearing a uniform.

"Buddy, it's time to go. This is the last stop. Where you get off," he said.

I uncurled from the high-backed chair, eyes of fear and confusion reflected in the dark window. My arms were wrapped not around my sleep-talking brother but around the backpack with the DC logo. The smuggler, Solomon, had given me the pack, filled it with a puffy coat and food.

Someone will tell you when to get off, he had said.

"You okay, man?"

I nodded. I understood he meant for me to leave the bus, but the words he spoke were gibberish. My muscles ached when I stood. The top of my head felt disconnected from my body, as if my skull had lifted open, and my brain was floating above it.

I had fallen asleep on the bus with a slave girl beside me and awoke alone, an old man, heavy with aching limbs who must grab the top of seats for balance as I followed the wolf man down the aisle of the empty bus.

"Go that way," the wolf said. He pointed to a ragged line of people scuffing through a corridor, shoulders curled beneath the weight of their possessions. Some had headphones clamped to their ears like the girl on the bus. Acrid smoke drifted from lit cigarettes. The sulfur of burning matches. A woman clutched a squalling infant that arched its back as if to do a backflip from her arms. Her wrist twisted when the bag she rolled behind her flopped onto its side.

Calgary Terminal, the sign said. I knew the word "terminal." The end.

Calgary. The end.

The line of people spread and filtered into a large room with a glass ceiling. All around, handshakes, hugging, kissing, walking arm in arm, holding hands. Exclaiming. Laughing and crying. So many white faces, fat and thin, pink and pale blending all into one. Smiling. So much smiling. Just like the airport in Toronto. And so much English, even the children could speak it. So few words I knew.

Who was here to collect me?

I stood alone, a little to the side. No one approached.

What now? Where do you go when you are at the end? When no one comes for you?

I spotted the slave girl from the bus, black sweater with

hood pulled up, her back to me, talking to elders. She would help. She would know the customs.

Through the crowd, around the suitcases and boxes on the floor. I tapped the girl's shoulder and grinned.

"What?" The voice aggressive as she pulled away from me. It was not the girl with the Sweet Chili Heat. Where was she? Not on the plastic chairs all joined together. Not at the telephone kiosks, or at the blue metal cupboards. No slave girl with hair as black as Solomon's anywhere on the glossy brown tiles. Where had she gone? Like Ishi reflected in the bus window, she had vanished.

I followed the people who trickled in groups through glass doors. One door, two. Doors that opened without pushing or pulling.

Outside, a frigid world of gray and beige, frosted with white powder. Rows of thick wires that carried electricity strung tightly between poles. Parked at the curb, a line of yellow presidential taxis, and above, a curved cement bridge on stilts with racing vehicles.

A dark sky stirred with heavy clouds. The air tasted cold and smelled thick with exhaust laced with the scent of clean clothes. The street glistened dark gray, edged with white. A snake pit of roads writhed with a tangle of shiny cars, SUVs and pickups. One blue wall. A sign. *Chevrolet Buick, GSL, Certified Service.* English letters, but what did they mean?

A train stacked with metal boxes and decorated with street art rumbled like a tank. The screech of metal wheels on rails. Doors and trunks slammed.

How could this be real? How could this *not* be a dream? Wake up! Wake up and let this strange delusion end.

A dagger of ice cut from the west, the setting sun a thin red line. The chill reached through my shirt and jean jacket to clench my bones, yet I remained standing on the bricked edge of the road. Like a rock in a river. Not like a boy who has lost his mother, his brother, and his home.

Remain visible. Someone needs to find you.

Who would come? Who would welcome me in a language I knew? Kiss me on each cheek and take me to a safe house?

People flowed around me. The vehicles pulled away slowly, one after the other. To the right. Only to the right. No vehicles traveling left.

No one approached. Day faded into curfew.

You need to go. Far away, Solomon had said. *So far that they cannot find me.*

But where? How far? What country?

You are safe here, he said. *In this country. Even if you are caught.*

Why could I not have stayed in Canada, where it was safe?

Where was I now? How many days had I been on the bus? Three days? Four? Why had I not asked questions?

The people were gone. The vehicles gone, and still I stood, shivering and alone. My teeth clashed together as if they would break. My arms wrapped my chest, ears brittle.

Someone *must* come.

Only four presidential taxis left, tinted windows, top lights lit. Where were the officials, the ministers of government they were meant to pick up? The Ethiopian drivers lounged beside the cars, leaning on them, talking. The tips of their cigarettes fired red when they brought them to their lips.

I took a step forward.

Trust no one, Solomon had said.

One of the drivers noticed me. Expensive leather coat. Long face and hooded eyes. Short nose. Age of a university student.

Was he looking for me?

Another step.

Two small scars above the eyebrow. The flash of teeth of a jackal.

Tigrayan.

I froze.

The tribe in power. They took Gashe.

He blew smoke from his mouth as he studied me, dropped the butt and ground it into the pavement with his polished shoe. His movements slow and deliberate.

I turned from the wind. Legs shaking. Too heavy to run. Walk. Fast.

"Hey!"

If someone hunted you, it would be … to make a statement … I do not think they come for you. They lose interest.

A glance over my shoulder. He stood by the car. Arm in the air.

Not following.

I rounded the curve of the brick building, head up, as if I knew where I was going.

Get away. Keep out of sight.

Before me was a vast wasteland. Cars rushed overhead, but below, where I walked, there was nothing. No people crowding the streets. No shops. No animals.

Where was the life of this place? Crisscrossed roads, paved, with yellow markings in the center. Ramps and bridges. Which road in this stark landscape was I meant to follow?

The wind snapped a row of flags on tall metal poles, the sound like whips. A clang of metal on metal. A building shaped from glass, topped with a Mercedes-Benz symbol. A yard outlined with a shiny rainbow of luxury cars, so real I felt I could touch them. These had been Emperor Haile Selassie's cars. He liked them the way Gashe liked Peugeots. Why was I seeing the Emperor's cars?

Across the road, cone-shaped trees, dark green, like the ones I had drawn to win the international art prize. Others black-barked with outstretched arms and fingers, like feelers that grasped at the wind. Faded grass streaked with white. A path through it, worn by feet or hooves.

In the distance was a grouping of monoliths, like a futuristic sculpture that reflected the end of day.

Curfew would be soon, or perhaps it had already passed. Is this why the cars moved with such urgency? I needed to be off the street. Where would I hide?

There were no narrow spaces between buildings, no alcoves.

The plain buildings in the distance glowed yellow with electric lights. Electricity meant people. Would someone help me?

Pushed by the terrible wind, I followed the footpath. The wet grass cold on my ankles. A tight line of cement blocks beside the pavement. Cars swooped and flew in all directions, in and around, over and in front of me. So fast. Everything so fast. An orange fence of plastic. A low barrier of thick steel cable bolted to square wooden posts. Electric wires hummed.

Keep walking. Move away from the danger. The Tigrayan can drive his car only to the right. Focus. Walk. Quickly. Keep moving.

The cement path stopped.

Just stopped. A dead end. Across the road, nothing. No tracks, no path. The buildings in the distance, gray on gray, like something shrouded in fog. So close, they seemed, so real, but so far. How could I get to them?

Darkness loomed. Terrible things happened at night.

Nowhere to hide.

A bus roared past, the wind of it flapped my clothes.

The bus was safe. The warmth, the rhythmic hum of the motor would take me home. It could take me back to Yosef

where I could get a good job cleaning dishes. I had money.
I could buy a ticket. I would go back. I could wash dishes
beside Yosef. I could … I could …

I turned.

The wind snatched my breath, pressed my chest. I had to
get back to the bus. The tips of my ears burned to ice. My
hands froze into talons. Eyeballs on fire from the cut of wind
dripped tears.

I was almost there. I could see the building. Red bricks.
Curved wall. Not far.

Help me. Someone.

Etheye, tell me what to do.

How could it be so cold?

Toe of sneaker snagged the cement edge. Face slammed
the careful rows of bricks. Blood gushed as water from a
hose. Stained shirt and jacket, smeared the back of my hand
when I lowered it from my nose. My hands would not
unfurl. Without hands, my future was that of a beggar. I
sobbed like a child.

Crying will not help you. Gashe's voice in my head. *It is
through adversity that one learns best the skills of a man.*

Useless words, Gashe. Useless!

It is your time to be a man. Solomon's words.

I didn't want to be a man. I wanted to be a child who was
loved and taken care of by his mother. I wanted to be safe
and protected and told what to do in the perfect life I had
with my family.

I took baby steps toward my destination.

So cold. Let this nightmare end.

Three taxis remained at the curb, the drivers facing away.

Stay quiet. Invisible.

Past a wooden bench. A newspaper rack. Five metal
doors. Glass with steel edges, the one I had come out. IN

painted in large white letters. A lock but no handle. How to get in a door with no handle?

Three more doors beside those. Identical but with handles. OUT! OUT! OUT! they screamed. My claws gripped the freezing edge. I pulled. Door locked. I pushed. No movement. Locked.

All locked.

What if the drivers turned? What if they saw me? I had to get in.

I pounded with my fists on the glass.

"Kifeti! Kifeti!" I cried. No light. No movement within.

The door grew hazy through tears as I sank to the rubber mat. I forced the fingers of one hand against the other, but they did not straighten.

Crouched between a brick wall and a locked door. I drove the heels of my palms against my eye sockets.

Stop crying, idiot, think!

You must live, Etheye said.

I was too tired. So heavy. So cold. I rocked back and forth as I wept. I was worse than a beggar outside of Gashe's compound, lost and useless and alone.

"What's wrong?" The words in Amharic. My head snapped up. The taxi driver in the leather coat.

My back pressed hard against the bricks. I would tell this enemy nothing.

My eyes ran like a tap left open. Stop the embarrassing tears!

"Come, I will help you." The familiar mistakes, the *pse* of a Tigrayan speaker. Like Isaias.

He extended his hand. Palm up. "Come with me."

I swallowed fear, the taste of it like brass, and ran the back of my hand beneath my nose. A smear of mucus.

5

A single door slammed. A car drove away. Two taxis remained. Engines running. Exhaust seeping from the back.

The two drivers studied me, one in front of me with his hand extended, the other older, standing beside his car. Well-fed body, hand in pocket. He glanced sideways. Middle Eastern looks. A straight, attractive nose.

Eritrean.

Two men left in the world. Both enemies.

One whose tribe imprisoned Gashe. The other an enemy of war. A devious neighbor trying to steal my country bit by bit.

Neither could be trusted. Why were they together?

"Come," the younger man said. "You can trust me. No one here will hurt you because of the shape of your nose."

I rose slowly, but I did not take his hand. Tears stilled by fear. Eyes watchful.

The Eritrean was older, but not as old as Gashe. He would be the one in charge. The one most to fear.

The younger man spoke into a cellular telephone like Solomon's, then snapped it closed.

"I must go," he told the other driver. "He's all yours."

He pulled his taxi from the curb. *Alberta, Wild Rose Country* on the licence plate. Red tail lights disappeared.

Just one left. The Eritrean.

"What's the matter with you?" He spoke Amharic with surprising fluency and only a slight accent. His tone was fierce and gruff.

"I don't know where to go," I said. My eyes felt like the eyes of my youngest brother trying to avoid punishment. Kato's tears dripped down my cheeks before I could wipe them. I was failing miserably at being a man.

"Get in my car. I will take you home," he said. He circled the back of the vehicle and got in.

Solomon had been kind. Yosef had been kind. The girl on the bus had been kind.

But this man, how could I trust him?

The passenger window slid down. The driver leaned across the seat.

"Get in!" he commanded. "I don't have all night."

If he left, I would be alone. On the street. In the dark. In the freezing cold. Past curfew.

I opened the front door. Checked the rear seat. Empty, as was the floor. I sat on the far edge, pressed against the door. My left hand clenched the straps of my backpack, my right hand poised over the door handle. Every muscle tensed.

Heat rushed from the vents in the dash. It smelled pleasantly of a flowery perfume with a hint of spice. Warm, at least.

The man picked up the handheld radio, the cord coiled and tangled.

Abrupt English words. "Ahmed here. I'll be off the air for thirty minutes. I have a small errand."

An identification card on the visor, held there by an elastic band. The name said *Gabriel Bakir* and the picture was not of this man.

The man switched to Amharic. "Where do you want to go?"

"I don't know," I said. How much to tell? Be careful what you say. "No one came for me. Someone should have come."

I shrank into the seat when he reached over my right shoulder, ready to bite if he grabbed me, and to bolt out the door. He yanked the belt and clipped it in place so I couldn't escape. He pulled from the curb.

I was trapped.

"Where do you live? I will take you."

"You will take me home?" I asked. The nightmare would end.

"Yes. Tell me where."

"It is far, I think. Addis Ababa." I said.

"Yes, I know by your language. But now. Where now?"

My home was with Etheye. Was she still in Addis?

"I don't know." Etheye had to pay the smuggler. Did she sell the house? Where would she go?

The driver sighed. A long, slow, dramatic exhalation.

"Why are you so scared? I will not hurt you. You can trust me," he said.

Trust an Eritrean? He must think me a fool. I would be careful, watchful, ready to escape.

The streets curved and rose. We drove toward the towering buildings with lights that I had tried to reach on foot. So quiet after curfew. So empty.

"You cannot go from Ethiopia to Canada on the bus. You know that. I know that," he said. "You think I don't know you are running away from something?"

"I came on a bus," I said. Ahmed said nothing. His mouth became a straight line. "And an airplane," I offered.

"So? You want me drive all night while you tell me nothing? I don't want to know. I have enough troubles. I don't know why I brought you." He pulled into a car park, stopped and released my security belt.

"Get out," he said. He made a sweeping motion with the back of his hand, shooing me like a bad smell. "Go! Leave! You cost me money." Before me was emptiness lit by streetlights.

"Here?" my voice squeaked. "But there is nothing."

A woman's gravelly voice on the radio called cars and read numbers.

"I have work. Customers. Money to make. You think I have the night? You think I want to help you?"

He couldn't leave me here, could he?

"I cannot go home. They will kill me," I said.

He shook his head. "Why I do such things?" he muttered.

He shifted the car into gear and pulled onto the street. Where was he taking me now?

A streetlight switched from yellow to red. He slowed the car and stopped.

"Kids think their parents will kill them. But fathers forgive. Whatever you did can't be so bad, okay?"

"I did nothing wrong."

"Of course. It's always someone else who caused the problem. If you did nothing wrong, what gives you such fear?"

"I want to sleep. Where can I sleep?"

"You tell me nothing. I take you to police. You sleep there."

I knew what the police would do. I squeezed the door handle and pushed. The streetlight flicked green. Ahmed gunned into the intersection. The door flew from my grip. Pavement rushed beneath the open door. Ahmed grabbed the shoulder of my jacket. I flung my DC backpack at his face. The car swerved.

"Shut the door! Idiot!" he screamed. I dragged the door

closed. The cords in Ahmed's neck were visible. "What are you doing? Trying to kill us? What's wrong with you?"

He looked as if he might hit me. I shrank against the side, out of his reach, and pulled the pack to my chest like a warrior's shield.

"Why are you scared of police? What I supposed to do with you?" he asked. I remained silent and watchful. I did not think he expected an answer. We crossed a river.

"What is in the pack?" he asked suddenly.

"A thick coat." I *was* an idiot. Why had I not put it on? Ahmed remained silent but turned his head to look at me.

"And?" he asked.

What had Yosef called them? "Tubes for the feet."

"Socks?" the driver used the English word.

"Yes, *socks*! And food. Injera. Water. Gloves for a mechanic, a hat of wool."

"Why do you have these? It is spring," Ahmed said.

"Solomon?" I said. Did he know Solomon?

He muttered to himself in Tigrigna. "That makes no sense. Kids have books. Music. A calculator. Maybe chocolate." I caught parts of what he said.

"Why do you have those things?" he asked me. The fan shot hot air, the woman's voice called on the radio.

"To stay warm?"

"But it is spring," he said. "You come now? You just got here?"

"Yes, on the bus."

"I don't believe it. Money? You have money in that pack?"

"No." The paper money with the number ten was folded in the pocket of my jeans with my birth certificate.

"Papers? Documents?"

"No." Not in the backpack.

"You came on a boat? Where did you land? Vancouver?"

"English China, first," I said. "Then Toronto, Canada."

He spoke quietly to himself. "Vancouver, then. But why Toronto?"

We drove in silence. I recognized the buildings. We were driving in a large circle.

"How did you get in the country without papers?" he asked me.

"The smuggler spoke for me."

"How many others?"

"Two. A woman and a girl."

"His wife? His daughter?"

"They were like me."

"Ethiopian?"

"No."

"So this man pretended to be your father, brought you to Canada and put you on a bus? And now you are here?"

"Yes."

"You must have papers. They do not let you in without papers. A passport."

"He took them."

"To use for someone else ..." Ahmed spoke out loud again, but to himself.

"I don't know what to do with you," he said. He stopped in front of a large square building with big windows all along the front.

The air inside the brightly lit shop smelled of old coffee and a type of food that made my stomach feel sick. There were racks and shelves overflowing with colorful packages of chocolate and other sweets. An entire wall of glass displayed drinks, such as Coca-Cola, Fanta, bottled water and the boxes of milk that I had seen in Canada.

So much, so much of everything.

Ahmed and another man spoke in Tigrigna. About me, and my lack of identity papers. I was able to follow parts of it.

"We need to find out who he is and how he got here. You don't just walk across borders. You don't get in without documents," the other man said.

This man, too, was near the age of Gashe, but he did not wear the mark of success. His shirt did not fully cover the bulge of fat that hung over his belt. His fingernails were grimed with grease. He smelled of gasoline, and beneath that, the stench of an unwashed body. The name on his shirt said *Neguse*.

"That is what I told him, but he kept saying he came on the bus. From Toronto."

"There is more to his story. He could be someone important. Good thing you brought him to me," the man said.

"You'll keep him, then?" the driver asked.

"For now, he stays here where I can watch him. Come back at the end of your shift. I'll figure out what to do."

When night lifted to morning, Ahmed drove me on the smooth roads without life. We passed rows of tidy houses with square patches of grass, each with a lone tree. Cars and pickups parked in front or to the side, but not a single guard was visible, nor a cement wall to protect property.

He took me to a street lined on each side with a row of deep holes dug in black dirt, like a graveyard waiting for the corpses of well-fed giants. Amid the field of rectangular craters were the wooden skeletons of cheap buildings not meant to last. Far beyond, on the horizon, were the tips of mountains. Like Addis, this place was edged with mountains, but these were farther away, as sharp as spears and tipped with pure white. Mostly it was a flat land of emptiness.

Where was he taking me? Where was this place called Calgary? This country called Wild Rose? Where on a globe of the world were mountains such as these? I had been in Canada with Yosef. I had traveled several days by bus, crossed no oceans. The road signs and those on buildings were all in English. This must still be North America, but where, exactly, on the globe?

At the end of the street — amid all of the nothingness — was a tall plastic house with a massive door on the front, so big that a car could drive through, maybe two cars. We entered through a smaller door. Inside was a huge cavern with high ceilings, like the interior of a cathedral, but without the benefit of curved arches. The walls were plain white, without cracks or signs of repair. It was mostly bare of furniture and it smelled of fresh paint.

He took me down a short flight of stairs. He shook a blanket onto a sofa like the green one in Toronto, but this one was patterned in rich shades of brown, and covered, all along the back, with a row of cushions.

"You will sleep here," he said. Ahmed climbed the stairs and put out the light. I heard him lock the door.

6

The voices were above me, raised in anger.

"He cannot stay here!"

A wooden spoon striking a metal bowl.

"He has nowhere to go. He has no one."

"What were you thinking? Bringing him here?"

Shuffling feet. The creaking of wood.

"He was alone. His face covered with blood."

"What if the authorities find out? What if he is a spy?"

The happy sounds of small children running.

"He cannot stay here! He will ruin our chances. Ruin everything!"

A door opened. Ahmed stood in silhouette. A blinding light strobed.

Ahmed pulled me close, like a brother.

"You will come with me to work. Until I can think of something," he said.

He took me as he had the night before to the shivering cold shop that also sold gasoline. I drifted in and out of sleep on a stiff metal chair behind the counter where Ahmed grinned like a simpleton, nodded and took money and plastic cards from customers. In the evening he drove the taxi and Neguse kept his eye on me like a hungry hawk waiting to strike. I remained still and invisible and useless, and drifted time and again, home to Addis. I jerked awake when I drifted too far ahead in the chair, all senses on alert, and once, I fell to the floor.

"Stupid boy! Get up!" yelled Neguse when the bells on the door signaled the customer had left. "What do you think you are doing? Do not draw attention!" He flipped back his hand as if he would hit me, but dropped it before he swung.

I sat up as straight as if I was in school and focused on keeping my eyes open. But it felt as if I was in a maths class in which the teacher droned the same simple lesson over and over again. Why wouldn't they let me sleep? Why couldn't I just lie down among the cardboard boxes in the back room? Or even here? Behind the counter, where Neguse could watch me? If only I could sleep, I could think. If I could think, I could find a solution. Why wouldn't my brain work?

Ahmed returned during the rising of the sun. We drove to his plain plastic-covered house to eat the food his wife cooked and to sleep in quivering darkness that gave me no rest.

"Who are you? What do you want?" Ahmed and Neguse asked in each of the days and nights that blended together in a heavy gray fog. The same questions every day, one following the other. Did they expect different answers?

I repeated my name, but what did I want? I wanted what was impossible. I wanted to go home. To all that was familiar and comfortable. To the brother who was the other half of me.

7

The waking of the sun colored the horizon pink, the moon still visible as I drove with Ahmed to his house. I pointed out the window.

"The moon. It's wrong!" I said. The crescent curled to the right, like an ear. "What has happened?"

Ahmed leaned forward and looked up.

"It looks fine to me," he said.

"It's on its side," I insisted. "Do you not see? It has tilted."

"The moon in Canada, it always looks like this."

"In Canada?"

"Yes. Where do you think we are?"

"In Wild Rose country."

"In wild ... Ho-ho," Ahmed laughed. He slapped the steering wheel with his palm and wiped a tear from his face. "I can hardly wait to tell the others," he said.

He glanced at me, then explained. "It is a slogan for the province. The province is Alberta. The country is Canada."

"We're in Canada?" Canada was a safe country. It gave aid to the world. No one would hurt me.

"Yes, this is Canada." He pointed to the sky. "That is the moon. Anything else you need to know?"

"The moon at this phase should look like a smile. My brother and I watch it all the time." Ahmed did not look convinced.

"You know, how it is on a mosque?" I asked.

Ahmed parked the car in front of his house. He gazed at the sky and scratched his cheek.

"You are right," he said. "The moon does look different in Africa. It has been a long time for me. I had forgotten."

He pulled the keys from the ignition and opened the door. "But the mosque I remember."

At the shop Ahmed allowed me to refill the shelves with chocolate and shiny bags of crisps when it was his shift, and to clean the machine that dispensed syrup and ice, but he had stopped looking at me and stopped asking questions.

The two of us rarely spoke these days. It was as if I had become a heavy piece of luggage to be dragged from his house to the shop and back again. But I didn't mind the quiet.

I noticed tiny leaves now on the trees that had been bare sticks when I first arrived, bright yellow-green that twitched in the breeze like the sequins on Etheye's best dress when she walked. I wanted to roll down the window of the car to listen to their sound.

"My wife," said Ahmed. He removed his hand from the wheel, glanced at me quickly. "She says to get rid of you."

I studied his profile. There was no laughter in his voice. His wife? Why would he care what she thought?

Ahmed stared straight ahead, as if it took all of his concentration to keep the car on the empty road.

"Because of the sister. You understand," he said. "An unmarried man cannot be in the house with an unmarried woman. It is haram. She comes soon, the sister. Very soon."

I knew it wasn't only his wife who wanted me gone. Ahmed, too, was tired of me, and Neguse had never disguised his dislike. They had figured out no way to make money from me.

The silence in the car grew as heavy as clouds before hail. Ahmed switched on the radio, to a chirpy woman's voice speaking rapid English.

I didn't know why Ahmed kept me as long as he did, or even why he had picked me up in the first place. I wanted to leave, but where would I go? How would I live?

Ahmed stopped in front of his house and cut the engine.

"What will happen to me? Where will I go?"

Ahmed lifted his shoulders and dropped them. "This, I do not know. I want to help you, but ..."

The slam of the car door jolted me like the explosion of a bomb. He walked up the stairs without looking back.

Did he mean now? That I should walk away?

Ahmed strode back to the car. He rapped a knuckle on the window.

"Hurry up!" he said. "Don't keep my wife waiting. The food will be cold."

I stayed awake as the sun warmed the day, huddled in the cold darkness of below ground, trying to make a plan. But what was a boy with no skills — who did not speak the common language and who did not have identity papers — supposed to do?

The children scurried beneath the high table where Ahmed's wife had put steaming bread, sour cabbage and orange cheese for my mid-day meal. The boy had the same sparkling brown eyes as my young brother, Kato, who liked best to be chased. Their voices turned to high squeals when I lowered my head beneath the surface to peer at them with my eyes bulged and mouth twisted. They dashed, helter-skelter, from the room with grins on their faces, and flapped their arms as if they were bat wings. When I looked up again from

COLD WHITE SUN

the food, I caught them peeking around the corner of the doorway, popping out of sight as my brothers and sisters did when they were caught.

Ahmed's wife scoured the cooking surface, pressing hard to the rhythm of the drums and whistles that came from the radio. She watched the children and she watched me. Ahmed was in the next room, speaking into a telephone.

"You keep him then!" Ahmed yelled. His voice lifted over the music and the laughter of his small children playing. "I have kept him long enough!"

His wife stopped the circular paths of her scrubbing. The children froze. We all stared at the doorway.

Ahmed stormed into the room. My body twitched when he smashed the phone on the table. He wore his taxi-driving clothes. These were not the clothes he wore for the afternoon shift at the shop that sold sweets and gasoline.

"Come on," Ahmed said. "Let's go!"

The chair scraped on the floor when I stood. I had eaten little of the food. His wife would be insulted and hate me more. I looked at her to offer apology, but she was looking down, having resumed her cleaning.

"My backpack?" I asked Ahmed. Would he allow me to retrieve it? Or must I leave that, too?

"Go! Hurry!" he said, his voice and his face gruff.

Ahmed maneuvered through the patient lines of cars and pickups but did not take the proper turn for the sweet shop. He drove straight and fast until he stopped in front of a plain cement building with a flat front.

"It grieves me to do this to you. But you must understand, I do not want trouble," he said. "Yes? You understand?"

I nodded but I did not understand. "How do I get to the next place where I am supposed to go?"

Ahmed shrugged.

206

"That is not my business," he said.

"But Solomon …" I said. "He made the arrangements."

As soon as I said the words out loud, I realized they were just words, that the smuggler had disappeared and that he had made no arrangements.

Ahmed was the only person I had. I followed him into a room with a low ceiling and outlined by a row of matching chairs.

"I have a boy here. For you," Ahmed told a woman behind a tall counter.

"Stay here," he told me. He pressed his hand on my shoulder and turned to leave. "Be well."

"Hey, wait!" the woman called in English. Ahmed stopped and turned. "You can't just drop him off! He's not a dog. This isn't the SPCA." Ahmed approached the counter.

"It is with my eyes I see he is not a dog," he said calmly. "He is not my son. I do not know him. I have no responsibility." He turned again to leave.

"Wait. You can't go! You have to …" She withdrew a sheaf of papers from a slot and waved them in the air above her head. "You have to fill out some forms."

"You fill them out," he said. "I have work." He was nearly to the door. The woman's chair rolled behind her when she stood.

"It is against the law," she said. "I will call the police."

Ahmed stopped.

"They will come and take you," she said.

He strode to the counter and leaned over it, his face close to the woman's face. "I know this not to be true!" he said. He and the woman glared at each other like two goats about to fight. The woman picked up the handset of the telephone.

"Who will pay for him? Me? Why should I have to pay for this beggar who has come at my door?" All eyes in the room turned to the conflict.

"Paying isn't the problem," she said, her voice calm. Gently, she put down the telephone. "But we need information. Fill out these forms and take a seat."

"I will lose a whole day of work because of this? Who will pay?" Ahmed asked.

"Fill out the papers and take a seat," she said.

When the woman turned to face the computer, Ahmed left me.

8

I picked up the sheets of paper Ahmed had placed on the chair. Everyone sitting in the room held a set. They were covered in small blocks and tiny English words. A thin man with shoulders curved inwards appeared at intervals, said a number, and someone holding the long papers followed.

I saw no Ethiopian to explain this custom. Not even an Eritrean.

When I stood again before her, the woman who had given Ahmed the documents looked at me as if I had walked across a clean floor with muddy feet.

"Yes," she said, but her voice did not sound like one of agreement.

"I do not know," I said in English.

"You do not know what?" she asked. Three parallel lines cut deep into her forehead.

"The writing of it?" I said. She sighed.

"Give those back to me." She flipped the pages over and pushed them toward me. "French. This side."

"I have no understanding," I said.

"You don't know English or French?"

I shook my head. "No. I speak a small bit of the English."

The way she looked at me, I wondered for a moment if I had grown two heads. "Amharic?"

"Amharic? What are you saying? You need an interpreter?"

I shook my head. If only I could understand her swift words.

"Take a number." She pointed with her index finger to a red plastic device attached to a pole. "Sit. Over there."

My ticket ripped when I yanked it as I had watched others do. I wiggled my fingers into the opening to get out the other piece and sat on a chair, holding the torn number.

"7-8-6," the man called.

I followed him to a small fabric enclosure that did not reach to the ceiling. I sat on one side of the metal desk, the thin man with hair that grew around his head in a circle sat on the other. He arranged the papers and picked up a pen.

"Name?" he asked.

"My name is Tesfaye."

"Is that your last name or your first name?"

"It is my name."

"Yes, but it is your given name, or your surname?" The man dipped his head and looked at me over the top of glasses that sat low on his nose.

His stare was hard. "Well?"

"I do not know this last name," I said.

"Okay, 'Tesfaye,'" he said. His voice was heavy with sarcasm. "We will skip that question for now. What is your birthdate?"

"Birth-date," I repeated.

"Yes, on what day, in what month, and in what year were you born?"

Such a difficult question. I knew there were only twelve months in North America. But I did not know the names in English. I could not even guess.

"How old are you?" he demanded.

I paused to think, not because I did not understand, but because the issue of my birth was complicated, and my age? It was of no importance once I had reached the time to begin school. I was born near to the Great Famine, but how did I translate that? The calendar in North America was off by how many years? Seven? Eight?

"Do you understand English?" The man's voice grew louder, the words slower, more distinct. "Do you need a translator?"

"Yes," I nodded. "No." Every answer I gave seemed to be the wrong answer. "Yes, I understand."

Then, there were the ages on the documents I had carried. What year was written on the certificate of my birth?

Which age was the right one? Which number should I tell him?

"Then answer the question!" he grunted. "I don't have all day. How old are you?"

"I have passed fourteen years," I said. This felt truthful. I must have lived fourteen, and so had Francis Marin and all of the other names I had been.

"Place of birth. Country of origin?" he asked.

"Addis Ababa, Ethiopia."

"Are you a Canadian citizen?"

"No."

"Are you a landed immigrant?"

"I do not know this immigrant."

"I'll take that as a no. When did you enter Canada?"

"I do not know."

"Where did you enter Canada?"

I smiled. I knew this answer.

"English China."

"There is no 'English China.'" He stared at me.

The city where Yosef stayed.

"To-ron-to?" I said. He wrote on the paper.

"Were you lawfully admitted to Canada?"

"Yes?" What were these questions? So fast. So confusing.

"Have you remained in Canada continuously since your entry?"

"Yes?" The "yes" answers pleased him.

"Do you wish to remain in Canada permanently as an immigrant?"

"Yes?"

"Are you currently in possession of a valid passport or travel document?"

"No." Solomon had taken the ones he had made. I had my birth certificate in my back pocket with the ten-dollar bill. Should I show it to this official?

"How much money did you have in your possession when you arrived in Canada?"

"When I came to To-ron-to?"

"Yes. That was your point of entry?"

"I had no money."

"Are you receiving welfare? Do you have any relatives in Canada who can support you financially? Upon arrival in Canada did you present a passport or travel document to a Customs or Immigration officer? Upon arrival in Canada did someone else present a passport or travel document to a Customs or Immigration officer for you? What is that person's name? What is that person's connection to you? Did you intentionally avoid examination by an Immigration or Customs officer to enter Canada?"

Questions, questions, questions. So many I did not understand.

"Sign here. Go sit over there. Someone will call your name," he said.

The second man pressed my finger in ink, then on a piece of paper, the way it was done when one votes in an election. He told me not to smile when he flashed me with a camera. He copied some items from the first paper.

"Okay," he said. "Do you have *any* documents with you?"

I unfolded my birth certificate. The man examined it and printed neatly in the little boxes on his paper.

"Perfect. What is your address in Calgary?"

"I do not know this."

"That's fine. What is your address in Ethiopia?" I still did not understand the question.

"Where do you live? In Ethiopia?" This was easy, something we had practiced in school.

"My family lives in Addis Ababa."

"Yes, but where?" He paused. "What is the address?"

"My sisters have a dress." I pictured them in my mind, dancing, with all of the colors swirling together. The man stretched his neck toward me and squinted.

"No, you don't understand. Where is the house?" The man held his Bic ballpoint pen as if it was a spear that he meant to throw at me. "If I went to Addis Ababa, how would I find it?"

"There is a wide gate with four holes."

"What is the name of the street?" The only street name I knew was the famous Bole Road that led from the airport to the center of Addis. He held his blue pen above the paper.

"Bole Road," I said.

"And the number?"

"The number?"

"Of the house. What is it?" His face looked like a sweating pomegranate so full of rot that it might explode.

What should I say? Ahmed's house had a number on the front.

"1-6-0-5," I said. The man wrote the number on his paper.

"Who is your next of kin? Who cares for you?"

"Etheye." The man repeated the syllables slowly and wrote down the English sounds.

"And she lived with you? At this address? 1605 Bole Road?"

"Yes." This man had strange questions. Of course Etheye lived with me. Where else would she go?

"And so, you would like to claim refugee status?" I did not want to stay in a refugee camp, but to answer "no"? Would they send me back to the Special Police?

"Yes," I said. "A refugee."

"What is your mother tongue?"

"My mother's tongue?"

"Yes, what language?"

"Etheye speaks Gurage and Amharic." He expelled all of the air from his lungs.

"But *you*. What language do *you* speak?"

"I speak in English."

"Yes, but English is not your *first* language. In ..." he consulted his paper. "In Ethiopia, what language do you speak? At home."

"Ah," I said. "Amharic. Amharic is my *mother tongue*."

He asked unusual questions about marriage, education, occupation, diseases, crimes and debts. He also asked how much money I had.

Was this the time I was to offer him a bribe? Why had I not paid more attention to how this was done?

I unfolded the paper money with the number ten that had a picture of a man with no hair on the top of his head, and a nose as large as an Italian's. I put it on the man's desk and flattened it with both hands. I nodded as if I knew what I was doing. Gashe sometimes paid with a roll of bills.

Was this enough?

The man recoiled as if I had given him a poisonous snake. "What is this?"

"A gift," I said. "For you. For your hard work." I smiled the way Gashe and Kofi did when they presented such gifts.

"Is this all that you have? Ten dollars?"

"Yes." It was not enough. The bribe was too small. Would I go to jail now for coming to this country with the wrong papers?

The man pushed the bill with the ugly man across the desk toward me.

What had I done wrong? Perhaps he did not understand. He wrote the number ten on his paper.

I slid the money back. "For.you," I said. "For your family."

"Are you trying to bribe me?"

"Yes!" I said. "It is everything that I have."

"It is an offense to offer bribes in Canada."

He was offended? How, then, in Canada, did one get power and influence?

"It makes me sorrow to cause this offense," I said. He passed the money to me.

"Put it away. We'll pretend I didn't see it." Ah, it was important to keep it concealed!

There were more people who asked questions with no answers. The same questions, sometimes. The same answers, but it was as if they did not believe that Solomon had brought me to this country and sent me on a bus.

I was glad when a man named Rob came and took me away.

Rob parked in front of a two-level house, white with a thin metal door fitted at the center.

"Come on," he said. "This is where you're going to stay. For now, at least."

He dragged a plastic market bag from the backseat. It contained the clothing he'd taken from a shop after he displayed a small plastic card like the ones I had seen at Ahmed's gasoline shop.

"I will have work here?" I asked. Etheye said I was to be a slave in this country, but so far, no one had asked me to do anything except fill shelves with sweets and answer ridiculous questions. No one beat me when I made mistakes.

"No. No one is going to make you work. Not here."

Inside, we stood in the middle of two sets of stairs. One set went up, one set went down. Along the side and at the top was the type of wooden railings that should be on a balcony, and on its top edge, a small camera pointed at me.

"Melissa! We're here," Rob called. He used the toe of one shoe to pry the heel from his sneakers. A woman with frizzy hair the color of faded brass appeared at the top of the stairs, wiping her hands on a cloth striped with red and blue.

"Hey," she said. "Welcome, stranger. I haven't seen you in

a long time." They hugged briefly. Rob beckoned for me to climb the stairs. I removed my shoes as he had, toe to heel and pried. Why did they not have Velcro here? Velcro was much more convenient.

"This is Tesfaye," said Rob. "Tesfaye, Melissa." I tried for a friendly smile and waited for the woman to embrace me. She stuck out her hand the way I had seen Gashe do when he completed a business transaction. We moved our hands up and down. How long was I supposed to do this? She pulled back her hand.

"We're going to have to work on that handshake," she said. It was then I remembered the good English manners I had learned in school.

"Hello, my name is Tesfaye," I said. "Are you okay?"

Melissa twisted her face when she looked at me. "Ah ... yeah ... I'm okay."

I grinned. I had gotten it right.

"You've read his file, then?" asked Rob.

"Yup. Got it. No history? No priors?" she asked.

"Nothing we can find, anyway. No real info. No ID. He had a worn-out piece of paper he said was a birth certificate." Rob shook his head. "Pretty amateur."

Rob glanced at me. I smiled like a child who had been given a square of chocolate.

"He seems co-operative, but he refuses to give his last name, anything to identify him. The address he gave was bogus," he said. He turned back to Melissa. "Delusional. He thinks he's from Africa."

"Ethiopia," I said. "In the north and in the east." I waved my right hand to show them on an imaginary map, the way I had shown the slave girl on the bus.

"Well, at least he's the right color for his delusion," said Melissa. "Drugs?"

"Seems clean. Nothing in his pack. Just clothes and some weird sort of food, which we disposed of."

"So, what's the story? A runaway who showed up at Immigration claiming asylum that nobody knows what to do with?"

"That's about it. He said an Eritrean taxi driver dropped him off."

Melissa shook her head slightly. "What's an Eritrean taxi driver?" she asked.

"More farther in the north," I said. I waved my right hand again, but higher up on the imaginary map, then moved my hands as if I was steering a car. Rob and Melissa exchanged a look that I did not comprehend.

"The truly weird thing is that there was a small package of cookies in his pack from Kenya Airways. I don't know what to make of it," said Rob.

"Maybe that's *why* he thinks he's from Africa," said Melissa.

"Yeah, maybe," said Rob. "The good news is he understands English, speaks some," said Rob.

"Hooray." Melissa's sarcasm was apparent, even to me. "I can tell he's going to fit into this loony bin just fine. Come on, you," she said to me. "I'll show you what goes down 'round here."

The room Melissa showed me had the smell of a medical clinic. It had two narrow mattresses on wooden frames. There were cameras in the corners of the room, like eyes.

This was a prison.

"You're sharing with another boy. You're what, fourteen? Fifteen?"

A question, but what had she asked? What was 1415? I did the friendly smile again and nodded.

"His name is DJ. He's not here now. He's at Calaway for the day. Probably good. We'll get you settled in. Go over the rules." She slung the bag of clothes on top of a mattress.

"This one is yours," she said. "Got it?"

Another question. I nodded.

"Bathroom down the hall at the end. I'll get you a set of towels. Clean up after yourself. We don't have any slaves here. No servants, either. Not even your mother."

"No slaves?" I asked.

"Uh, no," she said. "That was outlawed a long time ago, like a century ago. Actually, I don't know if there ever were slaves in Canada ..."

"No slaves?" I asked again.

"Not a one," she said. "You have to look after all your own sh ..." Melissa glanced at me. "Sorry. Stuff. You have to look after your own stuff."

"Stuff?"

"Yeah, like your clothes and sh ..." She paused again. "Shoes. Like your clothes and shoes. Stuff. Don't leave it around for someone else to pick up, or there will be hell to pay. Understand?"

What were the words for "speak more slowly?"

◆

Three boys and two girls sat around a table in the cooking area the next morning. Everyone seemed to be my age or younger. Two boys did women's work at a basin beneath a window. They flicked soap and water at each other and fought with their elbows, the way my brothers and I sometimes did when we prepared for the Sabbath.

"Get a bowl. Eat," said Melissa.

On the table was a box of milk and a brown-and-yellow carton with a fat bee drawn on it. I mimicked a girl. Small, hard rings tumbled too fast and overflowed my bowl.

"Hey, slow down, there. You're wastin' the good stuff," the boy named DJ said.

"Leave him alone," the girl said. She reached for the milk. I swept the zeros from the table and piled them on top. I took milk, too, even though I felt no sickness. The zeros shot from the bowl again.

"Hey, I told you not to do that," said DJ. The others laughed.

"Ignore him," the girl said. I pinched the dry bits into my mouth. Sweet. Crunchy. Very sweet. The milk was so cold it made my fingers numb when I stuck them in the bowl to sift the wet bits.

"Man, I've never seen anyone eat Cheerios like that before!" said DJ. The metal spoon clattered to the table. He plunged his hand into his bowl, not just his fingers, and lapped at the milk like a thirsty cat.

What would Etheye say? This did not seem a polite way to eat, with one's tongue hanging out. But then I heard Gashe's voice in my head when he first sent me to the Catholic school. *Go, and learn their ways*, he said.

Like DJ, I sucked noisily from my fingers, too, and licked them clean.

DJ punched me on the shoulder. "Com' on, Africa Boy. We'll show you 'round."

I was glad for the chance to use my legs. I had been trapped too long at Ahmed's house, his taxi, the sweet shop, and the rooms where people asked questions. A football to chase would be magnificent. I wanted to run and jump and to explore every single thing.

But DJ and a boy named Jason shuffled their feet and moved as slowly as crippled men awaiting imminent death. It did not appear they had a destination.

"We should take that bike," said DJ. A bicycle was wedged into a metal apparatus bolted to the sidewalk. It was a good one with metal fenders and a wire basket in front to carry things.

DJ shook a match and inhaled deeply, the smell reminding me of the old soldiers at the mill.

"Bum a smoke?" said Jason.

"Get off," said DJ. "Get a job." DJ hooked four fingers of his left hand in the front pocket of his jeans and reclined against a lamppost. He pinched the cigarette between his thumb and index finger and smoked in short sips.

"Com' on, man," whined Jason. "Toss me a dart. You got plenty."

"Not for you, loser," he said.

I liked the look of that golden brown bicycle. I had longed to try one, but Gashe would not pay the extravagant price to ride in a small loop on the street.

"Africa Boy, you like that bike? You know how to ride?" DJ asked.

"I am not ever on a bicycle," I said.

"Not ever?" DJ's eyebrows shot to his hairline. He passed the burning cigarette to Jason. "This is your lucky day, man!"

"Take this one." Jason inhaled and huffed a cloud of smoke. "Consider it yours."

"I have no money," I said. The purple ten was safe in my backpack under the bed.

"You don't need money. You're in Canada now, dude. It's free!"

"Take it," said DJ. He pushed off the lamppost and snatched the cigarette. "We'll teach you."

"You can take a valuable bicycle?" I asked.

Jason put his hand on my shoulder. "Like, yeah! If it's not locked up, anyone can take it. Go ahead."

I lifted it from the rack. The wheels made a satisfying ticking when it moved. A ride in a Pathfinder, an airplane, a train, now a bicycle? I could hardly believe my good fortune.

"Well, get on, stupid. We'll show you," said Jason.

The front wheel wobbled when Jason let go of the handles. I was glad DJ still gripped the back of the seat. He let go. I fell to the street with the bicycle stuck between my legs.

"Priceless!" they laughed. Jason helped me up. "You really don't know how to ride."

"We need to find a hill. That's how I learned," said DJ.

The hill was a mountain. "Now, just hang on," advised DJ. He pushed me and released.

I shot down the hill like a bullet on an uncertain path. The front wheel shook. I tightened my grip and held it straight. Air rushed past my head and flapped my shirt.

I was riding a bicycle!

"Pedal! Keep pedaling!" the boys yelled.

Faster and faster. I was free! I was a bird with air beneath its wings. I was an airplane, lifting off.

Suddenly, I was in a line of traffic stopped up with cars and pickups.

How to stop? How to slow down?

A woman stood on the street, shaking her fist in the air.

"Stop! Thief!" she cried. I sped past her, rolling faster and faster. I turned to see this thief and what he took and collided with a receptacle meant for garbage.

It was not difficult to hear the hooting laughter from DJ and Jason.

◆

"Well," said Melissa when we returned to the house. "You have a fine way of introducing yourself."

I should introduce every time? I extended my hand to shake hers.

"Hello," I said. "My name is Tesfaye. Are you okay?"

"No," she said. "I am not okay. Stealing bikes is not acceptable." Jason and DJ kept their heads down, but their smirks were apparent.

"It makes me sorrow to cause you pain," I said.

"What the f ..." She stopped. "You cannot take things that are not your own. Got it?"

"Yes," I said.

"Windows," said Melissa. Jason and DJ groaned.

"Man, tha's not fair," said Jason. "You can't make us do your dirty work."

"We din't do nuthin'," said DJ. "Africa Boy. He took the bike."

"All of them," said Melissa. Her voice was low and loud. "Inside *and* out."

Now I knew why the house sparkled with cleanliness. Millions of tiny spongy bubbles formed when Jason squeezed a stream of soap into the bucket and added water. I inhaled the scent of lemons as my arm moved the cloth in circular patterns across the glass.

It was the work Ishi and I so often shared. We had complained that our house had too many windows.

This time I did not complain. It felt good, finally, to be useful.

10

A few days later Rob and I stood in a jumbled line before a wide counter where four uniformed workers smiled like dolls behind computers. The room was furnished with plastic tables and chairs. It was noisy with alarms and smelled of old grease.

"What do you want?" asked Rob.

I did not know what I wanted. To stay in Canada? To go home? To have the simple problems of DJ and Jason?

"To eat," said Rob. "What do you want to eat? Big Mac? Fries? Milkshake? Chicken burger?"

He was saying too many words I did not know. It was like going inside the clothing store at the too-bright indoor market where there were rows and rows of fancy stalls with name-brand clothing and happy shopkeepers.

"What do you want?" he had asked then, just like now. There was so much selection. How was I to choose? Buying clothing was Etheye's job in the thirteenth month. New clothing appeared just before school resumed. Each of us wore what fit us best. The only exception was the monkey shirt. I would snatch that first, even though I knew Ishi preferred the green T-shirt with Teenage Mutant Ninja Turtle.

"Hel-lo," said Rob. He tapped my shoulder. We had moved to the front of the line.

"Hi, may I take your order?" asked the girl.

"I'll have a Big Mac, fries, a chocolate shake," he said. The girl pressed buttons on her machine. "And a pie. Apple."

Rob turned to me. "So, what will it be? What would you like?"

"I do not know these things. Do they have injera?"

"No." Rob laughed.

"Make that two," he said to the girl. "He'll have the same as me."

The girl loaded enough food on a plastic tray to feed my entire family. Rob carried it to a corner table and slid into a plastic seat. He divided the food evenly and poked wide straws through the X's in the top of the containers.

"Go ahead," he said. "Dig in!"

I bit into a hot finger with squared edges that poked from the open red package.

"Potato?" I asked. Rob nodded.

"Yeah. Fries." He gripped the thick bread with meat, opened his mouth wide and bit into it. He sucked on the straw before he swallowed.

The potato tasted of too much salt and left a film of grease on my fingers.

"Like it?"

"It has an unusual taste," I said.

Rob shook his cup side to side. "I can't believe you've never had fast food before." Around us children gobbled food the way I had at home, before my sisters came to push me away. But I did not see any mean sisters ready to hit.

On the other side of a large window, children climbed a colorful plastic apparatus. When the door opened, it was as loud as our garden when everyone played football.

I opened the small hinged box. Inside was round, soft bread sprinkled with seeds. It was filled with two large pieces

225

of pressed meat and an extra piece of bread. I separated the layers to examine them: Meat. A thin square of orange plastic. Strange-colored slices of cucumber. Chopped onions, lettuce. I dipped my finger into the red sauce and licked it. Sweet.

"All of this? For me?" I asked.

"Yeah," Rob said. He stuffed several fries into his mouth. "Take a bite. You're going to love it."

"It is kidus?" I asked.

"It's hamburger. From a cow," he said.

"Yes," I said. But what if a Muslim had slaughtered it? "How is it prepared? Who killed this cow?"

"How am I supposed to know? It's fried, I think."

"Ah," I said. I nibbled another fry. The salt burned my tongue. Everything here had too much salt or too much sugar. I sucked on the straw until my cheeks collapsed and I nearly swallowed my tongue. Slowly, the liquid pumped. A jolt of cold blasted the roof of my mouth that caused pain in my forehead.

"Cold!" I said.

"It has ice cream in it. You do know what ice cream is, right?"

"Yes," I said. Cream with ice. Everything in Canada was so strange.

"Are you going to eat that?" asked Rob. He meant the Big Mac. My stomach felt sick wondering if it had been handled by a Muslim. I lifted off the top piece of bread with the seeds and took a bite. It had the taste and consistency of paste.

"Not like that. Like this," said Rob. He opened his mouth wide again and took a huge bite.

"I do not think I am so hungry," I said. I tugged at the lettuce and bit off a small piece. The milkshake tasted of sugar rather than of chocolate, but I liked how the coldness melted in my mouth.

"You're not, like, a vegetarian or something, are you?"

"I do not know what that means. I am Ethiopian."

"No, like, someone who only eats vegetables and fruits and stuff."

"I like these things very much. Etheye prepares the wat with many spices."

"What?"

"Wat," I said. "It is the name. How do you say it in English?"

"I don't know. What do I look like, a dictionary?"

"I do not know."

Rob shook his head. He squished the box from his Big Mac and moved the paper cup with the lid closer. He resembled a South American anteater when he sucked on the straw.

"If you are going to take that apart piece by piece, we're going to be here all day."

"My hunger is not as great as yours," I said.

"You don't have to eat it," he said.

"Maybe later." I closed the box, admiring how it fit together with such precision. "Or we can give it to a beggar?"

"We don't have beggars here. At least, not ones that want cold hamburgers." He piled the uneaten food on the tray and stood up. "Keep the pie. You're going to love the pie." He passed the elongated package of thin cardboard to me, then tipped the tray into a receptacle near the door that overflowed with packaging.

"What will happen to it?" I asked.

"The garbage?"

"Yes. If not for beggars, then for … animals?"

"No, it just goes to the dump," he said. "But animals would be a good idea."

I pictured the people who lived in the Korah outside of Addis, where Gashe threatened to send us if we did not obey, how the best shelters were built with scraps of scavenged wood with rusted tin roofs. How happy they would be to have this food, even if it was cold and had too much salt, even if it tasted like paste, and the meat had been slaughtered with the wrong prayers.

11

On the days I was not in an airless room attempting to correctly answer questions about who I was and how I came here, I wandered the streets with DJ and Jason. I listened to their talk of the need for money and their desire for beer and tried to get used to being punched in the shoulder for no reason.

In the background was the hollow *thwapping* of the cardboard cups that drummed against buildings when the wind swirled low. People driving cars had the giant cups, and most often, people walking on the street carried them, too.

"They're for coffee. You don't got coffee in Africa?"

"We have coffee. Etheye makes it."

"Well, duh," said Jason. "It's the same thing."

I did not think it was. How to describe the enticing aroma of roasting coffee and incense that meant food was coming? I could think of no way to explain in English. I caught a paper cup between my feet and dribbled it as we walked. When neither of them tried for a steal, I passed to DJ. He lifted his foot and squashed it flat.

The leaves on the trees that bordered the streets grew bigger every few days, and the color transformed from lime to the shade of the skin of a ripe avocado. Bright flowers popped from the ground, and men, women and children wore T-shirts and short pants.

DJ and Jason begged on the streets for coins to purchase cigarettes. I sat nearby and watched. Clutching their stomachs and telling people they were hungry was most effective. When they didn't have enough money, we scavenged the streets for cigarette ends. I suggested they kneel, bow their heads to the cement and put a small cup nearby to collect coins. They laughed as hard as the day I learned to ride a bicycle. Jason fell to his side, then rolled off the bench by the blue-green river.

"You're like the funniest dude ever, man," he said. "But I still wish I had a smoke."

"Maybe we could use him. He's skinny," said DJ.

"To smoke?"

"Yeah, man. We're gonna smoke ya." Jason pealed again with laughter. When he regained his breath, he said, "It's because yer so scrawny and hungry looking. The old ladies would fall for it. Make us rich."

D.J. worked a toothpick with his tongue. Vertical, horizontal, vertical while he appraised me.

"We'd hafta work on him. Teach him some things. He stands out too much," he said. "Obviously not from here."

I was eager to learn. I wanted worries as simple as collecting money to buy cigarettes and learning how to break rules and not be caught.

"You hafta blend," DJ instructed. "Be cool, like us."

I would be a strong student.

"You have to hunch more, like this," said Jason. He rolled his shoulders forward to demonstrate. I copied his poor posture.

"Yeah, that's better," agreed DJ. "You can't go 'round like you got a stick stuck up your ass."

"And what's with the shoes?" asked Jason. My high-top

sneakers were tied precisely with a bow with equal-sized loops. Jason lifted his foot. His shoe hung loose, the laces sprawled and tucked beneath the thick tongue.

"Here, man," he said. He bent before me and loosened my laces. It felt now as if the sneakers were three sizes too big. "Try that."

I curled my shoulders and tried to press my belly button into my spine as I walked. The sneaker flew from my foot in a low arc.

DJ and Jason cackled. "Slower, Africa Boy. You goin' too fast."

Hunch. Slow.

"Hands in your pockets," called DJ. I scuffed on the ribbon of pavement that ran through the grass, trying not to dislodge the shoes again.

It was a most unnatural way to travel. A person would get nowhere walking like this.

"Wait!" said DJ. He hobbled beside me. The crotch of his jeans drooped nearly to his knees. He took the hat worn by baseball players from his head and pushed it onto mine. The curved brim was so low that I could see only the cement path beneath my feet.

"Now," he said. "You at least look like you belong, Africa Boy." DJ punched me in the shoulder. I stayed head down, hands in pockets.

If I looked cool and did everything they said, would it stop me thinking of my family? Was Gashe being beaten? Now, while I slouched on the street of a foreign country learning to be a beggar? How ashamed he would be.

"Hey! Man! Africa Boy." Jason nudged my arm with his elbow.

"Next thing, we're gonna teach you are some new words," he said. "Improve your vo-cab."

12

The days blended, one to the other, and still I had not discovered my purpose. DJ and Jason had purpose as my teachers. Melissa had purpose cooking and overseeing the house. Rob's purpose was to take a boy named Kenny and me to many different places, and to teach us how to boil Italian noodles and to open tins of food.

But my purpose eluded me.

I was on my side, facing a white wall, alone in a bed with perfumed sheets that made me sneeze, a soft pillow beneath my head. Electric lights flashed on. The blind snapped up. Around me, I could hear movement, now-familiar English words, scuffling feet, a yawn, and a loud fart that dribbled like air releasing from a balloon.

"This is such fuckin' shit hole," Jason's voice outside the room.

"Shut the fuck up. Who the fuck cares what you think?" said DJ.

The sharp smell of the insecticide DJ sprayed on his body each morning.

"Go fuck yourself," said Jason. A skirmish in the room. A toilet flushed in the distance. Someone shoved so hard against a wall it vibrated.

"Break it up, boys! Break it up!" Melissa's voice yelled down the hall. The revolting smell of sizzling pork. The clinking of dishes. The struggle between DJ and Jason continued. Flesh struck flesh.

"Hey! Hey! Hey!" Rob's voice in the room. "Melissa said break it up."

Dragging feet, mumbled phrases. The word "asshole" clear and low.

Around me, the house was filled with the noise and smells of life, but I remained as still as a corpse, allowing gravity to press me into the mattress like a heavy anvil, to crush me so thin I could vanish. As if I had never existed.

What was the use of being alive if you contributed nothing? Why had Etheye saved me?

If I could sleep, and never wake ...

I dragged my knees toward my chest and tucked my hand beneath my shoulder. The warmth of touch, even if it was my own arm holding my own body, gave me comfort. I wrapped the other arm over my shoulder. Shallow breath. A thin line of pain around my skull.

I was just a beating heart in a shell of bones and flesh. Could I slow down my heart? Until it stopped beating? I would lie here until death took me, until the wire that squeezed my brain cut off the supply of blood.

I never forget about you. Never. You are my soul, Etheye whispered. But she had forgotten. She had pushed me away, sent me so far that I could never get back.

I survived, Etheye! I live.

But I am a coward who would rather die.

"Hey, Africa dude!" called DJ.

I held my breath and my silence.

"Hey, I said. You hafta get up." He shook my shoulder. "Them's the rules. You know them. You don't get to sleep in," he said.

I was dying. Already, almost dead. Like Gashe.

The room emptied.

What had happened to Gashe? Why did he speak for unity and democracy when he had everything to lose? His position. His family. His life.

My life.

If he had remained silent, he would be busy counting his money. Sponsoring students. Giving alms to the poor.

I would still be in Addis.

Education is the only way to change a country. How often had he said that? But it was the university students who were attacked and rounded up and taken away. How could knowledge change a country if the educated were imprisoned?

I shifted in the bed. Had they killed him immediately? A bullet through his skull? Or were they doing it slowly?

I stared at the wall dimpled like the skin of an orange. My heart beat its sorrow. How could I be sad? Had I not wished he would pay for the suffering he had caused Etheye? That I would be free to choose my own life?

"Hey, Tesfaye. You have to get up." Not Jason's voice this time. Rob's. He shook my shoulder and peeled off the blanket. "Come on, buddy. Get dressed. You have an appointment."

I wasn't even allowed to die.

◆

Rob took me to a building where I had not been before, to rooms as bland as all of the other rooms where I had been questioned. He told me not to worry, that I was not in trouble, and that he would return for me.

"Just tell the truth," he said. "Everything will be okay."

Did Rob think that I had not been telling the truth?

The walls of the room were painted rainy-day gray that matched the furnishings, a cheap metal table and three chairs. A man of heavy build, a glossy scalp and thick glasses had an open file folder on the table with the familiar sheets of paper covered with little boxes. His hands were meaty and large. Beside him, a man with a lined pad of yellow paper. His pen was poised, ready to write things down.

I waited to be invited to sit.

"So you entered Canada illegally? And you would like to stay?" the bald man asked. His voice was pleasant and comforting.

I wanted to return to Addis. More than anything, to go home, to stop the questions, but I knew that returning to Ethiopia was certain death.

"Yes. It would please me to stay," I said. It was my first lie. Rob would be disappointed.

The questions made me want to rest my head on the table and close my eyes. Why did they ask me the same things?

"Why are you here?" he demanded. His voice echoed in the bare room.

A new question.

The large man, angry now with a red shining face, stood across from me. His weight rested on his hands splayed on the table. He strained his head toward me, our faces close enough for him to strike. I braced myself for the attack that must soon come, alert to the danger of quick movements, ready to dodge.

"These are not difficult questions! Why won't you answer?"

But the questions *were* difficult. What answer did he want?

The man threatened me with his eyes. One hand curled into a fist. I knew the feeling of being beaten, the sickening sound of flesh hitting flesh.

Bang! He slammed the table. I jerked as if the blow had hit me and not the metal surface.

The other man bent to pick up the pen that vibrated from his hand and rolled across the floor.

"Do you even understand English?" the man shouted.

"Yes," I nodded. "Yes, I understand English."

"Do you know what I am asking?"

"Yes."

He sighed heavily, scraped the chair across the floor, and dropped into it. He spoke as slowly as if I were an imbecile.

"Then why. Don't. You. Answer. The. Questions?"

"I do not know why I am here."

"You know that I know that you are lying." His voice was soft, but he stared at me without blinking. He stopped speaking. It was a most uncomfortable feeling. I pressed against the back of the chair. I blinked and blinked and blinked. His eyelids did not move. My lungs squeezed out all of their air. Should I say something? He had made a statement. He did not ask a question.

"I am telling what is true." My voice squeaked. I cleared my throat. "I saw many happy Chinese people. Some were in the uniforms of police. Or maybe guards."

"What else did you see?" I closed my eyes to better remember, then opened them to speak. It seemed so long ago that I came here.

"Moving belts that carry people inside a shining market, and many, many people in all the colors of pink."

He fell into the chair and crossed his arms over his chest.

"You expect me to believe this? You're kidding, right? You think I'm stupid?"

"Some people were also brown," I added.

"You expect me to believe you entered this country by air and landed at a major international airport?"

"Yes."

He shook his head and then yelled, "Wrong! It. Does. Not. Happen. Do you hear me?"

"Yes."

"We have document scanners. We have security devices. And you want to tell me you just breezed through it all? Just walked into this country like you owned it?"

"Yes. The China man said, 'Welcome to Canada.'"

"Why don't you answer the questions truthfully? Why not make it easy for everyone?"

"I answer the questions." I flinched when he raised his hand as if he might slap me.

"Who are you trying to protect?"

"I protect no one."

He sighed deeply, pushed back the chair and left the room.

The man with the writing pad did not move or speak. We sat in silence. My foot began to wiggle. A jug of water on the table sweated. Beside it were two empty glasses upside down. My dry throat felt as if it had been scraped of its flesh. Was there a polite way to ask this man for water? There were only two glasses. The water, I realized, was not meant for me.

The room was undecorated except for a dull mirror and a door. The only things to look at were the water jug or the man. My foot jiggled faster. I needed a toilet. Now, before I exploded. I wished the man would say something, so that perhaps I could ask. He glimpsed at me when I looked at him, but otherwise his face held no expression. I lowered my eyes, focused on the man's notebook. He had thick fingers and a plain gold ring tight on his left hand. He moved his fingers in a slow pattern, smallest to index, smallest to index, smallest to index. He stopped moving them when he noticed I was watching.

The door burst open. My foot stopped shaking. The angry man raged in. He clutched a pale beige folder. He slapped it on the table.

"We know all about you," he said. "We know who you are, and why you are here. We know how you got here. We know *all* of your plans."

My teeth gripped my bottom lip. What was he talking about?

"It's all here. In this report." He tapped the folder.

"It is in the report?" What report did he have? Had Solomon been caught? But Solomon said he would deny all knowledge of me if he was captured. Even if we were in the same room, he said he would deny knowledge of me. Had I made a mistake?

"That's right," he said. He smiled, now, with the patience of an elder. He slid the folder to the side. "Now, why don't you start telling me the truth?" He slouched in his chair and touched his fingertips together in a triangle.

I remained silent. The police interrogator pumped his steepled fingers in a slow, languid manner.

"No rush," he said. "Whenever you are ready." I pressed my lips together to moisten them. Prepared for what? What did he want me to do? He reached for the jug of water and poured slowly into a plastic cup. He took a small sip. He raised his eyebrows and smiled. "Want some?"

"Yes," I said, even though the drinking of water might cause my bladder to overflow.

"So," he said, sliding the filled cup toward me, "it seems you can tell the truth when you want to." Another comment. Should I respond? I tasted the water. I would live as the desert lives when it rains. I sighed deeply, then bent my head and closed my eyes.

"It has been clearly established that you are involved in illegal activities," he said when I looked up. His voice was gentle, the voice of a teacher. "I think that you acted out of desperation. That you were in trouble. That you needed money. That you saw no other way."

I translated the words that I knew, and nodded to indicate that I understood — desperation, trouble, money. He did know about me, after all.

"So, tell me. In your own words, tell me the plan." I preferred this reasonable man to the angry one he had been before, but I did not know what he was talking about. What plan? My eyebrows drew together.

"I did not know the plan. It was arranged," I said. I took another sip of water. The two men exchanged glances.

"Who made the arrangements?"

"The arrangements were made by Solomon," I said. "The arrangements were bad when I came here. At the bus ending."

"What do you mean?"

"No one came to take me."

"Take you where?"

"I do not know this."

The room fell silent again. I rubbed the metal arms of the chair.

"Okay, this is what I think." He leaned toward me across the table. "What I think is that there is only one reason to sneak into this country. And that reason is to kill people. Was that your plan, Tesfaye? To come here and to kill?"

"No! No!" I leapt to my feet. He rose, too, and pressed closer to me, his fingertips on the table. I stepped back. His mouth twisted into a snarl.

"There is no doubt in my mind why you are here." He sneered. "Tell me. Did you come with explosives? Maybe some little incendiary devices? Something easy to assemble with a few electrical wires and fuses? Is that it? Or would you get all the parts here?"

"No! No!" My voice rose louder than it should to speak with an adult. I knew who killed. The police.

"Gashe," I said.

"Gashe. Your father?"

I nodded. How to explain? "The police. They took him."

The man kept his eyes fixed on me and bobbed his head in a slow, knowing way.

"He did nothing wrong!" I said.

"It is my experience, that when a man is arrested, he has done something wrong," he said.

"That statement is not correct," I said.

"You have broken the law in Canada. You are in a lot of trouble. And I mean, a lot." His words hung in the silence like a low, dark cloud. "You know what happens in Canada when people sneak into the country?"

I closed my eyes and shook my head. I did not know what happened in Canada when people were perceived to break the law, but I knew what happened in Ethiopia.

"Sit down," he said, "and tell me what you know. I am in a position to help you, but first I must hear the truth coming from your lips."

"You must hear the truth?" I asked. He nodded. The other man readied his pen.

"Have you done this many times before, or was this just the first time?"

"This is my first time in Canada."

◆

The words he spoke were kind and soft. *Tell me what you know.*

I couldn't see his face. He was in the backseat of the car, me in the front.

The words, so tender, so soothing. Yet the wire tightened around my throat. The weight of Ishi was beside me, asleep. I had to wake him. He needed to get away. Too late for me, but not for him. They wanted only me.

I struggled for air, unable to move my head.

I reached for Ishi, dug my fingernails into his arm and shook him.

"Wake up, Ishi! Wake up!" I screamed. I kicked him. He did not stir.

"Ishi!" My cry was too thin. The wire twisted. "Ishi!"

No movement. Ishi, beside me, was already dead. They had killed him first. Ishi! The scream tore my throat.

I curled into emptiness. I was alone. There was no reason to live. Hot tears cut my face. Every muscle quivered. I gasped the high pitch of mortar shells before they explode.

"Hey, man." A hand, warm on my shoulder. "You okay?" His touch as gentle as Etheye's.

"This is a shit hole, man, but you're safe here."

My eyes clenched. What was real? Why couldn't I breathe? My breath shuddered. Let me die. Let it be over.

"Sit up," DJ said. His hand at my back, lifting me. Feet on cold floor. "We'll get a drink of water or somethin'." One hand holding mine. Down the long hall. We circled the common room that overlooked the street. Around and around. My eyes open, but not seeing.

Blind. So powerless. Ishi!

DJ pressed a cool glass against my fist. My fingers opened. He cupped his hands around mine.

"You got it?" I nodded. "Come on, now. Take a drink. Just a sip. Tha's it."

On the sofa. Feet on the floor. Head drooped over knees. Arms encircling shins. Pain. How could I feel such pain?

I twisted from DJ's touch. Leave me! I want to die.

"Com' on, man. It's over. Just a dream."

No dream this.

"Come on. Back to bed, okay? It's all chill." DJ pulled the warm feather blanket over my shoulders. "We all been through it. I won't tell nobody."

My eyes wide now in the darkness. Could I ask him to lie close beside me?

I focused on breathing. One in. One out. One in. One out. How many breaths equaled a minute?

A nightmare. Only a dream that ripped out my throat.

And my heart.

Only a dream.

13

The next week when Rob picked me up, the boy with the name of Kenny was with him. DJ and Jason never came with Rob and me, but often, Kenny came with us to the massive indoor food markets to purchase highly polished fruits and clean vegetables. We used huge metal baskets with wheels to collect the food, then walked along the blue-green river, or played games popular in Canada.

Kenny laughed as much as a young child, and he spoke slowly with simple words so I could understand. I watched Kenny and copied what he did. I wanted to be him, to not think about the past and to think only of the succulent, creamy taste of ice cream.

Kenny had chosen chocolate, but he was not licking the coldness fast enough. He turned his head and lapped rapidly with his tongue, but the ice cream was faster. It poured over his hand and down his shirt and made a small brown beard on his chin. Rob passed him a napkin.

"I've been thinking," Rob said to me. "You don't really belong here, do you?" His ice cream was green pistachio, mine was coffee.

"I belong in Ethiopia," I said. I twirled the cone in my hand, letting my tongue clean the edges before they dripped.

"No, I mean in the group home. There is nothing wrong with you, is there?"

"No, nothing is wrong. Melissa treats us well."

Kenny shoved his cone in his mouth and crunched. Melted ice cream drooled from both sides of his lips.

"It's just your English that's not perfect. You don't always understand," Rob said.

"Sticky hands," said Kenny. He pressed his fingers together, then popped them open to demonstrate.

"I understand Kenny." I grinned at my friend. "Sticky," I said, and copied his motion with my fingers.

"Yes, I've noticed that you get along well with him. That's why I thought ..."

Kenny and I played with our fingers as if they had glue on their tips.

"Sticky," I said.

"Sticky, sticky bubblegum," sang Kenny. Rob spat on a napkin and wiped Kenny's fingers.

"But you also get along with DJ and Jason," said Rob as we walked to his car.

"They are my friends," I said. I also wanted to be like DJ and Jason, but often they were angry.

"It doesn't add up. I really don't think you belong."

Rob reached into the backseat of his car. He withdrew an elongated brown ball with a line of wide stitches at its center.

"You like it?" he asked.

"It is a most attractive ball," I said.

"You want to play?" He held the ball with his fingertips on the stitching, and drew his arm back as if he might throw it. "I thought we could go to that field over there, practice a few passes ..."

"Football!" said Kenny. He bounced up and down.

I remained silent and watchful.

"What's wrong? You told me how much you like to play football with your brothers. Remember?"

"That is not a football," I said.

"Yes, it is," Rob said.

"You must make it rounder," I said. I spread the fingers of both hands and curved them to demonstrate the spherical shape of a football. Rob looked confused.

"It must roll. When one kicks it," I explained.

"No, no. Football is about throwing and catching and running," Rob said.

"No, no. Football is kicking, and scoring goals," I said. Rob was kind, but he knew little of sports.

"Goals? Hang on a sec." Rob opened the trunk and rummaged through the contents. He withdrew a proper football.

"Yes, that is it!" I said. It was Umbro, just like the one Isaias had given me.

"Soccer," said Rob. "This is a soccer ball." It felt so good to hold a football. It had been too long since I had played.

"Soccer. Soccer. Soccer. Let's play soccer," said Kenny. He ran around the car and pretended to kick.

"In Canada, football is an entirely different game," Rob explained.

I didn't care if he called it soccer or cricket or hockey. The field had perfectly trimmed grass and the plump ball spun as we chased it and fought for the chance to kick it.

Later, when we were breathing hard from all the running, Rob gave us each a plastic bottle filled with water.

"We may have a placement for you," he said. "How would you like to go live with a family?"

"Will Jason and DJ come?"

"No, just you. But the family is a good one and they have other kids," he said.

"Can Kenny be with me?"

"Kenny is a little different," he said. "I'm working on something for him, but no, he won't go with you either."

Why was it that every time I made friends and learned new things I had to go somewhere else?

"I'll still be around, but I'll see you less often," said Rob. "Mostly you'll live with the family and learn from them."

"I will have work?" What kind of work could I do? I had seen no goats to tend. I had seen no chickens laying eggs, and I had seen not a single coffee cherry to pick. How would I pay for all I had been given?

"Well, maybe eventually you could get a job. Maybe in a year or two. When you're older."

Dare I ask for what I really wanted? Not to learn how to prepare dried noodles that came in a box, not to taste all the flavors of ice cream, but to use my mind for something of value.

"Will there be school?" I asked.

"Yes," said Rob. "You will be *required* to go to school."

This was the best day in Canada. A real football and the promise of school.

"I would like to go to this place," I said.

◆

Three days later, Rob took me far from the city of Calgary to a place where the land was flat and the sky grew to enormous proportions. The large clouds in a bright blue sky were puffy on top, flat on the bottom, and low enough, it seemed, for me to reach out the window and touch.

Rob drove at more than 100 kilometers per hour on the

smooth, wide road marked with yellow and white lines. The cars, pickups and trucks drove at great speeds all in one direction, easily passing Rob's car. On the road opposite, they flew toward the city.

We passed kilometer after kilometer of wires that carried electricity to nowhere. It was enough time for us to share boiled egg sandwiches thick with mayonnaise and scattered bits of raw onion.

He slowed when we came to a village of narrower roads that twisted, and that were lined mostly with houses and low buildings.

"Well," said Rob. "We're finally here. What do you think?"

"This is where I will go to school?"

Rob had stopped in a field with a grid of tin boxes with windows and pointed roofs. It was a most terrible place.

"Not exactly here. Not literally. This is where you will live."

There was nothing here but a few tall trees — no mountains, no cows, no goats, no sheep, no chickens — only yellowed grasses and sky. Yet when we stepped from the car, the air reeked of fresh animal dung. The wind swirled and lifted dirt as it did in Addis, blasting so much grit I could taste it coating my tongue and clinging to my teeth.

"That smell," I said.

"Packing plant. You'll get used to it. Soon you won't even notice it."

A crazed and vicious dog lunged at me but was yanked back by the chain tied to its neck. It kept a wide stance, barked and bared its teeth.

"Don't worry, it's tied," said Rob. Spit dribbled from its jowls. It leapt and leapt. What if the chain broke? A man with a large protruding belly appeared at the door two steps from the insane dog.

"Hey! Hey! Killer! Shut up! Shut your goddamn trap!" he yelled. He braced an arm on the doorframe and kept watch over Rob and me.

We picked our way through a small garden where marigolds grew in rubber tires painted white. Naked dolls with hair knotted into dreadlocks, toy cars and trucks, a worn-out sofa and a small bicycle with an extra set of wheels littered the yard. A smaller building of faded tin was on the left. For cooking? Or for animals?

Rob led me to a wooden lean-to attached to the low metal structure. Music and a babble of loud English punctuated by laughter sifted through the walls.

The noise stopped suddenly when the metal door rattled, then banged shut. The room we entered was small and the air stale. It was crowded with furniture and with people holding red plastic cups.

All the faces stared at Rob and me.

A man with thick black hair to his shoulders, and forearms covered in blue tattoos heaved from an armchair.

"Welcome home!" he said, shaking my hand and clapping the other on my shoulder.

Someone pressed a glass of juice in my hand, and a woman named Janis showed me a table full of pastries and cheese, vegetables, crackers and pressed meat.

A small boy, of an age almost for school, peeked at me from behind his mother. He pointed at me with one finger.

"Look," he said. "A chocolate man!"

"Shhh," his mother said. "That's not nice." Yet his comment made me happy. A chocolate man would be a delicious thing. Later, the boy came beside me and licked my hand.

"You don't taste chocolate," he said.

I wondered could I lick him back. Would he taste of salt or sugar?

After the guests left, Janis showed me a small room with a bed and explained this private room would be for me alone. She embraced me, tight in her arms, as Etheye would.

"Welcome home," she said. "We hope you will be happy here in this crazy mixed-up family."

She was kind, but she was mistaken. This was not my home. This was not my family. I was here only to learn.

14

I hunched into the feather-filled coat Janis called a parka. A knitted wool cap over my head to protect my ears. Head tucked into a hood edged with fur. Fists plunged deep in the pockets. Still, invisible swords sliced my face into strips. I was a walking corpse, kept alive only by shivering and the quickness of my steps.

There were things worse than people trying to kill you. At least that death would be swift. But this death by freezing was slow and painful.

How could anyone live in a place this cold? Who would live where they could not grow food? Truly, all of the religions had it wrong. Hell was not a place of unending flame. Hell was a country called Canada.

I pushed into the building that held Mrs. MacPhail, the loud and bossy woman I had met the day before.

"Good morning!" she called. She carried a steaming cup. The smell of coffee filled the room that was warm and moist with the making of coffee and the breathing of many people.

"Help yourself to coffee," she said. "Then come see me."

I rubbed my hands together. I did not like this woman who yelled at people and said, "Get your crazy ass to work! Now!" Her voice so loud and sharp it hurt my ears. I also did not like the way her flecked green eyes penetrated the round lenses of her glasses and saw my soul.

I poured transparent coffee from the clear glass carafe. No roasting of beans here, no grinding with pestle and mortar. No ceremony. Coffee in white Styrofoam, not in tiny glass cups. No one gathered together. No one encouraged to drink one cup, two, three.

Here, tasteless coffee was consumed to stay warm.

I stood before this teacher's desk, my hands wrapped around the cup, pulling it to my chin, hoping for warmth from a lukewarm liquid. Why was it not hot at least? Why did they pour cold milk into tepid liquid and call it coffee? Did they not know to heat the milk, add butter and stir slowly?

"You look cold," she said. "Take off your coat. You'll warm up quicker."

She made no sense. To take off my coat would mean putting down the plastic cup. Taking off the coat would be like removing the fur of an animal. How could it stay warm without its thick layer of skin?

"It's insulating you from the warmth of the room," she said, seeming to read my mind.

My teeth clattered.

"You'll get used to it," Mrs. MacPhail said. "This is what we call a hint of autumn. Once winter comes, you'll think this was tropical."

Winter? The rains would be colder?

"Listen, I've got to place you, so I'm going to have to give you some tests. Then you are going to go to the high school."

Janis had taken me to the high school yesterday. They did not want me there. Mrs. MacPhail raised her hand, palm facing me to stop my protest.

"My husband teaches there," she said. "Social studies. You'll just sit in on his classes, sit at the back of the classroom.

We'll call it 'cultural immersion.' Good for you. Good for his students."

She spoke slowly and clearly, much better than most people, but still I missed some of the words. The tests she gave were simple.

And this school? How could they call it a school? Open to the street. No fence. No guards. No desks. No teacher at the front. No order. No discipline.

It looked more like the mill of Kofi's cousin than a school. Boys and girls of all ages together. Mostly white, but I noticed an Asian, a Somali, a few Sudanese. Music played, people danced and talked. Others sewed or wove strips of leather and string. Only two people studied with books and pencils. How was this a school?

The high school was an equally poor learning environment. I sat up straight on the tattered sofa at the back of the class. The students were my age. Only one person with brown skin, and it so light, I could not tell the nationality. How to tell the different tribes or religion with these people? Everyone here looked the same and wore clothes with the most expensive logos.

It was true that everyone in North America was cool, and everyone was rich.

But this school had none of the ordered discipline of the Cathedral School in Addis.

"You may have noticed we have a visitor with us today." Mr. MacPhail's voice boomed into all parts of the room. "His name is Tesfaye. He is from Ethiopia. When you are finished your assignment, you may go talk with him. But *not* until you hand in your papers."

A girl with corn silk hair slithered beside me, so close I could smell her flowery scent.

"Where's Ethiopia?" she asked. "Is it somewhere in Canada?"

"It is a country in Africa."

"I've seen people from Africa before, you know. And from China and Korea and Japan and the Philippines. There's tons of them here, but I've never talked to one before. I like the color of you."

The remaining students gathered around the sofa, one perched on each end and one plunked on the other side of the girl.

I felt like a museum exhibit. I was afraid to move.

"Can I touch you? Feel your skin?" Before I answered, the girl caressed my arm, her skin like the petal of hibiscus.

"Can I touch your hair?" Another girl, leaning in front, displayed breasts that nearly leapt from a tight shirt.

They touched and I touched, the hair and skin of these girls so smooth and so clean. I liked the girls, but Gashe would not be pleased that I was associating with such immodest women.

"Hey, you're from Africa, right? What's it like to shoot a lion?" asked a boy with hair as black as mine.

I had never shot a lion. I had never seen a lion, except in a book.

"It is nice," I said.

"Oh, do you have zebras where you live?" asked the girl who rubbed the top of my head as if I was a prized cow.

"Monkeys and gorillas!" someone shouted.

"You live in a mud hut, right? How big is it?"

"He probably doesn't even understand English, you dope!" said another girl. She slapped the boy's arm with the back of her hand.

I was surrounded by kids, all of them talking so fast and saying so many things. It was as if they spoke a language other than the English I had learned at school. Neither was it the English of DJ and Jason. I grinned and tried to look more stupid than I was.

I had learned that sometimes in Canada, it was better to appear not to understand.

◆

"Look, whatever happened before now, it doesn't matter," said Mrs. MacPhail.

How could it not matter? How could the disappearance of Gashe not matter? How could my family being left with no one to provide not be important?

"I'm not going to ask you about it. What's important is *now,* the choices you make *now,*" she said.

She could see inside of me, my blood, my bones, my thoughts. Could she see what had happened? Did she know about the list that carried my name? That I was a coward who ran away? Did she know that I had left my brother to fend for himself?

"Do you understand?" she asked.

"Yes." I nodded.

"Okay." She adjusted her glasses. "Now we have to get to work. You scored extremely well on the tests I gave you. Extremely well. The next step is to build a plan for you. We need to determine your needs and decide how to help you succeed. You are with an excellent family who will provide for your physical needs. They have a boy about your age. You've met him?"

◆

Spencer was the son of Janis and Tomas. Of all the cool boys I had met in Canada, Spencer was the coolest, with a type of hair that stuck from his head like the spokes on a wheel. My room and his room shared a thin wall.

Spencer knew everything about everything, and he taught me in the way that I had taught Ishi when he had come to live with us. He had a car held together splendidly by corroded metal. He allowed me to sit in the front seat. Like Gashe, he waved to everyone, but he did not throw alms onto the street.

Spencer had a wife who, he explained, was not a forever wife. He called her a "girlfriend." Spencer said I should have a girlfriend, too. First, he showed me pictures in magazines he kept beneath his mattress. He was most excited about the women with starving bodies and breasts heavy with milk. I wondered what their fathers would do if they saw their daughters in Spencer's magazines.

I let my hair grow into an afro so I could copy Spencer's attractive style. We painted the spikes on my head yellow, green and red — the colors of the Ethiopian flag.

Everyone liked this style. They became happy when they saw me, especially when I remembered to walk in the manner that DJ and Jason had taught me, shuffling and dragging my legs as if I was a cripple. I liked the swooshing sound made by the leaves on the ground when I walked this way, and how the crisp leaves rose in waves like desert sand. I also liked how yellowed leaves drifted from branches, made as bare as they had been when I first came to Canada and met Yosef.

The wind I did not like. The cold of it stole my breath and froze my lungs. I was happy to seek shelter at school.

Pumpkins were everywhere. Every shape and every size. On tables, in a box beside the door. It looked like the preparation for a feast.

"Grab a pumpkin!" yelled Mrs. MacPhail when she saw me. I chose the best one. Small and heavy, the kind Etheye would choose to make the best wat.

"And a knife. We're going to make jack-o'-lanterns for Halloween. Have you ever seen one?"

"It is a type of food?"

"More like a lantern," she said. "A little lamp for decoration." Another strange custom. Who would use perfectly good food to make a lamp?

The students taught me to stab the top of the pumpkin, cut a circle and pull out the slimy seeds that they shook into the garbage. I scraped the inside clean.

"Now, make a face," a boy told me. I made my eyes big and let my tongue fall from my mouth.

"Not like that," he laughed. I scrunched up my lips and crossed my eyes.

"In the pumpkin! You get to carve a face now." He had used triangles to represent eyes and sharp teeth and was peeling the thin outside skin from the face. "You can make it anything you want. Happy. Sad. Scary."

My hollow pumpkin leered, eyes looking left, in a frightening way. I added a poorly sewn scar. Mrs. MacPhail gave me a tiny candle.

"Tonight, when it gets dark, you light the candle and put it in the window or on the doorstep," she said.

"The candle flame will cook it?"

"No, it's just a decoration. Tomorrow, you throw it away."

"Excellent food is thrown away?" How rich would be the street beggars of Addis if they came to Canada. "Everyone does this?"

Later, Spencer stepped into the room where I slept and where I studied.

"Come on, bud. We've gotta go," he said.

Darkness had fallen. Books with difficult English words were open on my desk.

"Now?"

"Yes, and bring your pillowcase. Hurry. We've gotta pick up the others."

The candle flickered in the face of my pumpkin that someone had put on the step, causing it to glow like a low moon. The door of Spencer's car screeched open.

"Tesfaye! Come on! What's taking you so long?" he asked.

A massacre had occurred in the next house. The windows were splashed with blood, the word HELP written on the glass. A body hung from a tree. My heart quickened. I ran to the car.

"We must go back inside. Lock the door," I said.

"That's nothing," he said. "We'll find some way better houses."

"We must *do* something."

"Yup. But we can't do anything standing around here. Get in!"

Why did he not appear afraid?

Everywhere I looked were corpses and skeletons hanging from trees and houses. Front gardens were turned into burial grounds. It was as if the clock had turned back to the time not long before my birth, when Mengistu first took power in Ethiopia. Our teacher had told us how the bodies of men had swung each morning from lamp posts, the birds pecking out their eyes.

"Spencer, where will we go?"

"I'm not telling, but you're going to love it," he said.

He stopped in front of a brightly lit house. Three other friends crawled into the backseat. All of them had pillowcases, and one of them had the type of paint that girls spread over their faces. One boy wore a black sweatshirt with a skeleton printed in white.

Spencer drove quickly on the familiar streets. He did not stop at the sign that said Stop.

"We'll escape? All of us together?"

"Escape? Are you kidding me? This is like the best night of the year."

"The deaths," I said.

"You don't think it's real, do you?" Spencer asked. "The blood and the bodies?"

The boys in the backseat cackled. I remained still, silent and watchful.

Mike rolled down the window and flung a beer can. It hit a postal box.

"Woohoo!" he yelled. "Did you see that? Fuckin' A, man!"

Spencer, Mike and the others howled like wolves. I twisted the pillowcase into a tight rope that curled into a knot.

"Tesfaye, you okay?" Spencer glanced at me. "It's all pretend. Totally fake. Like a game. You know how to play pretend, right?"

I was an expert at pretending.

"It's like when you play with my little brother and you act like a lion or a bear or something and chase him like you're going to eat him. It's just a game."

Mike growled in the back street and batted the spikes of my hair.

"Why would you do this?" I asked.

"Because it's fun! It's Halloween, man."

"Why the bodies in the trees? And the graves?"

"To make it spooky. Everyone loves to be scared, right?"

I thought of mean-faced soldiers with AK-47s, military trucks stuffed with ordinary people, and the fear of not arriving home by curfew. I thought of my weeks in hiding, the pounding of a fist. *"Open! Open de deur!"*

I did not like to be scared.

Spencer parked in front of the food store. He went in but left the engine running. The other boys dipped their fingers in the colored paint and smeared it on their faces.

It was just pretend. A silly game. I dipped the three middle fingers of my right hand in the yellow paint to make curved lines across my cheeks and to my chin.

Spencer returned with a stack of narrow cardboard cartons. He gave one to each of us. Inside were twelve perfect eggs, all clean, and all of the same size.

"All of this, for me?"

"Yup," he said. Spencer reversed from the parking lot and drove to a street where monsters and witches and Ninja Turtles and beggars ran from house to house.

"Those are children? In the disguises? Pretending to be something else?"

Mike snickered. "What a fuckin' doofus," he said as he climbed from the car.

"None of this is real. The blood is fake. Ketchup or something. On Halloween, you can do anything you want."

I placed my eggs carefully on the seat. The other boys carried their cartons under their arms.

"Bring your eggs," said Spencer. "So, what you do is go up to a house and press the doorbell. Someone will answer and you'll say, 'Trick or Treat.' Then you hold out your bag like this. The person will put candy or chips or maybe pop in the bag."

"Okay," I said.

"Yeah. Then you go to the next house and do the same thing."

"How many times must I do this?"

"As many as you want."

"Do I use the eggs to pay?" The boys exchanged glances.

"Kind of. You see, when you say, 'Trick or Treat,' if they don't give you anything, or they say you're too old or something, then you give them an egg."

"Like this!" said Mike. He threw an egg at a street sign. It smacked, then dribbled like mucus from the nose of a bull.

"You would waste a valuable egg?"

"Oh, yeah. I'd easily waste a dozen valuable eggs," he said.

"But those eggs would feed many people. My whole family!"

"Well, in case you haven't noticed? You're not in Africa anymore," said Mike. "Let's hit the first house."

It was like a miracle. House after house gave us sweets. I wanted to eat the chocolate, but I didn't want to waste any time. I ran from house to house, careful to avoid the pretend bodies that swung from trees.

"This isn't any fun," said Mike.

"Free chocolate!" I said. I imagined all of my brothers and sisters with me. So many sweets we could get. And no cost!

"Who are you supposed to be?" a man asked.

"I am Tesfaye," I said. "Trick or Treat." I held open the sack for the pillow.

"You look like a punk. Besides, you're far too old for this …"

He slammed the door. I heard the lock turn.

"He give you anything?" asked Spencer.

"No."

The boys pelted the man's house with a hail of expensive eggs.

"Woohoo!" they yelled. "Woohoo!"

"That's enough candy." Spencer shoved the carton of eggs at me. "We have work to do."

We pelted the school, the police station, road signs, the windshields of cars and park benches.

It was extremely satisfying to feel the egg fly from my hand, watch it splatter and dribble away to nothing.

15

It was a strange manner in which the nights stretched longer than the days and the sun was not overhead at midday. Rain came in crystals that Spencer's small brother taught me to catch on my tongue. On other days, the wind whipped my face as if with shards of glass, the air so brittle that surely my face would split if I did not press it together when I ran to and from school. Sweaters, coat, scarf, gloves, mittens, hat, wool socks, heavy boots — none of it could prevent the ice that replaced the marrow of my bones.

The only warm place was curled on my side beneath a feather quilt, listening to the hum of hot air that blew the curtains printed with horses and cowboys with ropes.

Winter was a terrible thing, but it was not the only problem.

Living with Janis and Tomas and Spencer was fine. School was fine.

How could I not be happy? I was in a safe place. I had enough to eat. I had challenging work at school. I was helping other students at the outreach school. My English was improving.

But I did not deserve this life. I had not earned it. I hated every good thing that happened to me.

I acted the way happy people did. I smiled and nodded and laughed and said all the proper things. But inside, I was an old man, longing for the past. It was as if by pleasing everyone else, I had lost who I was. I was an actor. Or worse, I was a cartoon, a line drawing without substance.

Ababa's saying was true: *Living is worthless for one without a home.*

I was no one here. An orphan without prospects. A person who could see the warmth of the sun but not feel it. I did not belong and I never would.

The only thing I wanted was to sleep, and to let the creeping fingers of death take me.

The bossy principal of the school defied my wishes. Mrs. MacPhail came to the house of Tomas. She threw open the door to my room and stomped in.

"Get up!" she ordered. I burrowed my head beneath the pillow and drew the cover over top. She tore off the blanket and exposed my naked body. I leapt into the clothing folded on the floor, glad that she had turned her back.

"Brush your teeth! Wash your face! We are going to school," she said. Her glare was as severe as Gashe's. She pointed to the door, then her car.

"Get in!" Waves of hot anger rolled off her.

She came to the house every morning to force me to the plan I had helped her make. She waited outside and blared the horn if I took too long.

I hated how this woman saw my inner core, the falseness of my smile, my act of belonging, my agreeing to anything and everything. No matter how smooth the façade or how layered, she saw what lay beneath.

I refused to look directly in her eyes the way Rob had taught me was proper in Canada. I kept my eyes busy with other things. I did not want her to examine my worthless soul.

Weeks passed in this manner. I became punctual. I did the work that was expected. I avoided conflict with Mrs. Mac the way I had learned to avoid conflict with Gashe.

But still, she found me. I was in plain sight at a table not far from her desk.

She walked toward me.

"Listen, Tesfaye." I kept my eyes on the bits of purple glitter stuck to the table. They winked in the sunlight that came through the window when the clouds shifted.

"My daughter needs some help," she said. I felt her stare and glanced up. "She's bright. Super bright. But she doesn't exactly thrive when it comes to mathematics and physics."

Why was she confiding this? Why to me? Teachers did not speak in this way to students.

"I thought that maybe you could help her," she said.

"Me?"

"Yes. You have a gentle manner and you are exceptional in the sciences. I think she would listen to you."

My eyes dropped to the Shakespeare book face down on the table. I thought of the times I tried to teach Ishi. I was a terrible instructor who preferred to play football in the garden or pelt salamanders with pebbles or create wars between ants. Ishi's grades had not improved.

"I am a poor teacher," I said.

"Just a few hours a week after school. I will pay you."

I wanted to tell her No.

"Hey!" she yelled across the room. Two boys argued. One, on tiptoes, held a cigarette package above his head. The other leapt on a chair to snatch it. He toppled to the floor when the tall one slid the package inside his coat. "You want to graduate? Get to work or get out!"

She returned her attention to me.

"Your daughter, she wants this?"

"She will," said Mrs. Mac. My eyes darted to hers.
"Agreed, then? You know where I live?"
I nodded.
"You can start tomorrow."

16

How could a hot white sun offer no heat? How was it that the same sun that caused coffee beans to grow did not melt the thick layer of snow that covered the naked branches of trees?

The eye of the sun flashed on the ice as I walked to Mrs. Mac's house, a blinding combination of white reflected on white. Even the green trees with prickly needles were cast in crystal. The snow squelched like breaking Styrofoam with every step. The ice was as slippery as the mud in the garden during the winter rains, the mud that made Etheye so cross because it took longer to wash our clothes.

Etheye would like the powdery snow, how it rarely stuck to clothing, and when it did, how it would simply melt into water, rather than dry to a crust.

My brothers and sisters would be amazed at how snow could be shaped into balls. We could have the biggest snowball fight ever, as big as that football match we had with Isaias' ball. And the snow. It could be caught in a cup and dribbled with Fanta or Coca for a satisfying drink.

Breath fogged from my mouth. Ishi would never believe any of this, how dripping water froze into spears that clung to the edges of buildings, how the wind felt like needles, how the cold at first took away the feeling in your fingers and toes, and then caused them to burn. He would not believe what I was seeing now, a rainbow around the sun, with two bright spots, like brothers to the east and west. The stark beauty stole my breath.

"Three suns. How could this be?" I asked Devina. We sat together at a large table in the house of her father and Mrs. Mac. Schoolbooks and binders and graph paper were spread over the table.

"Sundogs," she said. "I suppose," she snapped off the end of a carrot with her teeth, "you've never seen them before."

"What causes them?"

"How am I supposed to know?" She broke the carrot in two, passed the half to me that had not been bitten. "Something to do with ice crystals." We both looked out the window, admiring the prisms that shot from the infant suns. "It means a change in the weather. Same as a Chinook arch."

"Oh," I said, even though her explanation did not explain anything. "To make it warmer?"

"You got it," she said. "You catch on quick."

"What happens when the cold goes away?"

"It gets warmer, you dope."

"Ah, so you can grow coffee?"

"Man, what planet are you from? Coffee does not grow in Canada. It doesn't even grow in North America. South America? Yes. North America? No."

"Ah," I said. Then I remembered the heavy bags at Kofi's mill stamped with the name and flag of Canada. "Grain. You do not grow coffee here, but you grow grain."

"You're a genius."

I smiled, even though I understood the sarcasm. "Wheat?"

"And oats and barley and canola and peas, and all sorts of other boring things."

"Teff?"

"What?"

"Teff. Do you grow it here?"

"Teff? I've never heard of that. You must have it wrong."

"Teff. For injera." I cupped my hand like a bowl and made a stirring, mashing motion with my other hand.

"Would you speak English? How am I supposed to communicate with you when you speak African?"

"Amharic," I said.

"What-ev-er," she said. She rolled her eyes in her head as if she was dying.

Devina peeled a banana. She gave me half. Ishi also would not believe the food, how much there was everywhere, all the time, and how you could eat whenever you wanted.

"Are you mental?" she asked. Her voice and the way she slanted her head told me she was teasing. "Is that why they had you in that group home? Because you are not so smart in the head?"

I ate my banana slowly and watched her. She tapped the side of her head with one finger.

"Huh?" she asked. She made me think of how Ishi always says the things that are on his mind. I wished Devina liked to play football. I would like to beat her at something, maybe accidentally trip her while she was running.

Her drooling and stinking black dog loped into the kitchen. It laid its giant head on her foot. She stroked its ear with her other foot. I shifted my chair farther into the corner.

"I don't know why you don't like dogs," she said.

I did not respond. I saw no reason to explain how a dog appearing so calm could turn as quickly as the wind to tear off your hand and drag it away.

"You are just like one, you know. A dog."

"Do not say that!" I said, then added the word Canadians used often without sarcasm. "Please."

"Why? What's wrong with being a dog?"

"It is an insult. A dog cannot be trusted."

"Well, anyway, you are just like a dog," she continued. "Or a pig. A pig will do the same thing." She used her ruler to make a straight line and measured it, then looked up at me. "You follow people around with those big sad eyes. You do anything anyone says. It's like you're trained not to think."

I heard the whine of Gashe's switch and felt it burn across my back. *Obey!* he commanded with each stroke. *Obey! You must obey. You do as I say!*

"And," she said. "You like to run." She looked up from her schematic drawing of levers and pulleys. "Dogs like to run."

I wanted to say I did not like to run, but that would be untrue. Running, feeling the rhythm of my heart, was freedom.

"You should take Charlie. Go for a run." She fondled the dog's ears and stroked the top of his head.

"I must go now to study," I said. I left her there with her open book on the kitchen table, the untrustworthy animal at her feet. Should I have told her the drawing she made was wrong? That the configuration would never lift a load?

No, there were some things she needed to learn for herself.

◆

I held the metal door at the house of Tomas as I closed it, so it would not rattle and bang shut. I felt the need to wash from being so close to the breath of the filthy dog. A ridiculous clown looked at me in the rectangular mirror above the bathroom sink.

What had happened to me? I lived in a free country where tribe and religion did not matter. Here, even women carried the same rights and the same choices as men.

I had been given everything. Enough food, a free education and a place to live. I wore perfectly fitted clothes with the best logos, with hair in colorful spikes.

Is this who I was? A mannequin? A puppet?

When I tried to learn inline skating, I told Yosef that I did not want a wife, that I wanted to study. And yet I spent my time being a child and looking good to attract girls. Everything about me was as false as Gashe strutting in his finest clothes and best car, concerned only for his image.

We are the same, you and I. Cut from the same cloth.

No. Gashe, I would never give away a child to increase my influence. I would never inflict cruelty on another.

I would no longer pretend.

I removed the long-bladed scissors from the cabinet. One by one, I sawed the ropes of my hair and dropped the spears in the trash. When I was done, Ishi looked back at me from another world, but without the sparkling eyes that sought mischief.

The eyes in the mirror were as serious and sad as the eyes of Ababa's best cow.

I cupped my palms, let water fill them from the tap. My hands so like Gashe's, the bowing of the fingers that bound us. I bore his hands, his love of learning.

I dipped my head, washed my face. Water streamed from forehead to chin.

I had everything Gashe dreamed of for Ethiopia.

I dropped my head again, the water cool and cleansing. I heard Gashe's prayerful voice, *In the name of the Father, the Son and the Holy Ghost, One God.*

I saw him bent in humility, hands covering face, forehead to the floor. A third time I dropped my head. *In the name of the Father, the Son and the Holy Ghost, One God.*

The washing away of sin. Baptism. Renewal. Oneness with God. I hid my clean face with Gashe's clean hands. He would be so ashamed of me.

17

A snow blizzard raged its anger outside the windows of the school. I was the only student who had come to stick to his plan. Mrs. Mac stood beside the small table in the corner where I worked. She touched my shoulder.

"Are you all right?" she asked. Her voice and her eyes were not harsh when I stole a glance at her.

"Yes," I said. "I am fine."

"Look at me," she said. I swiveled my head in her direction, but I did not look at her. She lifted my chin.

"Look at me," she repeated. She was like Etheye, hard to ignore. "Tell me what's wrong."

"Nothing is wrong." Nothing was ever wrong in Canada. It was the perfect place.

She pulled a chair beside me and sat, close enough that I could smell the spicy soap she used.

"You can trust me. I will not judge you. I will tell no one," she said.

What would I tell her? Of fear? Of worrying that this would be my eternal resting place? That I was dead to my family? Of knowing I could never go home?

Snow whipped the windows, so much that I could no longer see across the street. Knives of cold sliced beneath the door. My ankles ached from the draft. Chicken flesh raised beneath my jeans. I lifted the hood and zipped my coat to the chin to cease the shivering.

Mrs. Mac was not moved by the cold. She sat. She observed me. Without a word.

She knew parts of my life, but not all. Should I tell her about my family? About Etheye? Her fingers gentle on my face. *I never forget about you. Never. You are my soul,* she said.

But had she? Had she forgotten me?

I huddled my shoulders, slipped my hands into my armpits and clenched my eyes. The wind whistled a high-pitched whine.

Should I tell her about Ishi, the part of me that made me whole? How I never said goodbye?

"I understand," she said. She touched my arm. Left her hand to rest on my sleeve.

I curled tighter. Head to chest.

Hold. Hold it in.

She could not understand. No one could.

She could not know how it was to live without love. Or belonging.

A grader shunted and chugged outside. Its blade scraped unyielding pavement. Beside me, Mrs. Mac's breathing was even and slow. Her hand warmed my arm as she rubbed it.

"Your family," she said. My head snapped toward her, eyes open. "Do they know where you are?"

I closed my eyes and shook my head.

"No," my voice a whisper.

"They need to know."

Eyes open, back straight. "It is not possible," I said.

"Your *mother* needs to know. Think of her."

I thought of little else. Etheye, Ishi, Tezze, my sisters, my small brothers.

Gashe.

"I don't know how we'll do it, but we'll find a way," she said.

"They told me that I must have no contact with my family. They told me I must forget about them."

"Who told you?"

"The authorities at Immigration, and CSIS. The police. The people who asked so many questions and did not believe my answers."

"Well, I believe in you, and what's *impossible* is to forget your family. Your mother needs to know you are safe."

"I cannot take this risk," I said. "There is too much danger."

"Do you trust me?"

I nodded.

"If you want this, we'll find a way." She crossed the room to get a pen and a pad of lined paper from her desk.

Could this bossy teacher find a way? I unzipped my hood.

"First things first. Do you know where your mother is?"

"No." Was Etheye pleading at the prison door for information about Gashe? Was she wrapped in a drab netela begging in the streets, seeking coins for food? Was Kofi looking after her?

"This task is not possible. I do not know where to look," I said.

"Anything is possible," said Mrs. Mac.

The windows of the school rattled. The edges were clouded with ice.

"Would she be at the house where you lived?"

"I do not know. She maybe sold the house to pay the smuggler."

"Would that take all of the money?"

I shrugged. Why had I not thought of this? Why had I not thought of the stacks of birr locked in the cabinet of Gashe's room? What did it cost her to save me? How much to bribe the guards that kept Gashe in jail? How much for his body?

All of it. Etheye would haggle, but she would give everything — the VCR, the television, the Persian rugs. None of it mattered to her.

"She would give everything, even cows if she had them," I said.

"Cows?" The teacher's eyebrows lifted in surprise. "I just love cows. I grew up with them, you know."

I did not know. But it made me feel good to learn this. Etheye would like this woman.

"Where would she go?"

A woman without means? To the streets? To the Korah? And what of my brothers and sisters? And the servants?

"There would be nowhere for her. She could not earn enough of a living in the city."

"What about the country, then? Could she go there?"

"Her father, he lives in a village. But it is a great distance to travel."

"But, if she had nowhere else ..."

It was where she sent me. Would she go to Ababa?

"She would not leave Gashe if he was living," I said. But was he living?

"So the city then? She would stay in the capital?"

"Yes."

"Can we send a letter? How do you get mail in Addis?"

"I do not know. Gashe receives messages. I think they pass person to person."

"But conceivably, we could send a letter."

"It might be a possibility. But Etheye cannot read."

"You can write it in Amharic," Mrs. Mac said. "It would be good practice. To help you remember your language."

"Etheye cannot read in any language."

The teacher looked up from her notepad. "Someone could read it for her?" she asked. "Your brothers? Your sisters?"

I thought also of the men who sat at small tables on the street writing things down and reading documents aloud for people who could not do it for themselves.

Mrs. Mac fetched a pen from the tin can on her desk and pulled two sheets of paper from the computer printer. She held them out.

"What you are going to do now is write a letter to your mother," she said.

I shook my head. "You do not understand."

"Explain it to me."

I rolled my lips inward, pinching them tight in the manner of Ishi when he held in emotion. Mrs. Mac waited. The overhead lights hummed. Hot air shot from the vents near the windows.

"By a letter they will find me. The police would see the stamp, the postmark. A letter would send my family to the jail."

"I see." Her head tipped to one side, eyes gazed at the ceiling. She tapped her lips with the pen. "There has to be a way. Maybe I can get someone to mail it when they travel to another country …"

Mrs. Mac thought all things were possible. But contacting Etheye was one thing she could not accomplish.

"I want you to write a letter anyway. Even if we can't send it," she said. "It doesn't have to be long. Just let her hear your thoughts. Tell her you are safe."

It was simple idea. Write the words. Tell Etheye I am safe. It was a waste of time, but to please Mrs. Mac, I held the pen to the smooth, white paper.

Where could I begin?

There was no beginning. The words inside my head were

English words. The sounds and flowing symbols of Amharic frozen in my mind.

I wrote one word.

Etheye.

◆

"I've been talking to some people," Mrs. Mac said several days later. Her cluttered desk was between us. I stood before her, a completed assignment extended in my hand. She nodded, dropped my work on a stack of papers and leaned back in her chair.

"There is the idea of writing a letter and having someone deliver it, but I don't know anyone who travels to Africa, let alone Ethiopia," she said.

She faced her palm to me when the telephone rang. When the call ended, she said, "Telephones!"

I did not respond.

"Are they common in Ethiopia?"

"In the city, yes. But they are not commonly used."

"Your mother? She has a telephone?"

I nodded. The ringing had startled me the night of the edire. Phone calls were rare. They were also dangerous. Etheye's speech had been rapid to keep the call brief.

"You know her number?"

"In Ethiopia, *people* do not have telephone numbers, *houses* do."

"So, the telephone number for the house would be the same, even if she didn't still live there?"

"Yes."

"Do you remember the number?"

"Yes. I know this."

"Oh, my God, Tesfaye!" Mrs. Mac leapt from her chair and put a hand on each of my shoulders. "We can *telephone* her!"

My heart pounded. A phone call from so far away? It was not possible. I had flown over the ocean. There were no telephone wires.

"She will not be there," I said. I could think of no way she could afford to stay in the house without Gashe.

Mrs. Mac rummaged through books on a shelf.

"We can *try*," she said.

She withdrew a book with a paper cover, licked her middle finger and whipped through thin pages. "I know it's here somewhere," she said.

She passed a colored map of North America. "Canada. USA. Caribbean," she said. "Here! Frequently called country codes." She ran her finger down a list.

"Ethiopia. 251!" she said. "The country code is 251, and if you know the telephone number of the house. Tesfaye! We can do this!"

She continued reading out loud: *"To direct dial all other international countries, dial 011 plus the country code, city routing code and number."*

"You do not understand," I said.

Mrs. Mac held her finger on the page and looked up.

"The telephones are monitored."

"Monitored? Every phone? All the time?"

"I think this, yes. It is another way the government can find information it wants."

Mrs. Mac tapped her finger on the book, then rested her chin on her hand. She flipped more pages.

"Let's at least figure out the time difference ..."

"The time," I said.

I pictured the house in darkness, Gashe turning the dial that lit the radio stations, *Tell no one what you hear.*

"The international radio stations work best late at night," I said.

18

It was another day when wind carved faces into leather and blew snow from rooftops. Another day when I was the only student left at school.

"The risk is small," said Mrs. Mac. Her words were slow, her tone serious. "People I trust have advised me. Today, right now, we are going to phone your mother."

My hands trembled, and my lips.

Phone Etheye?

Mrs. Mac lifted the receiver of her desk phone.

"Tell me the number," she said.

The phone rang over and over, the bells loud against the cement wall, the cord still, curled and twisted. My heart pushed so hard against my chest with every ring of the telephone that I thought my heart might fly out of me and across the room. My right leg vibrated.

Brr-ring. Brr-ring.

Who would answer? What would I say?

Brr-ring. Brr-ring.

No one was there. Everyone was gone. The phone echoed in a silent house, with me on the other side of the ocean, waiting.

"Allo?" The voice of Ishi.

Could it be possible? Mrs. Mac turned from the tears that trailed fire on my cheeks.

"This is Tesfaye."

"It cannot be! Who plays this trick?" I saw him in my mind, standing in the space between living room and unused North American kitchen, holding the phone to his ear.

"My brother, it is me." The words choked in my throat. To hear my language, to use the familiar words that flowed suddenly from my mouth like breath. His voice, so close, as if he were beside me.

"You live?"

"Yes," I wiped the tears with my fingers, but as much as I wiped, more came. More and more and more, until I could not see. "Can the dead speak?" I asked.

"He's alive! He's alive. Tesfaye is alive!" Ishi screamed. He dropped the phone. It spun on its cord and clunked against the wall and the floor. "Tesfaye is alive! Tesfaye is alive!" He ran through the house, and outside, waving his arms, flapping his hands and yelling while I dangled from a spiraled cord. Etheye's quick steps were next, bare feet slapping on white marble veined with black.

"Tesfaye?" Her voice enveloped me like a soft breeze.

Panting breaths. Mine. "Etheye," I breathed, my voice as high as a girl's. Mrs. Mac touched my arm. Her eyes overflowed.

Voices exploded around Etheye. Running feet as everyone gathered to watch the telephone.

"Etheye," I said to the phone. "You are well?"

"Thanks be to God our Almighty Savior! You live? Such good fortune has come!" I heard her spit three times. "I pray this every day that God protect you. That I do the right thing."

Sobs closed my throat. My hand sweated from squeezing the phone. I pushed it harder against my ear. Her voice in my head. So clear. Across the ocean. To this country of too much.

"Where be you?"

"In Canada. A very big country. In North America," I said.

"You be safe?"

"Yes. Safe. It is a good place. I live with a white family!"

"You be a slave? Ah, my heart, they treat you well?"

"Not a slave, Etheye. A student!"

"A student? You use your good mind?"

"Yes, and I have a strong teacher. A woman, Etheye. Can you believe it?"

"I cannot believe you live."

A man's voice in the background, lower than the fluttering excited sounds. Whose?

"Gashe?" I asked.

"Nothing. He be not returned yet."

"And you? How do you live?"

"I be well. Your brothers be well. Your sisters be well. How you talk to me from America?" she asked. "How it be that I hear you?" Her voice suddenly became as hurried as it had been the night she made me leave with Kofi.

It was his voice in the background. What was he doing there?

"I put away the telephone now," she said. Her voice fell to a whisper. "Do not use the telephone again. It be too dangerous, my heart. They find you. You must live."

The line hummed. Dead.

19

Ishi was alive. Etheye was alive. Everyone was fine. They lived still in Gashe's house. I could picture them there. The phone call had taken me home.

The man's voice in the background. Not Gashe, but perhaps Kofi. Gashe would trust him to care for Etheye. He would provide. He would be kind to her.

I imagined my family standing around the phone, necks jutting out — a phone call from so far across the ocean. I knew of no one who had received such a call. It was unfortunate they could not brag of it.

"What are you smiling about?" Iced fog frothed from Devina's mouth. I had heard her running to catch up, the sounds sharp and clear in the morning cold.

"There is no wind," I said.

Devina's eyes rolled. "Weirdo," she said. "Do you know how often you complain about wind?"

I lifted my chin and puffed frost into the morning darkness as we walked side by side. Devina copied me.

"*Choo. Choo,*" she said. She glanced at me, then rolled her eyes again. "Trains, stupid. We're olden-days trains. Our breath is the steam coming out the top. Don't you know anything?"

"There are no trains in my country," I said. "A short track. But no train."

The woolen ball at the end of Devina's hat swished to and fro when she shook her head. "Who builds a train track that has no train?"

I had no answer, so remained silent. I liked the crisp silence and the squeaking rhythm of our boots.

"Look." I pointed to the horizon.

The sun crept from its dark bed into the frigid stillness, and with it, the twin suns embracing each other in a halo that circled the sun. We stopped to watch.

"They are stretching as the sun rises," I said. "It is as if they are trying to grasp each other."

"I like how they are exactly the same," said Devina. She did not roll her eyes, and her voice carried no sarcasm.

"These sundogs make me think of my family," I said. "The big center one, that's Etheye, my mother. The little ones, they are my brother and me."

"Oh, puh-lease," she said. "You are starting to sound like Shakespeare. Besides, I thought you came from a huge family with a bazillion siblings, not just one brother."

"One brother is my twin. You would like him."

"Probably not," she said.

"We look exactly the same, but we are different in every other way."

"Well, that's something in his favor."

Devina was the rudest person I had ever known. She had no thoughts to protect another's feelings, but her honesty pleased me. She would not pretend to be who she was not.

Her school came first when we crunched again along the street.

"After school? We'll do homework again?" I asked.

"Like you were a lot of help. That last assignment? An epic fail. The teacher actually laughed."

I recalled her misguided diagram.

"I'll explain it," I said. "I'll show you. With strings."

"Fine," she said and rushed toward her school.

I also wanted to show her something else. I had filled two paper cups with the Orange Crush that fell and rolled from the vending machine at school yesterday when I inserted coins. I had stuck twigs in the sweet soda this morning and left them outside. They would be frozen solid after school.

In this country, we didn't have to wait for a special Holy Day to get one, or for the electricity to work.

We could have Ethiopian popsicles all winter, whenever we wanted.

Author's Note

It has been an honor and a privilege to be trusted with this story. It is a work of fiction, but it is based on a true story. Researching and writing it has taught me so much, and it has reinforced my belief that we must seek in each other what is the same, rather than what is different.

When "Tesfaye" and I first met to explore the concept for this book, I explained how honest he would have to be, the level of detail I would need, how we would go together to places I suspected were dark and possibly terrifying. There was something in his eyes when I spoke of the potential pain that called directly to my soul. The man vanished, and I saw, sitting across from me, the boy he once was, alone and afraid.

Memory is a tricky thing — the things we remember and the things we forget. Some parts of this story are as near to true as possible, given his age when certain events occurred, and some parts are purely fiction, based on embellished episodes from his life — historical events, or things that were likely. If there are mistakes, they are mine alone.

I know people will want to know what is true and what is not. I won't tell, but if you find yourself thinking, "That's not possible. That couldn't have happened," it's probably one of the true pieces.

The work became fiction to protect Tesfaye, even though he is now safe and thriving in his adopted country. The fear is for his family still in Ethiopia. No story is worth putting a life in danger.

Cold White Sun was never meant as political commentary, nor to disparage any country. I apologize to anyone who finds it hurtful. Rather, the goal was to tell the story of a refugee. My hope is that in learning about Tesfaye, we might take opportunities in our everyday lives to look beyond appearances, heritage and religion. That we might look more often for commonalities, the things that bind all of us.

I haven't words to express my gratitude to Tesfaye and to his family for their patience and their confidence in me. I would love to tell you who the real Tesfaye is. I would like to yell it from the top of a mountain and let it echo.

So sometime, if you are in the Alberta mountains — in Banff, or Jasper, or Kananaskis or Grande Cache — and you hear a name echoing, mountain to mountain, it might be me breaking my silence. Or it might be the echo of two strangers meeting, and forming a friendship destined to last a lifetime.

About Ethiopia

When I first started writing *Cold White Sun*, the only thing I knew about Ethiopia was a terrible famine in the mid-1980s in which millions of people of died. The news images from those days made me believe Ethiopia was a vast desert. The people looked like exhausted villagers, skeletal and dressed in rags. That's what I thought Ethiopia was.

Village life is part of Ethiopia, but certainly not all.

Ethiopia is a landlocked country located in northeastern Africa, in an area often referred to as the Horn of Africa because of the shape of the continent. Near its center is Addis Ababa, the country's capital. It is a huge, vibrant and rapidly growing city, with a population of more than 6.5 million — about the same as New York City.

Ethiopia is an ancient civilization and home to the Great Rift Valley, which is often called the "cradle of civilization" or the "birthplace of man," based on archeological evidence that dates back more than 3 million years. It is where the fossils of the pre-human "Lucy" were found.

One of the reasons Ethiopia is such an interesting country is because it was never colonized. While the country was invaded in 1935 by Italian forces led by Benito Mussolini, who *intended* to colonize it, the attempt was unsuccessful. It took five years, but the Ethiopians — with the help of the British — were able to drive out the Italians in 1941. The influence of that occupation remains. It is why pizza and spaghetti are not uncommon, and why the architecture in the Piazza District of Addis reflects Italian design.

Without a significant influence from outsiders, Ethiopia maintained its own culture, tribes, languages, traditions and religions. The country uses a different calendar than the Gregorian calendar used in North America. The Ethiopian year has thirteen months, and the years are calculated differently; there is a seven- to eight-year gap between the Ethiopian calendar and the Gregorian one.

At the time when this story took place, birth years were unimportant and age was not relevant. However, the approximate ages of children were kept in mind until they turned five, so parents knew when to send their children to school.

The primary language is Amharic, and all government documents would have been kept in this language, using the Ethiopian calendar. It's why Tesfaye has difficulty answering the questions of immigration officials.

Names are also different than they are in North America. Ethiopians have only one name. However, they will sometimes use their father's first name as a type of equivalent to a North American surname. So, if you were Ethiopian, you would use your given name, followed by your father's first name. Using Ethiopian "surnames" to trace ancestral lineage is impossible.

Ethiopians also did not have street addresses when this story took place. Only a few roads had names, even in Addis Ababa. Directions were given based on landmarks.

Ethiopia is a country rich in history and culture, and wound tightly into that culture is religion. The majority are Christian — primarily Ethiopian Orthodox Church — followed closely in number by those who are Muslim. The Ethiopian Orthodox Tewahedo Church (EOTC), the faith Gashe and Ababa practice, is an ancient religion that may feel familiar to those of other religions. The veneration of the Virgin Mary, for instance, will feel familiar to Roman Catholics; not eating pork will be familiar to Jews and Muslims, as will customs surrounding the slaughter of animals for food. Religious postures, such as kneeling with the head to the floor, demonstrate humility, unworthiness and the need for mercy. The EOTC faithful are required to pray seven times a day at prescribed times. Men and women worship at the same time but separately in the EOTC church.

Traditionally, Ethiopia was a monarchy. Perhaps its most famous emperor was Haile Selassie, who ruled the country for forty-four years. He was deposed in 1974, following a coup when a group called the Derg seized control. Mengistu Haile Mariam soon rose to power with a communist philosophy. This was a dark time in Ethiopian history. Mengistu was a cruel dictator who launched a campaign to rid the country of his opponents. Known as the Red Terror, it was marked by two years of horrific violence. Tens of thousands of citizens were murdered in the late 1970s.

Mengistu remained in power until 1991. This is the revolution that opens *Cold White Sun*. Mengistu fled to Zimbabwe, but although an Ethiopian court convicted him of genocide and sentenced him to death, Zimbabwe has never extradited him. Mengistu is now in his eighties.

In addition to the 1930s conflict with the Italians, Ethiopia has fought decades-long battles with its neighbors, Somalia and Eritrea, over borders. Following World War II, Ethiopia and Eritrea were united in a federation, with both sides being equal. In 1961, Emperor Haile Selassie ended the federation and made Eritrea — with its important access to the Red Sea — a province of Ethiopia. Eritrea did not like this arrangement and began its fight to gain full independence. The war created a deep-seated bitterness on both sides. Ethiopia wanted to keep Eritrea; Eritrea wanted to be its own country. The war lasted for thirty years, until 1991. The United States was involved in the negotiations, and that's why we see the uprising outside the American embassy in Addis. Eritrea officially gained its independence in 1991.

Tensions between the two countries remained high, with a second war breaking out shortly after independence. A peace agreement was signed in 2000 but was never honored. Borders remained closed, with not even telephone calls allowed between the two countries.

The good news is that relations are improving. On September 11, 2018, the border crossings between Eritrea and Ethiopia reopened.

Originally from Cape Breton Island, Nova Scotia, Sue Farrell Holler comes from a culture rich in storytelling. She believes in the power of story — the stories we tell and the stories we listen to — to bring people together. She writes for children of all ages, and sometimes for adults. She lives in Grande Prairie, Alberta.
www.suefarrellholler.com